HOMECOMING

Published by Simon Publishing®
Simon Publishing is a registered trademark.
    https://www.simonpublishingllc.com/

ISBN: 979-8-9926895-1-8

Library of Congress Control Number: 2025920332

Cover Design by Melissa Waters

Printed by Ingram Spark and KDP Amazon
First Edition

2 0 2 5 1 1 1 1

*To my family, with all my love,
and in memory of my mom, Judy*

HOMECOMING

Suzanne Eisinger

SIMON PUBLISHING

PROLOGUE

Peter tipped his face up to the darkening sky, concern lining his forehead. Soon there would be no light left to find her. He quickened his pace, his attention alternating between the uneven road at his feet and any signs ahead of her car. He called her name, his voice growing more breathless with each attempt. But there was no answer. Eventually, the winding road reached its plateau, a graveled lot overlooking the gaping canyon below. Her car was there, as he knew it would be, perched at the edge of the lookout.

She sat in the driver's seat, the front door open, as if waiting for him to arrive. He smiled in relief, scrambling the last few yards to where she was parked. He called out, his arms extended in a ready embrace. Only then did she glance up, her blank expression changing to scorn at his approach. Spurred to action, she slammed the car door and reached for the ignition. The next thing Peter heard was the grinding of gears and the sharp metallic sound of the accelerator being floored. The car lurched toward the abyss, the engine's shrill scream drowning out the ones wrenched from Peter's throat.

Peter awoke with a start, his heart pounding and body heaving as his lungs strained for air. He swung his legs to the side of the bed as he fought to regain control of his consciousness, then dropped his head as the realization set in.

Eve was back.

Chapter 1

Of all the days to be running late, it had to be the first day of class.

Natalie half-walked, half-jogged down the sidewalk leading to the Psychology building. She checked her watch, but not before having to unwrap several layers of clothing to find it. The cold usually didn't bother her, but today was one of those damp, Midwest mornings that chilled her to the bone. Seeing the time, she swore to herself and quickened her pace to a full-out run.

Yanking open the doors to the lecture hall, Natalie was both comforted by the immediate rise in temperature and embarrassed at being the last one to arrive. Heads turned at her noisy entrance, leading Professor Spencer to do the same. She nodded sheepishly at him and searched for a seat—any seat—that would permit her to dissolve into the background as quickly as possible. However, this was one of Dr. Spencer's classes and there was barely a vacancy to be found.

Left with little choice, Natalie moved down the main aisle to the first row where one seat remained. She lowered her backpack to the floor and began easing into her seat when the girl beside her motioned for her attention. Professor Spencer, elbows resting on the podium, crooked a finger in her direction.

Natalie swallowed and rose, crossing the three steps it took to reach him.

Dr. Spencer's head cocked to one side, his expression one of mild irritation. "Traffic jam?"

Her face reddened. "No, I…overslept. Sorry—it won't happen again."

"Glad to hear it," he replied. "While you're up here, why don't you write down your contact information and details about the study session."

"Sure." She busied herself at the blackboard, while Professor Spencer turned to the class and cleared his throat. Natalie could almost feel the room sit up collectively and lean forward in their chairs.

"Welcome to Psychology 101," he began. "I'm Peter Spencer. If this is not the class that is printed on your schedule, now would be a good time to leave."

Of course, no one moved. This was a coveted class in the Psychology department, the first to fill up during registration and one of the few that remained at near-peak attendance throughout the semester. These students were right where they wanted to be.

"Before I begin, let me introduce my graduate assistant, Natalie Brooks." He motioned in her direction. "Miss Brooks will be teaching a study session once a week to go over any questions you may have. Time and location are listed on the board." He glanced at Natalie, who gave a self-conscious wave, chalk still in hand. "If you're interested in doing well in this class, I suggest that you take advantage of her study sessions."

Natalie returned to her seat and bent to the task of taking notes. For the most part, the information was nothing new: the definition of psychology, most prominent theories, and so on. She had taken this class years before as an undergraduate, sitting moon-eyed along with the rest of the coeds as the younger—but no less striking—Dr. Spencer lectured. Now, as the familiar words seemed to write themselves into her notebook, Natalie surveyed the students around her. Most were freshmen and sophomores, a nearly equal mix of male and female, although the females seemed to be paying particular attention to the speaker. Little had changed, she thought. Women were still drawn to him. Now, surrounded by students at least five years her junior, Natalie couldn't help smiling at their whispered exchanges.

"Wow, he's pretty hot."

"He's old enough to be your father."

"My dad *never* looked like that."

These were among the tamer observations she had heard over the last few months. Some were beyond suggestive, prompting Natalie to shake her head at the audacity of today's undergraduates.

She looked up from her notes as Dr. Spencer wrote a definition on the board. He was still just as handsome as those early years: tall, with brown hair that curled up at the edges and a slim but solid build. His standard classroom attire was also unchanged: khakis, white button-down shirt and conservative tie. His only visible alteration was the closely cropped beard that now adorned his face, an addition which seemed to further enhance his appeal. Natalie recalled the awful crush she'd had on the man throughout her four years here.

But this time, things were different. Now in the second semester of her graduate program, Natalie was back at the University of Wisconsin and pursuing the field she had grown to love in this very lecture hall. Dr. Spencer may have been the initial draw, but psychology was her dream. She was in this for keeps.

The bell rang and Natalie began packing up her things, her mind already focused on the busy day ahead. As she prepared to leave, Professor Spencer appeared beside her, briefcase in hand.

"See you this afternoon?"

She nodded. "2:00—same as last semester, if that works."

"Fine." He made way for her in the aisle and then continued to walk alongside her toward the exit. "I'm starting a new chapter. I'll need some articles from the library."

"Okay, see you then."

With a half wave, Natalie watched him climb the stairs to his third-floor office as she began the long trek to the student union.

She'd never expected to be working for Peter Spencer. During her first week back in Madison, Natalie had been surprised to learn he was in need of a new graduate assistant. Not unusual, as she realized later. Dr. Spencer was reputedly difficult to work for, with an exacting nature and little tolerance for errors or laziness. Of those assistants who lasted the year, most didn't return the next fall. Still, Natalie rushed to apply.

The result was a non-stop day from beginning to end—back-to-back classes in the morning, a few stolen moments for lunch, and afternoons helping the professor with research and teaching his undergraduate study sessions. Evenings were reserved for homework and perhaps dinner with her roommate if their schedules overlapped. In the morning, more of the same.

She wouldn't have traded it for anything.

***

Peter dropped the stack of photocopied articles into his briefcase and snapped it shut. For a moment, he almost wished Natalie were as efficient as his previous assistants, who were, by any measure, anything but. At least with them, his evenings were free from the specter of catch-up work. Not so with Natalie. When handed a list of articles he needed for his current manuscript, she always managed to return by 5:00 with the requested stack. Considering many of these were decades-old articles long shelved away in some of the most remote areas of the library, that was a feat in itself. Peter knew. Since the previous summer, he had been researching early cases of Post-Traumatic Stress Disorder dating back to World War I. He'd done his share of hunting down obscure articles and was glad to hand the task to someone else. Although, in the future, perhaps he would start making her lists a little smaller.

Yanking on his coat, he turned off the light and shut the office door behind him. Two doors down, Neil looked up as Peter passed by in the hallway.

"Hey, leaving so soon?" Neil leaned back in his chair, a ready smile on his face.

Peter stopped and leaned up against the doorframe. He readjusted his grip on his briefcase. Thanks to those articles, it felt five pounds heavier.

"It's after 6. Don't you have a wife?"

"Yep," Neil acknowledged. "I just wanted to finish grading these tests. There's no way I could concentrate on them at home with those two rugrats tearing up the place."

Peter gave a short laugh. The antics of Neil's two preschool boys were a ready source of amusement around the office coffee machine. Neil was at turns exasperated and completely enthralled with the pair.

Neil glanced at Peter's briefcase. "By the way you're holding that thing, you've got plenty of homework yourself. Natalie keeping your nose to the grindstone?"

Peter shook his head. "She gets the research done faster than I can use it. I should be more careful about what I wish for."

"You've met your match with that one," Neil grinned. "Better get to it or she'll have your job before long." Neil began turning in his chair, then stopped and called to Peter's retreating figure. "Hey—you still up for Friday night? Tip-off's at 8."

Peter nodded with recognition. The UW Badgers were playing at home in the Kohl Center and, while he was too damned old to stand for an entire basketball game surrounded by 7,000 screaming fans, he also refused to miss it. Any bar would do so long as there was a TV and a pool table. "Sure. We can figure out a place to meet later this week." He gave a brief wave and continued to his car, pulling his cell phone out of his pocket as he walked. He had two messages, the first from a number he didn't recognize.

"Hi, Peter," a woman's voice began. "It's Amy. It's been a while. A few of us are getting together for dinner at Maggio's and I was wondering if you'd like to join us. Friday night?" She left her number, perhaps hoping that his recent neglect was simply the result of a misplaced scrap of paper with her name on it. Peter reached his car just as the message ended. He remembered Amy, a pretty twenty-something blonde he'd met at a State Street bar a few weeks back. What he didn't remember was giving her his number. He wondered how she'd managed to track him down. *Friday.* Well, that one was easy, at least. Badgers, hands down. He briefly considered calling Amy back with his regrets but thought against it. Better to just let that one die on its own.

He recognized the second number. Tossing his briefcase into the backseat, he listened to his sister remind him of dinner on Sunday. Before she hung up, a little girl's voice shouted, "Hi, Uncle Pete!" from the background, bringing a smile to his lips.

Peter climbed behind the wheel and drove the two blocks to the campus fitness center. Taking a tired breath, he reached for his sports bag and swung out of the car. After a long day of teaching and the prospect of more work at home, he knew even the slightest hesitation would derail his workout tonight. And a hard workout was exactly what he needed if there was any chance of sleeping through the night.

***

"Hey, can you listen to this for a minute?" Peter swiveled around in his chair and faced Natalie, who sat across the office from him. He began reading aloud from the legal pad in his hands. Natalie listened closely, her expression becoming more confused as he continued. Peter finished and looked up. "What?" he said with concern.

"That doesn't make sense." Natalie walked over and took the legal pad from his grip. She scanned the page until she reached a particular paragraph.

"What do you mean it doesn't...."

"Here," Natalie pointed. She grabbed a pen from his desk and circled the offending sentence, then drew an arrow connecting it to an earlier paragraph. "Try this. It sounds better." She read the revised construction out loud and, with a look of satisfaction, handed the legal pad back to him.

Peter looked at it again and, finding no argument, shrugged. "Okay, yeah, that sounds better."

Natalie grinned and began to walk back to her desk when she glanced at her watch. "Oh, I've got to go. You don't mind if I leave a few minutes early today, do you?" Without waiting for an answer, she began slipping files and her laptop into the backpack on her desk.

"Big plans tonight?" Peter asked.

"Kind of," Natalie replied vaguely. "But don't worry. I'll have these articles summarized for you by Monday."

"That's fine. Have a good weekend."

"You too," she responded, grabbing her coat and heading out the door with uncharacteristic haste.

Peter wondered about her evening plans, but only briefly. He had plans of his own—Neil and the Badgers were awaiting him at Flannery's in a few short hours. Besides, he had learned early not to interest himself in the social life of his graduate assistants. 'Keep it professional' was his personal mantra—no sense in wrecking a good working relationship over misunderstandings and drama.

Especially with this one, the first decent assistant he'd had in years.

CHAPTER 2

The sky was in its final transition of the day—a deep, charcoal blue—when Natalie and her roommate pulled into one of the last spots left in the parking lot. They sprinted toward the main entrance of Flannery's, their hair blown by the wintry gusts, and yanked open the door. While outside temperatures had plummeted into the teens, inside was decidedly warmer, owing in part to all the bodies assembled there for happy hour. Surveying the room, Natalie spotted the faces of their friends who had arrived early and taken possession of one of the corner booths. She waved and alerted Gina, who continued to look around the room, then headed in their direction with a bounce in her step.

"Happy Birthday!" two of them cried in unison, sliding to the edge of the booth. Natalie and Gina unpeeled the layers that protected them—scarf, gloves, coats—and sank down onto the cushioned bench.

"Waiter!" called Theresa. "We need some drinks!"

Gina glanced at the empty beer bottles scattered across the table. "Been here awhile?"

Theresa just smirked. "It was the only way we could keep the booth."

"Now, you two need to catch up," Molly added, holding up her bottle.

Eventually, a fresh batch of drinks was ordered. Natalie, universally acknowledged as the weakest drinker of the group, sipped her first beer.

Gina watched her with a knowing smile. "Girl, we'd better order you some food or you're going to be under the table in less than an hour." Without waiting for an answer, she popped out of the booth and retrieved a menu.

"Anything," Natalie said when the waiter arrived with yet another round. "Just fast," she added. "These girls are out for blood." The waiter gave a bewildered look to Gina, who supplied him with an order of chicken wings, bread sticks, and potato skins. "That should coat your stomach for a few hours, at least," she declared.

The music seemed to get louder as the hour wore on, compensating for the general noisiness in the bar. Though not especially large, the dance floor was crammed with students dancing to the latest pop and rap hits. Natalie, well into her second beer and awaiting the arrival of her appetizers, stood up with resolve and asked who would dance with her. Three friends sprang up and half-led, half-pulled her toward the pulsing crowd.

***

Peter yanked open the door to Flannery's with difficulty. The vast difference in temperatures created a vacuum-like seal between the entrance and the room inside. Walking in, he was struck by the sheer wall of noise, heat, and light. He cringed at the mass of bodies moving on the dance floor and, head bent down against the cacophony, made his way to the bar that lined the far wall. Neil was waiting for him, beer in hand, prepared for Peter's reaction.

"Christ, Neil—what were we thinking?" Peter muttered as he sat down on the stool beside his friend. "I came here once when I first moved here and never came back. Now I remember why."

Neil nodded. "It's pretty packed tonight. Students just came back from break and don't have too much to do yet at school. Perfect time to go out, I guess."

"How the hell are we going to hear the game with this *music*?" Peter gestured as he said the word, implying that it sounded like anything but.

"There's another room in the back. Pool tables, a TV. It's a lot quieter in there. But no bar, so we'll have to bring the drinks in from here."

"I'm fine with that," Peter said in relief, already dismounting his stool. As Neil ordered a pitcher of beer, Peter absently scanned the crowd, many of whom were moving onto the dance floor for a new song that had just begun. The bass and percussion were so overpowering he could barely hear the melody of the song—if there was one, he thought with disapproval. And the words might as well have been in another language from what he could understand. Wishing for some classic country, Peter was beginning to feel decidedly ancient when he spied a familiar face.

Ten steps away, surrounded by at least thirty other dancers, was Natalie, looking like he had never seen her and dancing as if she were the only one in the room.

He couldn't help staring. Natalie twisted and turned to the music in a way that was both playful and seductive, her arms held out above her head in abandon as she let them sway along with the rest of her body. Her eyes—at times staring off into space, at others, completely engaged with the person before her—never sensed that she was being watched from the bar. Even if she had, Peter suspected that she wouldn't have cared. At that moment, it seemed her only interest was feeling the music and moving in sync with it. In all the months they had worked together, Peter had never seen this side of her.

"Hey, is that Natalie?" Neil startled him back to reality as he returned with the pitcher. "She cleans up nice, doesn't she?" Neil grinned, glancing at her ever-so-slightly tighter shirt and jeans and the absence of the hair clip that she wore at the office. Tonight, her long auburn hair tumbled down her back giving her a gypsy-like appearance. Turning to Peter, he saw that his friend had noticed the same thing; in fact, he seemed captivated by it.

"Whoa, Buddy," he joked. "She's off limits." Hands filled with pitcher and mugs, Neil nudged Peter with his shoulder as he proceeded toward the back room. "Come on, the game's about to start."

Peter accepted the nudge without complaint and, after a final glance at the dance floor, followed his friend into the back room. Illuminated by hanging lamps positioned above each of the two pool tables, the room was dimmer—and considerably quieter—than the one they'd just escaped.

Neil switched the corner TV to the Badgers game while Peter racked the pool balls. Then they filled their glasses, awaited tip-off, and began to play. The noise next door was audible, but tolerable. *It might turn out to be a good night after all*, Peter thought.

***

Natalie sat down in the booth with an exhausted grin. She knew the alcohol had kicked in but experienced little of her earlier concern over how she would feel in the morning. On the contrary—she was having the time of her life, dancing like she hadn't in months and feeling downright sexy in the new top she had bought for the occasion. Not bad for a brand new 25-year-old.

Her friends had all migrated to the dance floor, other tables, or parts unknown, so Natalie had the booth to herself for the time being. She sat back luxuriously and stretched her legs until they reached the bench on the other side. Nibbling the last potato skin on the plate, she turned her attention to the dance floor. One young man, with whom she had danced several times that evening, gestured for her to join him, but Natalie shook her head. At that moment, all she craved were a few moments of relative peace and the rest of that potato skin.

Gina walked up and began reaching behind Natalie for her purse. "Having fun?"

"Oh, yeah." Natalie grinned. "Best birthday ever."

"Glad to hear it." Gina retrieved her purse after a few sharp yanks and sat down. "Now, I have to go to work. Jessi is going to take you home tonight, okay? Don't forget."

"Jessi's taking me home. Right."

"Have a great time and slow down on the drinks. I'll see you tomorrow."

"Okay," Natalie nodded, a bit more emphatically than she had intended. It gave her a bobble-head kind of look.

Gina noticed, but only smiled. She already could predict the shape her roommate would be in by the time she saw her tomorrow morning after her shift. Then again, it was high time Natalie got out and had fun with the girls. Between school and work, they rarely saw her anymore. Gina gave her friend a final hug and climbed out of the booth.

Natalie surveyed the crowd around her, trying to locate her friends. There was Jessi—her ride, she dutifully reminded herself—dancing with the same guy she had been seen with earlier. Theresa and Kim were heading toward the bathroom, clearly enjoying the glances being thrown their way by the collection of unattached guys lining the hallway. Where was Molly? She scanned the room again but didn't see her. Oh, there by the bar. Molly was laughing at something the bartender was telling her as he deftly mixed a drink.

A glass of water wouldn't be a bad idea at this point, Natalie decided. She slipped out of the booth and headed up to the bar while Molly still had the bartender's attention. However, getting there was tougher than she had expected. A crowd of new arrivals blocked her way as they stood removing their coats and looking for available tables. Natalie found herself at a standstill as the newcomers fanned out in different directions. Spying an opening, she plunged through, expecting to reach the bar at the other side, but instead ran headfirst into a wall—rather, a human wall.

"Hey! Watch where you're going--" she scolded, attempting to right herself, but finding it impossible without holding onto the offending body which had knocked her backwards in the first place. Two hands shot out and steadied her, all the while holding an empty pitcher. Looking up in aggravation, she was stunned at the familiar face staring back.

"Professor!" Natalie's scowl transformed into a bright grin. A slow smile replaced Peter's equally annoyed expression.

"Hello there," he said. His hands lingered at her side for a final moment to ensure she stayed upright. "What's the rush?"

"I have to get to the bar," she said. Then, seeing his uplifted eyebrows, she added, "To get water. I wasn't expecting a traffic jam, though."

Peter gave a short laugh as he took her hand. "Hang on. I'll get you through."

Together they wove through the mass of bodies until they reached the bar. Natalie hopped up onto a recently vacated stool while Peter signaled the bartender for another pitcher.

"So, what's the occasion? Or is this how you normally spend your Friday nights?"

Natalie sat up tall. "It's my birthday."

"Well, happy birthday." Peter gave an exaggerated bow. "How old are you, anyway?"

"25."

"Wow, a grown up," he replied with amusement.

"You betcha." There was obvious pleasure in her smile.

A fresh pitcher was placed before them, and Peter ordered a water before the bartender slipped away. As it arrived, so did three of Natalie's friends.

"Nat!" Kim called, grabbing her friend by the arm and nearly yanking her off the stool. "Where have you *been*? Molly just got another round for us!"

Natalie took the glass of water Peter offered her and gave a melodramatic sigh. "Back to work." She hopped off her stool.

"Keep your wits about you, Birthday Girl."

With the help of her three equally inebriated friends, Natalie was whisked away.

***

Peter and Neil wrapped up their pool game just as the Badgers game was ending.

"I'm taking off," Neil said. "Peg will be wondering what happened to me if I don't get home soon."

Peter didn't need much convincing. "I'm right behind you," he answered.

The men left the quiet confines of the back room for the clamor of the main bar. Peter scanned the dance floor for Natalie but didn't find her there.

Neil followed his gaze and pointed to a girl in the corner booth, alone and sound asleep. "Is that who you're looking for?"

Peter gave a half laugh. "I'd better make sure she's taken care of. See you later, Neil. Say hi to Peg."

"Will do. Have a good weekend."

Peter headed for the booth where Natalie sat, her body upright against the cushions, her head listing to the side. She stirred as he sat down, regarding him sleepily. "Hey, Professor."

"Hi. You look a little tired. Where are your friends?"

"Everyone else left. Jessi's my ride home." Natalie sat up straighter, craning her neck to locate her friend. She pointed in the direction of a tall brunette tightly entwined with her new love interest on the dance floor. "But she's kind of busy right now."

Peter took her by the hand. "Come on," he said. "I'll give you a lift home."

"Oh no, I don't want to bother you," Natalie protested, all the while allowing him to ease her out of the booth.

"It's no bother," Peter reassured her. "Why don't we go tell Jessi that you have another ride?"

With Peter's arm beneath hers, Natalie made her way to the edge of the dance floor. From there she went on alone, hugging herself tightly to protect against flailing limbs until she reached Jessi. Tapping hard on the girl's shoulder, Natalie got her attention. Jessi seemed pleased at the prospect of more time with her new friend. Still, she marched over to the sidelines to see for herself whether this strange man was trustworthy enough to take her friend home.

"I'm her boss," Peter patiently responded to the girl's clumsy attempts at interrogation. "You have nothing to worry about."

Jessi turned to Natalie for confirmation but received only a sleepy nod of agreement.

"Okay," Jessi answered skeptically. "But I'm calling you in the morning." She directed her words at Natalie, who by this time was beginning to fall asleep again, and then at Professor Spencer. "No funny business."

"Absolutely no funny business," Peter answered with mock severity.

And then they left. Peter navigated the noisy crowd, his eyes trained toward the door while Natalie leaned on his arm, completely unaware that she was the object of envy for more than a few unattached women that night.

***

Natalie rested her head on the seat as Peter drove. He glanced over at her frequently. In fact, he found it hard to look away from her at all. Her half-closed eyes, dark wisps of hair falling across her face, and arms clasped around her made Natalie appear far younger than her 25 years. He sat up in his seat and shook his head, as if to rid himself of a ridiculous thought. This was Natalie, he reminded himself with irritation, the student who assisted him on weekday afternoons. Nothing more.

It had been six months since Natalie first knocked on his door. There were other applicants for the assistantship, most with far more experience. However, there was an earnestness about this girl that singled her out from the pack. A returning graduate student on partial scholarship, Natalie made it clear that she wanted this job more than anything—a flattering prospect for the professor in a position to offer it. Ten minutes into their interview, Peter made his choice.

It turned out to be a smart decision. Natalie was hardworking and conscientious, and, given the rave reviews from students in her study sessions, she was turning out to be a gifted teacher as well.

However, tonight Peter saw a side of Natalie which he'd never known existed—a playful, spontaneous side completely at odds with the professional demeanor she showed at the office. And she was *beautiful*, a fact that had somehow managed to escape him in all the hours they had spent together. Considering his natural abilities in not only spotting a beautiful woman, but landing one as well, Peter was surprised at how this girl had slipped under his radar for so long.

Until tonight. Despite the noise and crowds, Peter had found himself returning to the main room more often than he had any reason to. Sometimes he spotted her in a crowd of girls singing along with the lyrics. At other times she was dancing in the arms of some random guy, oblivious to the glances cast her way. Watching her gave Peter a guilty twinge, though for the life of him he wasn't sure why he should feel guilty for the simple act of watching her.

Which he was doing again.

Peter pried his attention from Natalie just in time to pull onto her street, slowing down to scan the addresses on each house. He found the number she'd mumbled to him before falling asleep and pulled into the driveway.

As with many of the houses in this neighborhood, Natalie's home had a distinct student-renter appearance about it—small, shabby, and bare of the typical clutter that characterized more permanent households such as lawn furniture, flowerpots and the like. A full front porch—for which Madison was known—opened out to a small front yard.

Gazing at the sleeping figure beside him, he gently squeezed her shoulder. Natalie's eyes fluttered open, visibly disoriented.

She sat up abruptly. "I... are we there already?"

"Hold on—I'll get the door."

Natalie began to protest, but he slammed his door before she could utter the words. In a moment, he had circled around and was helping her from the car.

"God, I'm a lightweight," she muttered.

Peter smirked, guiding her up the stairs to her porch.

Natalie searched her purse for her key ring, which turned up after only a few moments. However, unlocking the door wasn't as easy. She fumbled with the keys, first missing the lock entirely and then inserting the key upside down. After watching her frustrated attempts, Peter took the keys from her and opened the lock himself.

"Thanks, I'll be okay now." Natalie began to enter the house, but her foot caught on the step, and she lurched forward.

He grabbed her just in time. "Why don't I just walk you to your room."

Natalie exhaled in defeat. "Last door on the left."

They moved down the hall in tandem–Peter's arm wrapped around her waist, Natalie's head resting on his shoulder. By the time they reached the end of the hall, she was dozing off again.

"All right, sleepyhead, we're here." Peter opened the door to her room and turned on the light. He steered Natalie toward the bed and sat her down, where she slumped sideways onto the pillows. With an exasperated breath, Peter pulled off her shoes one by one, lifting her legs onto the bed. He unfolded a blanket lying nearby and covered her with it.

And then he just stood there.

The room was small and cramped. A wicker chair sat in one corner, a colorful afghan draped across its back. Beside the bed was a small desk—cluttered with books and framed photographs. Stealing one last glimpse of Natalie before leaving, Peter found, to his guilty surprise, that her eyes were open once again. She was watching him with a sleepy, curious expression.

"You know, in all those years that I had a crush on you, I never dreamed one day you'd be tucking me into bed."

Peter cleared his throat. "Well, don't let it get around," he replied, a gruff edge to his voice. "I'm not in the habit of doing this for my assistants." He turned toward the door.

"Wait," Natalie said, all traces of humor gone from her voice. "Don't go." She held her hand out to him.

Peter hesitated in the doorway and then—inexplicably—was drawn back to the sleepy figure. He took her hand and placed it back on the bed. "That wouldn't be a good idea."

"Why?"

Peter stood at the edge of the bed. "If the circumstances were different, I'd be in there already. But they're not." Impulsively, he bent to kiss her on the forehead, but as he did so, she tilted her head upward and met his mouth directly. Before he knew it, he was returning her kiss, his momentary surprise barely registering before it evaporated into a haze of new sensations.

A sigh, almost imperceptible, escaped from Natalie's mouth and Peter pulled away. Natalie's eyes fluttered open, a faint smile touching her lips.

"Your eyes are brown. I always wondered about that."

It was just the distraction he needed. Peter straightened and began to back away.

"Get some sleep," he said. Without a backward glance, he left.

***

On Monday, Natalie knocked on the office door.

"Come in," Peter's muffled voice replied.

She opened the door tentatively. "Hi," she greeted him, trying without success to wipe the look of embarrassment from her face.

"Good afternoon." He glanced at her a moment longer before returning to his papers.

Natalie entered the room and sat down in the chair beside his desk. "Professor Spencer, I...." She stopped, feeling ridiculous, but then realized she had already passed the point of no return. "I think I owe you an apology for the other night."

Peter swiveled his chair around, giving her his full attention. The expression on his face was a disconcerting mix of seriousness and amusement. "Oh?"

She took a deep breath and plunged ahead. "Actually, I don't remember much of what happened, but I'm afraid I may have acted inappropriately."

Peter crossed his arms over his chest. He was enjoying this. "But you're not sure."

"Well, no."

"So, what *do* you remember?"

Natalie shifted in her seat. "I remember you brought me home. And I remember you were in my room. Beyond that, not much."

Peter rocked back in his chair and tapped his fingers together, smiling all the while.

"That's all?"

"Oh, come *on*," Natalie became exasperated. "You know what happened. Put me out of my misery, will you?"

Peter grinned and sat up, turning again to the papers on his desk. "No apologies necessary, Natalie. Nothing happened."

She let out a sigh of relief. "Oh, thank goodness." She began to rise from the chair.

"Except for the kiss." Peter's face was still turned to his work. "But we'll just forget about that."

"The kiss?" Natalie repeated, sitting back down. "We kissed?"

"Well actually, you kissed me. You forgot that, too?" Peter turned and asked with mock surprise. "I'm not sure if I should be offended by that or not."

Natalie's hand covered her face, a hot blush spreading across her cheeks. "Oh God, I'm sorry," she began. "I…I obviously didn't know what I was doing…."

Peter laughed with obvious satisfaction, waving his hand dismissively. "Don't worry about it. Just forget it happened.

Now, where are the summaries on those articles you were going to give me?"

After a moment's hesitation, Natalie reached into her backpack and retrieved the work she had managed to complete—hangover be damned—with what was left of her weekend.

That night was never mentioned again, leaving Natalie with the vague suspicion that nothing had happened at all. Peter had brought her home—that much she knew. But his insinuation that she had kissed him? Impossible—the mere thought of it still made her cheeks burn with embarrassment. No, that was likely a practical joke to put her in her place—which wouldn't have surprised her in the least, given Dr. Spencer's delight in keeping the upper hand. Natalie quickly put it out of her mind and, for the rest of the semester, the two worked together as if that night had never happened.

Chapter 3

Friday was shaping up to be a spectacular autumn day. In the space of hours, maples and oaks exploded into brilliant hues of reds and golds, their leaves cascading across campus on gentle gusts of wind. The sun, less intense than the summer months, still radiated a gentle warmth. And the smell, smoky and damp, reminded Natalie of bonfires and chills to come.

She watched the spectacle play out in full technicolor from the large outdoor terrace behind Memorial Union. Lake Mendota shimmered in the sunlight, casting rainbow-hued prisms off the brightly painted wrought-iron chairs. The Terrace was one of the places that had drawn her back to UW. It brimmed with the constant hum of life: students at rest and at work at the outdoor tables, boaters tossed about on the lake in everything from canoes to double-masted sailboats, families and sightseers out for the day.

She spotted Andrew emerging through the exit, his tray laden with selections from the cafeteria. He squinted in the bright light, not seeing her. Natalie waved, then turned to make room for him.

Natalie's social life had taken a pleasant turn just before summer break. Andrew Parker, a graduate student in the Sociology Department, first noticed her during their frequent visits to the library. After exchanging glances, then smiles, then brief conversations over the copy machine, Andrew asked her to lunch. That she was two years older didn't seem to bother him in the slightest.

The relationship resumed after their return to school in August. Natalie enjoyed Andrew's company and breezy sense of humor and, while he wasn't *the one* as she and her best friend used to describe with dreamy-eyed romanticism, he was fun to be around.

The pair ate their lunch while Andrew described the research paper that had been consuming most of his free time lately. Less than an hour later, both food and conversation exhausted, they gathered their backpacks and rose from the table.

Natalie gave one final glance at the water. The early autumn colors bounced off the waves that rolled into shore. Gulls and ospreys flew past, framed by the foliage surrounding the lake.

It was time to work with Professor Spencer, one of the most enjoyable parts of her day. Yet, in the presence of such beauty, Natalie found it hard to walk away.

***

Peter watched Natalie get up from her desk and walk to the window, sighing as she watched the scenes unfold outside.

"What?" he asked.

"What?" Natalie turned around in surprise.

"That's the third time you've been at that window in the last hour. What's going on out there?"

Natalie gave a sheepish smile. "Nothing—just admiring the view." She returned to her desk. Folders lay strewn across the expanse of wood, all filled with journal articles that would need to be read and summarized by Monday.

Peter glanced at her and then turned back to his own work, though not for long. The seed planted, he was suddenly as distracted as she. Looking up, he could see the shafts of sunlight, the cascade of colorful leaves past the window's borders. It was ludicrous to waste a day this fine inside. He slapped his hand against the desk, causing Natalie's head to snap up in surprise.

"Come on," he said, pushing up and out of his chair. "Let's get out of here."

Natalie shot him a puzzled glance. "What…where?"

"There is no reason we should be stuck inside on one of the last decent days of the year. Get your stuff. We're taking a field trip."

For a moment, Natalie just stared at him, too startled by his spontaneous invitation to say anything.

"Well?" Professor Spencer stood in front of her desk. He grabbed a few of the files stacked there and handed them to her. "What are you waiting for?"

She stood up with a laugh and began collecting her jacket and belongings. Then, as he held the door for her, she hurried through.

They descended the stairs leading to the faculty parking lot. Ahead of them were dozens of cars, most only a few seconds' walk to the building's entrance.

"Oh, to have a parking spot this close," Natalie said wistfully.

Peter glanced over at her. "You bike to school, don't you?" He occasionally caught glimpses of her as she rode around campus, strands of hair escaping from her bike helmet, a look of complete freedom on her face.

"Usually, except when I'm running late, or have a lot to carry. Problem is, I never got around to getting a parking pass, so I've been relying on two-hour parking spots and hope no one notices when I'm there half the day."

He laughed. "I did the same thing when I was in school. By the end of the semester, my glove compartment was stuffed with parking tickets."

Peter reached the car first and opened her door, taking the backpack from her shoulder as she loaded the rest of her belongings into the car. He waited for her to sit down before returning the bag to her, which she accepted self-consciously.

Sliding into his own seat, Peter glanced over as Natalie buckled her seat belt. For a moment, her face changed, as if lost in thought. A faint smile touched her lips.

Curious, but none the wiser, Peter steered the car onto the main road. In a matter of minutes, the surrounding scenery transformed from bustling college town to sedate, cookie-cutter neighborhoods to pristine countryside—an endless sweep of cornfields dotted by occasional farm buildings and grazing livestock. As they drove, colors flashed by the window: faded greens and yellows of over-ripening crops in the fields, leaves of burnt orange and vermillion dotting the side of the road, pillowy white clouds framed by brilliant blue sky.

Twenty minutes later, Peter pulled onto a gravel road and parked. From its appearance, it hadn't seen much traffic in quite some time. Peter wasn't surprised. He hadn't visited this spot for years, certainly not since he'd returned to Madison.

The road was flanked by acres of corn on one side and an expanse of shade trees on the other. Weeds poked through the gravel at regular intervals. It all came back to him with such clarity, it felt like yesterday.

With an excited grin, Peter stepped out of the car. He peered through the open door at Natalie, who wore a perplexed expression on her face.

"Come on. I want to show you something."

Peter half-jogged down the path, searching for the opening in the woods.

"Where are you going?" Natalie called after him.

Peter motioned her along. "It's down here." Natalie caught up just in time to watch him disappear again through a space in the trees. Spotting the path, she plunged through and hurried after him.

It was like being in a different world. As they hiked, the woods thinned, giving way to patches of reeds and saplings. Peter suddenly stopped and stepped aside, watching for his companion's reaction to the oasis before her.

Natalie gave a small gasp.

A narrow creek, its bank lined by cattails and tall grasses, wound slowly past them. Mature trees in full color and sprays of wildflowers of every hue and scent imaginable dotted the landscape.

Peter watched her take it all in. "So?"

Her surprise was evident. "It's beautiful. How on earth did you find this place?"

Off to the side stood a weathered picnic table that had seen better days. Peter walked past her and sat down, leaning back on outstretched arms. "I grew up here."

Natalie hesitated, narrowing her eyes. "You're from Madison?"

"Just down the road. My family still owns the farm where I grew up."

"You're a farm boy? How is that possible?"

"Well, I had to grow up somewhere, didn't I?"

"I suppose," she conceded. "You just don't seem like the type…."

"To grow up on a farm?" Peter countered. "Isn't that where you grew up?"

"Well yes, but I'm nothing like *you*."

"Oh?" Peter's expression was a mixture of pique and amusement. "So, what *am* I like?"

Natalie paused, considering her response. "You're just very self-assured," she began. "You have this way of making people feel like they haven't experienced half of what you have."

He nodded. "Some would call that arrogant."

Natalie gave a neutral smile, saying nothing. Peter was well aware of his reputation among students for being stand-off-ish. He had cultivated it, appreciating the respect that came with it.

Natalie changed the subject. "So, you never left?"

"As soon as I could. I went to UW undergrad, and then UCLA for graduate school. I stayed there for almost seven years before UW offered me an assistant professorship. It was a good opportunity; plus, my family needed me closer to home."

Natalie brightened. "So, you must have just moved back when I was an undergrad."

"I've been back six years. Is that when you were in my class?"

She hesitated. "Something like that." She wandered over to a stand of wildflowers and began picking a handful.

Peter noticed her shift in manner, realizing too late the reason behind her look of disappointment. Two hundred underclassmen each semester, twelve semesters; that meant 2,400 faces since his return to Madison. Surely she could understand that he wouldn't remember her. And yet, right now he wished he could picture her as she was then.

He noticed the flowers she had selected, daisy-shaped with vivid orange and red hues. "Those are Indian blanket flowers," he said.

She nodded. "They're one of my favorites."

"There's an old Native American tale about them. Have you heard it?" She shook her head.

"One autumn, when the men of the village had gone off to battle, the wife of one warrior began weaving a blanket in the hope of giving it to her husband if he returned safely. She worked on the blanket day and night using only the brightest red, gold, and brown fibers. One night, while playing in the forest, their daughter got lost. The little girl, cold and scared, prayed to the Great Spirit for her mother's blanket to keep her warm. The next morning, they found her safe and sound and still covered by the thousands of blanket flowers that the Great Spirit had covered her with the night before."

Natalie smiled in approval. "That's nice. I'll remember that."

"Come on," he said, waving his hand. "The path continues for another couple of miles. It's a good hike." He walked a few steps toward a path that was barely distinguishable from the woods around it, except for the relative absence of branches and brush underfoot.

Natalie hesitated, watching him retreat from her. She took one more backward glance and, in doing so, spotted a weathered elm, its thick bark scarred with what looked like two sets of initials. She reached out and touched the carvings, EW + FS, outlined in a heart. They had clearly been there for some time, their edges softened as the tree continued to grow and swell around them.

Peter reappeared from the bushes, beckoning again. This time, Natalie ran to catch up, a spray of blanket flowers still clutched in her grasp, the initials already fading from memory.

***

The sun had begun its gradual descent as they made their way back down the path. Natalie was the first to reach the picnic table. She sank down onto the bench with a feeling of pleasant exhaustion. Peter sat down beside her, exhaling with satisfaction.

"This was an unexpectedly good day."

Natalie smiled. "It was." She gazed up at the sky, its blue vibrance diminishing with each passing minute.

Her phone's tinny ringtone jarred them from their shared silence. Fumbling for it in her pocket, Natalie cursed herself for not remembering to turn it off. Andrew's name appeared on the caller ID. "Excuse me," she mumbled, getting up from the picnic table.

"Hi." Natalie answered, all too aware of Peter's attention on her.

"I just finished the first draft of my research paper! How about helping me celebrate? God, I could use a beer." Andrew's voice was cheerful.

"Hey, that's great," Natalie responded. She knew how hard he had been working on it and wished she could muster up a bit more enthusiasm for his sake. "It's just that now's not a good time. I'm working with Professor Spencer. We still have a lot to do. Raincheck?"

Peter continued to watch her, a slight smile beginning at her obvious bending of the truth. She turned her back to him.

Andrew sounded disappointed, but not overly so. "Well, maybe the guys won't mind celebrating a little. If you finish up early, give me a call and we'll meet up. Okay?"

"I'll do that. Have fun." Natalie hung up and slipped the phone back into her pocket.

"So, we still have a lot to do?" Peter asked.

Natalie gave an embarrassed grin and sat back down on the bench. "I just wasn't up for a big night out. I hope you don't mind being my excuse."

"Not at all." Peter gave her a sideways glance. "So, was that your boyfriend?"

Natalie shifted awkwardly. "A friend."

"I take it you two aren't very serious."

"Not really."

"Why not?"

She shrugged. "I just don't feel that way about him, I guess."

Peter watched her for a moment longer and then shifted his attention to the sky. Natalie followed his gaze, marveling at how the sun could produce such exquisite colors in its final moments. Yet, it was Peter who ultimately proved more captivating to her, his serene expression fixed on something that she couldn't identify.

"You seem a million miles away," she observed.

"I was just thinking about the night that I brought you home."

Natalie said nothing, suddenly at a loss for words.

Peter continued, his focus still on the darkening sky. "I wondered what it would be like if we tried that kiss again." He peered over at her, a half-smile on his lips. "You know…now that you're sober."

So, they had kissed after all. She shifted nervously. "You said to just forget about that."

"Not a hard thing for you to do, since you never remembered it in the first place."

Perhaps it was the expression on his face—an almost puzzled amazement that she could have ever forgotten such an encounter—that made Natalie suddenly laugh out loud. "That bothers you," she challenged. "That I don't remember kissing you."

"If you weren't such a lightweight, you would have remembered," Peter retorted. "*Trust* me."

"My apologies, Professor." Natalie gave him an understanding nod. "I'm sure it was a very nice kiss."

Peter caught the sarcasm and straightened, eyebrows raised. "Seriously?"

Spurred on by Natalie's laughter, he shifted closer to her, causing her to shift farther away. Except that the edge of the picnic table was closer than she remembered and she began to lose her balance, arms flailing. Peter encircled her waist and pulled her closer. For a charged moment they locked eyes, silently searching for a sign of what should happen next. She was still smiling when his mouth found hers.

After a few moments, he relaxed his hold, their faces still touching. "Do you think you'll remember that one?" he whispered.

Natalie felt dizzy with sensation. "I'm not sure," she breathed. "Better try again."

***

The sky had transformed from burnt orange to darkening blue when Natalie raised her head and broke the kiss. She sat back on the bench and blinked her eyes hard, attempting to clear the fog in her head.

Peter appeared equally affected. He sat for a moment before standing up.

"Come on," he said, clearing his voice. "We should go." He offered her his hand.

Natalie accepted his help up. The feeling of his hand around hers—strong and possessing—was a new and welcome sensation. He continued to hold her hand as they walked.

"Where are we going?"

"I'm driving you home."

Natalie stopped. Peter felt the tug and turned around. She looked at him squarely, her back stiff as if bracing for an argument. "No, you're not."

"What?"

There was no mistaking the resolve on her face. "You heard me."

He hesitated. "Are you sure?"

Natalie nodded wordlessly.

"Okay. Let's go then." Hands still joined, they walked silently back to the car.

Chapter 4

The drive to Peter's house was made in silence, each occupant keenly aware that the wrong words might derail their tenuous plans. Peter detoured from the road they had taken from town earlier, this time turning onto a gravel road dotted with small farms. To Natalie's surprise, he pulled into a driveway along this road.

As the car rolled to a stop, she looked around in curiosity, eventually stepping out from the car to continue her examination. Before her stood a small ranch-style home, off-white in color with a wide expanse of land on all sides. The only visible neighbors were at least a half mile down the road and, despite the fading light, there appeared to be the remnants of a garden in the backyard. It resembled the other farmhouses she had seen during their ride together that afternoon, yet it was the ordinariness that surprised her most. Before today, she had imagined Peter driving home to a condo near the school, the quintessential "bachelor pad"—certainly not this quaint, faded dwelling on the edge of town.

They ascended the weathered concrete steps leading up to the front porch, flanked by a black wrought-iron railing. Peter unlocked the door and motioned for her to enter. Natalie stepped into the foyer, stopping to remove her coat. It was the smell of the house that first struck her—the slightly musty scent of a house that has been alive much longer than its inhabitants. It was a scent that reminded her of the countless family meals, children, and memories that had existed there before. In fact, very much like the home where she grew up.

As Natalie glanced around, she noticed an arrangement of framed photographs lining the walls. Under different circumstances, she would have eagerly studied the images, enjoying the connection it gave her to the person who had placed them there. Yet, all it took was the sound of Peter's footsteps behind her, a glimpse of his outstretched hands ready to take her coat, and her concentration was shattered for everything but the man who stood inches away.

Peter cleared his throat, his voice hesitant. "Can I…offer you a drink? A glass of wine?"

Natalie shook her head, her eyes never leaving him. Without a word, she circled her arms around his neck and continued the embrace they had started at the creek. Peter needed no further invitation. He returned her kiss, gently at first, and then more demanding, until Natalie felt herself being backed against the wall. An involuntary groan escaped her mouth from the impact. Peter whispered an apology against her lips, smiling at Natalie's breathless laughter.

Natalie untucked his shirt, reaching inside to touch his bare back, smooth and muscled. The sheer audacity of touching him flooded over her. *How could she be doing this?* Peter continued his explorations, pulling her shirt up and over her head before she had time to react. He bent to kiss her neck, her shoulders, her breasts, his beard tickling her skin and sending her senses reeling. A growing feeling of weakness radiated down her legs, leaving her wobbly.

"I need to sit down," she whispered.

Peter lifted Natalie into his arms and carried her into his room. As he laid her down on the bed, Natalie held tight, pulling him down with her. Peter's hands reached up and framed her face, his fingers fanning out through her hair until her hair clip stopped them. Loathe to stop his progress, Natalie reached back and deftly released her hair with a snap. Peter resumed his explorations, kissing her deeply as his hands continued beyond her hair.

In time, Peter sat up and began to undress, his fingers clumsy at the buttons. Natalie watched his progress, her heart beating with breathless anticipation. With a muttered curse, the final intractable button released with a yank, and the shirt fell onto the floor. Peter slid smoothly into her waiting arms, covering her bareness with his own.

*****

Natalie awoke with a start. Rising onto her elbows, she glanced around. The darkened setting gave her few clues at first, but as her eyes adjusted to the darkness, she began to recognize the outlines of the room. The events of the evening came flooding back.

She turned to the sleeping form beside her. Peter lay peacefully, arm thrown across his chest, his head and body turned toward hers. He was even more handsome in sleep, if that was possible. The serious expression he often wore in public was gone, replaced with a softer, almost boyish look.

Natalie closed her eyes in silent amazement. What had she been thinking? She had never been one to sleep around. But here she was, lying next to someone whose entire reputation was built on casual affairs. There was no reason to think she would fare any better than his many other diversions. Yet strangely, she felt little shame in being here.

Natalie listened to his deep, rhythmic breathing, letting her gaze linger on him a few moments longer before turning her attention to the clock that sat on his nightstand. *5:29.*

Despite having been up half the night, Natalie felt wide awake. She swung her legs to the side of the bed and slid to the floor. She searched the dark room for her clothing but found little except for a button-down shirt which obviously belonged to Peter. She pressed her face against it, breathing in the scent he had left behind.

Natalie slipped the shirt on, pausing to fold back the sleeves before setting off in search of the kitchen. Her body was beginning to feel stiff in places she had forgotten she had. Peter was exactly the kind of lover she had imagined him to be—bold, experienced, and very, very thorough. It had been an amazing night.

The refrigerator contained little in the way of food, but luckily was stocked with water bottles. Gratefully, she swallowed the cold fluid, which stung and shocked on the way down. Still holding the half-empty bottle, she closed the refrigerator door and padded toward the living room. On her way, she passed the hallway and the photographs she remembered seeing there. She changed course and turned on the light so she could examine them more closely.

The photographs had been taken in various places around the country: a two-lane highway set deep into the surrounding forest, sunlight shimmering through the branches; a prairie at sunset, its tall stands of goldenrod backlit by a sky as vivid as a firestorm; several ramshackle barns and small-town main streets. Some photographs contained people, too, although it was impossible to know if they were known to the photographer or simply locals from the areas through which he was passing. It occurred to Natalie that they must be a record of some long-ago road trip. And then she found one photo with Peter in it. He was considerably younger, probably in his early twenties, and he stood with his arms around two older men in front of a general store. Natalie stared at the photo, unable to tear her eyes from it. He was grinning, his eyes brimming with life, his face the picture of unbridled enthusiasm.

"I was wondering where you had gone." Peter's voice broke the silence, causing her to inhale sharply in surprise. She looked up to see him standing in the bedroom doorway. Apparently, he had managed to find only his boxers before venturing out to find her.

Natalie put a calming hand to her throat. "God, you scared me."

"Sorry." Peter crossed the room, stopping when he was only inches from her. He reached out and rested his hands on her hips. He swept an appraising glance over her. "This shirt looks a lot better on you than it does on me." He slid his hands under the shirt, caressing her up and down her back.

Natalie closed her eyes, giving herself up to the sensations. Peter began a trail of kisses along her neck, enjoying the contented sounds he elicited. "What are you doing up?" he whispered, moving from one side of her neck to the other.

She paused before replying. This felt too good to interrupt. "I couldn't sleep," she finally managed.

"Not tired yet? I must have been too easy on you." His tone had a wicked quality to it.

Natalie opened her eyes, feeling curiously shy all of a sudden. "You were…*just fine*. I'm just not used to waking up in a strange bed."

Peter lightly kissed her lips. "So, I guess you don't do this every weekend?"

"*Never*," Natalie replied, embarrassment spilling across her face. "I'm never like this," she finished awkwardly.

Peter saw her expression and lifted her chin with his hand. "We didn't do anything wrong, Natalie. There's no need to be ashamed." Bending down close to her ear, he whispered, "Did you enjoy yourself?"

She blushed. "Yes."

Peter smiled and returned his attention to her neck. "So then, no regrets."

Natalie wished she shared his carefree attitude, but already the consequences of their actions weighed on her. "And Monday?" she asked.

"Monday will be like any other day," Peter responded matter-of-factly. "Nothing has to change."

Natalie was not convinced. Maybe this came more naturally to him, but how could she work side by side with him and pretend that none of this had happened? Still, she said nothing, smiling instead with a confidence that was not quite there.

"Hungry?" Peter asked.

Natalie was surprised by the gnawing sensation in her stomach. "Famished."

"What do you say we have an early breakfast?"

And just like that, Peter released her and was striding into the kitchen, opening cabinet doors and taking out bowls and coffee mugs. Natalie followed him and began taking out the few staples she could find from the refrigerator. She in his button-down shirt and he in his boxer shorts, they were the picture of domestic harmony. At least until sunrise, Natalie thought, when her Cinderella spell would be broken, and she would return to being just his assistant.

***

Natalie inserted the key and gently nudged the front door open. It was just after nine in the morning, but she hoped that Gina might still be asleep.

No such luck.

"Well, where have *you* been?" Gina greeted her with raised eyebrows. She was pouring herself a cup of coffee, still in her pajamas. "Anybody I know?"

Natalie removed her jacket and hung it up in the closet. She then dropped her purse on the counter and sank wearily onto a stool near the breakfast counter. The evening's activities were beginning to take their toll on her. Natalie briefly considered trying to conceal the whole affair, but seeing Gina's face, knew she would never be able to pull it off. She was an awful liar, and Gina knew her better than anyone. "Peter," she confessed. "Peter Spencer."

Gina's eyes narrowed in concentration, apparently trying to place the name. Then her eyes widened, and she looked at Natalie incredulously. "*Professor* Spencer?"

Natalie gave a guilty nod.

"You *spent the night* with Professor Spencer?" Gina repeated. "Natalie, have you lost your mind?"

Well, there wasn't much she could say to that. So, she just kept quiet, waiting for the horrified yet well-intentioned lecture to begin. Amazingly, though, there was only silence. It was one of the few times Natalie ever remembered Gina to be at a loss for words.

"Well, go ahead," Gina ordered, shaking her head as she poured a second cup of coffee for Natalie and settled down on the stool next to hers. "Tell me what happened."

And she did. Natalie told her about the whole magical day and night, taking care to leave out a few precious details that she alone could savor.

***

On Monday morning, Natalie rode her bike across campus and parked in front of the Psychology building. Taking more time than usual, she scaled the three flights of stairs to Peter's office. *Professor Spencer's* office, she corrected herself. And today would be like any other day.

Right.

She had mentally prepared herself all weekend long for their first meeting together. Would he say anything? Should she? No, they had agreed that nothing would change. Still, her heart beat progressively faster as she neared his office door. She knocked lightly.

"Come in."

Natalie took a deep breath and entered. There he was, sitting at his desk as always, surrounded by files and photocopies. He looked up and nodded. "Good morning, Natalie. How was your weekend?"

"Fine. I managed to catch up on a lot of work. You?"

"Busy. There are some files on your desk that I forgot to give you Friday night. Be sure to get those summaries done by Wednesday, will you?"

At the mention of Friday night, Natalie tensed. "Sure." She walked to her desk and laid her bag down.

"Oh, here's another one." Manila folder in hand, Peter reached across to give it to her, brushing her hand with his as he did so. Natalie drew her hand away sharply, reacting as if she'd touched a hot stove.

Peter studied her face. "Remember," he said, his voice low and even. "Nothing has changed."

Natalie nodded and swallowed hard. She turned her chair to face the desk and willed herself to concentrate. But every sound he made—the scratch of his pencil against his notebook, the squeak of his chair—sent her thoughts scattering. She found herself re-reading the same paragraphs over and over again.

This is ridiculous, Natalie thought with frustration. She gathered up her files and stuffed them into her bag. She had to get out of this office, or she'd never get any work done.

"I'll be at the library," she muttered. Then, without waiting for a reply, she pulled on her coat and stalked out of the office. Her breathing did not slow down until she was halfway across campus. Had she turned and looked up, she would have seen Peter watching her from the window of his office, his expression unreadable.

***

The first week was the most difficult. The effort to stay detached took much of Natalie's attention and energy, leaving precious little to get her work done. Consequently, she found herself bringing more work home each night and working late hours as she tried to keep up with her coursework. She felt tired and distracted and out-of-sorts.

As Peter assured her, nothing changed in their outward behavior toward each other. They acted as before—professor and assistant. Only Natalie's emotions betrayed the truth, though they remained invisible to everyone but herself and, occasionally, Gina.

It was Gina who sat on Natalie's bed and listened as she struggled to make sense of what had happened; Gina who listened to her frustrated, jealous rants about the steady stream of female students who visited Peter's office for every conceivable reason—except academic ones. And it was Gina who patiently agreed with Natalie that her night with Peter had just been a mistake. Everything would become easier with time, she promised.

Natalie considered resigning her position but, in the end, decided against it. She would not give up the work she loved simply because she had made an error in judgment.

In the days that followed, Natalie found that time, in fact, did heal. Her emotions became less volatile, her mind less distracted. She was able to work in the same office with him and not listen for his every move behind her. She did not flinch at every accidental touch of their hands.

For his part, Peter appeared to behave as he always did; no change in his manner or tone with her, no furtive glances in her direction. He seemed so unaffected that at times she wondered if she had dreamt the entire thing.

Perhaps that was what bothered her most—that, for Peter, their night had been so utterly forgettable.

Chapter 5

———— · ⟨⟨⟩⟩ · ————

Peter's entrance into the farmhouse was stopped short by a small body rushing into his path and grabbing his legs. He managed to maintain his grip on the grocery bag, while simultaneously keeping himself upright. He looked down and tousled the preschooler's hair.

"Did you bring something for me?" she asked with a grin.

"Amanda!" her mother scolded. "Let go of your uncle. At least give him a chance to walk in the house before you pounce on him."

The little girl released her hold and plopped to the floor with a scowl.

Peter reached into his pocket and pulled out a plastic egg-shaped container, available for the cost of a quarter from the metal vending machine outside the grocery. It would be lost before bedtime, but her shriek of joy was reward enough. She opened the egg to reveal a tiny plastic dinosaur.

"How do you feel about apple pie for dessert?" Peter asked with a wink. He raised the bag with the boxed pie, prompting Amanda to pop up. "Why don't you take this into the kitchen?"

He didn't have to ask twice. Amanda grabbed the bag and ran into the kitchen, dinosaur and egg in hand. His sister shook her head. "You shouldn't encourage her, you know. She's going to run wild when she starts kindergarten next year."

"She's my only niece," Peter declared. "I can spoil her if I want."

Dawn rolled her eyes. "Mark my words, that girl's going to be trouble and it will be all your fault."

Peter walked behind her on the way to the kitchen, squeezing his sister's shoulders. "She's going to be trouble because you're her mother. You were exactly the same way."

Dawn ignored him. "Mom's going to be a little late. She's getting her hair done in town. Why don't you grab a beer and find Tim in the barn. I think he could use your help."

Peter was already headed to the fridge. The smell of roasting chicken and boiling potatoes filled the room. He made an appreciative sound and left through the back kitchen door, searching for his brother-in-law.

Tim was under the tractor, only his legs visible, when Peter reached the barn.

"Hey," Peter said, announcing his arrival. "You alive down there?"

Tim grunted in response and emerged a few seconds later, wrench in hand. "It wouldn't start this morning."

After running through several options, Peter offered, "It might be the fuel line. Did you check for a blockage?"

"That was the next thing," Tim answered, grabbing a rag from his back pocket and wiping his face.

"Here, hand me that wrench," Peter said, lowering himself beneath the tractor and loosening the fuel lines. Nothing ran out. "See this?" he called up to Tim. "It must be blocked. Maybe we can blow it out. Where's your air compressor?"

"In the shop. I'll go grab it."

Peter checked the fuel tank and tapped the lines leading to it. Within minutes, Tim was back, air compressor in hand.

The two worked side by side for almost an hour until the blockage was released. When Tim turned the ignition, the engine started up with a roar.

Peter stood up and dusted himself off, grinning. "Didn't your old man teach you about fuel lines?"

Tim shrugged. "Probably—not that I paid any attention. I never planned on running my own farm."

"Guess Dawn changed your mind."

"Guess so." Tim shook his head, but Peter knew better. Tim was crazy about his wife and little girl. He may not have planned this life, but it suited him well.

"Boys!" Dawn's voice covered the expanse from house to barn. "Time for dinner. Get washed up."

Tim climbed down, rubbing the oil from his hands with a rag and handing it to Peter to do the same. They walked toward the house.

"So, Dawn knows this girl from church that she'd like to fix you up with." Tim raised his eyebrows, clearly uncomfortable with the task he'd been handed. "She's cute, actually. Late 20's, works at a bank in Middleton. Just moved back from Minneapolis to be near her folks."

"Why doesn't Dawn ask me herself?"

"She figured you'd turn her down."

"She'd be right."

Tim glanced his way. "So, are you seeing someone?" he asked. "Just give me a reason and I can get off your back. You know your sister."

"Yeah, I know her." Peter gave a half smile. He hesitated for a moment before answering. Fleeting images of a certain Friday swept through his mind—the hidden creek, the kiss, the hours that followed. He cleared his throat. "No, nobody at the moment."

Tim peered over at him, a skeptical expression on his face. "Just not into the commitment thing?"

"You could say that."

Tim nodded and they continued their walk in silence. As they approached the house, he glanced up. "Look, Dawn just worries about you. She said you were pretty serious about a girl once, but it didn't work out."

Peter didn't meet his gaze. "That was a long time ago. I think things are better the way they are."

Tim dropped the subject and reached for the door, holding it open for Peter who swept inside without another word. Dinner proceeded without a hitch and nothing more was said about the new girl from Minneapolis.

Chapter 6

Weeks passed and life went on. Andrew continued to call, though Natalie was so busy she barely had time to speak to him, much less see him in person. Still, after Gina's repeated urging, she agreed to accept his next invitation.

"He may not be *the one*, Natalie, but he can get you out of the house and take your mind off things—it would do you some good."

Reluctantly, Natalie made plans to have drinks with him the following evening. Andrew was to pick her up at home, but as she finished up her work, she heard a knock on the office door.

She got up to answer it, expecting another in a long line of smitten freshmen. Instead, she found Andrew leaning against the door frame.

"Hey—what are you doing here?" A quick glance at her watch told her that it was an hour before he was due to pick her up.

Andrew gave her a kiss and strolled into the office. "I got off early, so I thought I'd give you a lift home. You're almost done here, right?"

"Um…right." Natalie looked around uncomfortably. Peter was in a faculty meeting but would be returning soon. She began gathering her papers and stuffing them into her backpack. Perhaps if they left now, they could avoid him altogether.

"So how about Dawson's?" Andrew suggested, hopping onto her desk as she rushed around. "I hear there's supposed to be a good band there tonight."

"Okay," Natalie answered distractedly, "as long as we can get a table. I'd rather not stand by the bar all night. Oh, and do you have room for my bike? I rode today."

She looked up in time to see Andrew's mouth open to respond, then glance at the figure in the doorway.

"Natalie." Peter's greeting was terse.

"Oh hi, professor," she rushed. "Do you mind if I leave a little early today? I can finish these abstracts at home." She managed to cram the final handful of papers into her backpack and zip it up loudly.

"Not at all." He continued to stand in the doorway, as if waiting for an introduction.

"Um—this is my friend, Andrew Parker. Andrew, this is Professor Spencer."

Andrew took a few steps toward Peter and extended his hand in greeting. "Pleasure to meet you, professor." Peter accepted it with indifference, his gaze never leaving Natalie.

"Andrew is getting his masters in sociology," Natalie continued, grabbing her coat and tugging it on.

But Andrew was in no hurry. "My SOC 500 class was just discussing your article in *Behavioral Psychology*, Professor Spencer. Great piece. But there were a couple of points I was surprised you didn't have in your conclusion."

Peter finally turned to face him. He raised his eyebrows. "Oh?"

Natalie cringed. This was exactly what she didn't need.

Andrew, appearing to enjoy his moment in the spotlight, gave his best summary of the professor's article and then listed the ideas that he felt were missing, ideas that could have made the conclusion a stronger one. Peter listened for a few minutes, a mask of bland amusement on his face. When Andrew finished, looking quite proud of himself, Peter launched into his own series of questions, catching the student off guard.

"How would you have applied the scientific method to prove that hypothesis? And did you consider that the control group would be denied treatment that might have helped them?"

"Yes, but in the interest of science…" Andrew began.

"Oh, I see. Perhaps ethics is unnecessary when it gets in the way of true science. Or perhaps your freshman class hasn't discussed ethics yet?" This last statement was delivered dispassionately, but the anger was not lost on Natalie.

"I'm a graduate student, not a freshman," Andrew said, his breezy demeanor suddenly turning defensive.

"Well, graduate students are certainly aware of the ethical guidelines in research. Or do you simply find such rules unnecessary?"

"I didn't say that," Andrew interjected. "I just meant that sometimes the benefits gained from such a study might outweigh the consequences of withholding treatment to a chosen few."

"I see," Peter continued. *"The end justifies the means.* A compelling argument for inexperienced students. Still, take care that you don't get caught up in the thrill of discovery. Those studies often cause more harm than good due to lack of proper restraint."

"I don't think..."

Natalie took Andrew by the arm and led him toward the door. "Come on, Andrew. We'll be late."

Peter stepped out of the way, nodding to Natalie as she filed past him. "Have a good time, Natalie," he said in a low voice. Natalie didn't answer. She was far too angry to trust herself with a response.

***

"What a piece of work!" Andrew fumed. "How do you stand that guy?" They were barely out of the office when Andrew began to vent his frustration.

"I'm sorry, Andrew," Natalie responded, trying hard to conceal her own anger. "He's not the most tactful guy in the world, but I've never seen him behave that rudely before."

"Does he talk like that to you at the office? Because if he does, he should be reported." They walked to his car, which was illegally parked in front of the Psychology building.

"No, never." Natalie said in his defense. "Professor Spencer is always very professional at the office." Natalie ran over and retrieved her bicycle which was locked nearby.

"So, I'm the only one? What makes me so special?" Andrew loaded the bike into his trunk and then unlocked Natalie's door. They sat in silence for a few minutes as Andrew navigated around the students walking home from class. As they neared her house, Andrew suddenly asked, "Hey, he doesn't have a thing for you, does he?"

Natalie flinched. "Excuse me?"

Andrew noticed her reaction. "Natalie, has he tried anything with you?"

Natalie shook her head emphatically. "Of course not, Andrew. Don't be ridiculous." Natalie shifted uneasily in her seat as he pulled the car to a stop in her driveway, saying a silent prayer of thanks for the distraction. Gathering her belongings, she got out of the car and walked hurriedly up the front steps, leaving the bicycle to Andrew.

***

While Andrew watched a football game in the living room, Natalie changed her clothes and freshened up. As she walked down the hall, however, she knew she couldn't go through with the evening. She was simply too upset.

"Andrew," she put her hand to her head. "I'm so sorry. I just don't think I can go out tonight. My head is splitting."

Andrew rose from the sofa and walked over to her. "Is this about Spencer? Because if it is, you should just put that jerk out of your mind. He shouldn't ruin our night."

"I know. Honestly, I just think I'm worn out from the week. I've been putting in a lot of extra hours lately. It must be catching up with me."

Andrew shook his head in disappointment, his expression less than convinced. He gave Natalie a chaste kiss on the cheek. "Get some rest. Maybe we can try again next week."

"Okay. Thanks for understanding."

Natalie stood in the doorway and waved goodbye, watching as he began dialing numbers on his cell phone. "Hey, Greg–what's going on? You headed to Dawson's?" Natalie had no doubt that he would be able to salvage the evening.

She closed the door and sat on the couch, her feigned headache threatening to become real. Her emotions shifted from anger to confusion and then back again. What had gotten into him? Andrew's questions made her wonder about Peter's motives. Was he angry at seeing her with Andrew? If so, he had *no right*. Peter had made it clear he wasn't interested in her. She could see anyone she wished.

The more she thought about it, the harder her head throbbed and the angrier she became. Impulsively, she grabbed her purse and keys, got into her car, and headed for the outskirts of town.

***

Peter was in the kitchen when the doorbell rang. And rang again. By the third consecutive ring, he shut the refrigerator door and followed the sound to its source. He opened it in a rush, as much to silence the annoying noise as to identify the visitor behind it. Seeing the face on the other side, his eyes opened in surprise.

"Natalie? What…"

Natalie didn't let him finish his sentence. "What in the *hell* were you trying to prove with that performance today?"

Peter was taken aback. "What are you talking about?"

"That little debate with Andrew." She imitated his voice, her tone dripping with sarcasm, "'*So, has your freshman class not discussed research ethics yet?*' Or, let's see—how about, '*I suppose that argument is very compelling with inexperienced students.*' You can be a real jerk, but you outdid yourself today."

Feeling more up to speed, Peter leaned up against the doorframe, his expression changing to mild amusement. "Now, Natalie, watch your temper."

Natalie exploded. "How *dare* you behave like that to a friend of mine!"

Peter waved his hand dismissively in the air. "The kid's an idiot. Maybe he'll think twice the next time he tries to show off for his girlfriend. You can do better than him." He turned and walked back into the house, leaving Natalie fuming on the front step. She followed him inside, more than ready to continue the battle.

"So, he was right. You *are* jealous!" she yelled, slamming the door behind her.

Peter's voice dripped with contempt. "*He* was right? That moron? He couldn't reason his way out of a paper bag. If I came down on him, it's because I have no tolerance for stupidity."

Natalie followed him into the kitchen, where he opened the fridge and, this time, retrieved a beer. She reached out and snatched it from his hands.

"It's more than that," she countered. "I've seen you when you disagree with someone. This was different. This was personal."

"Maybe," he conceded, grabbing the bottle back. "But either way, I was doing you a favor. You're wasting your time with that kid."

Natalie's mouth opened in reply, then closed just as quickly. She leaned her back against the counter and crossed her arms as he took a swig of the beer. When she finally responded, her voice was controlled, her words carefully chosen.

"You listen to me. It is *my* business who I choose to see socially. You do *not* have a vote."

Peter met her gaze. His expression was unreadable, though the tilt of his head dared her to disagree. "Maybe I should."

"What?" Natalie's tone was incredulous. "What gives you the..."

"Because I *know* you," Peter countered.

Natalie laughed out loud, the sound sharp and unnatural. "Why? Because we slept together? We both know that meant nothing."

The shock of her words left him feeling backhanded. He stared at Natalie, searching for some sign that they'd been uttered in haste, without thinking. But Natalie's face remained impassive, her chin tilted up in silent defiance.

"Is that how you feel?" he managed finally. "That it meant nothing?"

"Of course," Natalie replied, a spiteful edge to her voice. She stalked out of the kitchen but stopped and turned back to face him. Peter hadn't moved from his spot. His body was tight with anger.

"No," she admitted. "That's not how I feel. But you do, and I can't change that."

Peter's expression turned to surprise. "Why would you say that? When did I ever...?"

"You never had to," Natalie interrupted. "It's clear just by the way you've treated me since that night."

"But we were at *the office*!" Peter shouted, walking toward her. "What did you expect me to do?"

Natalie stepped back defensively. "It doesn't matter, Peter. I'm over it. Just stay out of my personal life and I'll stay out of yours."

Peter watched her leave, completely unprepared for the flood of emotions that welled up inside him. This wasn't the first time he'd hurt a woman with his indifference, taking what enjoyment was offered to him and then walking away. But, for reasons he couldn't begin to fathom, this time was different. Natalie was different. The clenching in his chest told him that, even if his mind couldn't make sense of it.

He caught up with her, grabbing her arm. Natalie swung around, startled. "I don't want to stay out of it, Natalie," he said, his tone hard, urgent.

Natalie pushed his hand away. "No," she said angrily. "You're just acting this way because you don't like to lose. You don't want me. You just don't want anyone else to have me."

"That's not true." Peter struggled to stay calm, reaching out for her shoulder. "Natalie, I do want you."

"*No.*" Natalie said, shrinking away. She put her hands up as if to fend him off. "Just stop. I can't turn my feelings on and off like you can. It's too hard for me."

"You don't have to," Peter said, studying her face. She looked tired all of a sudden, her initial look of anger replaced by a mix of emotions he couldn't identify. Disappointment? Resignation? He resisted the impulse to reach out again, afraid of pushing her farther away.

"You're right," he continued, offering a weak smile. "I've been a jerk. I thought we could go back to the way things were before. For a while, it seemed like we did. But then, I saw that kid and…I couldn't take the idea of you with him."

He paused, his eyes never leaving hers. "I don't want this to be over, Natalie. I don't think you do either."

Natalie shook her head. "I…can't do this." She moved toward the door.

Peter rushed ahead, positioning himself between her and the door. He made no move to touch her, yet his words had a heavy, soothing quality to them. "Let's try," he whispered. "Please."

Natalie remained frozen in place. "This is crazy," she said, her expression grave.

Peter couldn't deny it. Getting involved with his assistant, a student in his department—he knew better. It was reckless. Yet, he couldn't accept the alternative, watching her walk away.

Natalie continued, meeting his gaze. "You could lose your job. I could be expelled."

"We'll just have to be careful."

Natalie fell silent. She closed her eyes, exhaling heavily.

Her reaction, more than her words, told him what he needed to hear.

Relief taking over, Peter gave her no time for second thoughts. He took her purse and car keys and laid them on the table. Turning back to her, he smoothed a stray lock of hair behind her ear, his touch gentle and lingering.

"I hope we don't regret this," she whispered.

"We'll be okay," he whispered back, a reassuring smile on his lips. Hands cradling her face, Peter kissed her tenderly.

***

He lay beside her, head propped up on his elbow. A jumble of thoughts went through his head as he watched the sleeping girl by his side. He reached out and touched her hair, letting it fall through his fingers.

Natalie curled up on her side and drew the sheet over her. Her hair spilled out across the pillow and her face held a dreamy, innocent expression. Peter smiled. At this moment, she resembled a little girl.

A very different image than the one he had witnessed the night before, Peter mused. This woman made love with an abandon that took him by surprise. It was as if, having entrusted him with her heart, Natalie entrusted him with her body as well, which she gave completely and without reservation. Being with her filled Peter with a curious mix of desire and tenderness. He hadn't felt anything like this for a long time, and it was unsettling.

Natalie's eyes fluttered awake.

"Hi," she whispered.

"Hi."

"What time is it?"

Peter glanced behind her at the clock. "2:30," he answered.

"What are you doing up?" she asked, rubbing her eyes.

"Couldn't sleep."

"Must have been too easy on you," Natalie grinned into her pillow.

Peter laughed. He began to gently trace the contours of her face. Natalie's eyes closed as his fingers trailed lightly across her temples, nose and lips.

"That's where you hold all your tension," he said, his fingers resting on her forehead.

"It is?"

"Mm hm. I've seen it at the office. Your forehead always creases up when you're stressed."

"You noticed my forehead at the office?" Natalie smiled at the thought.

"You'd be surprised how much I noticed while you were tapping away on that computer."

Natalie's eyes opened, watching him briefly before replying. "You never let on."

"Of course not. You're my assistant," was his matter-of-fact reply. "It wouldn't have been appropriate."

"Well, I guess this *definitely* wouldn't be appropriate," Natalie observed.

Peter raised an eyebrow, an ironic twist to his smile. "Honey, this is the *definition* of 'inappropriate'."

Natalie giggled but said nothing, clearly enjoying his touch. Minutes passed before she broke the silence, her expression serious.

"Peter?"

"Hmm?"

"If you hadn't seen me with Andrew yesterday," she began, "would you have been content to leave things as is?"

Peter considered her question. "Content, no. Resigned, maybe."

"I should thank Andrew the next time I see him."

Peter rolled toward her on the bed until he was only inches from her face. His answer was gruff. "I'm not giving that kid credit for any of this. As a matter of fact, I'd prefer there not *be* a next time that you see him." He kissed her firmly.

Natalie returned his kiss, an amused expression on her face. "Okay, number one, you don't have a say in who my friends are," she returned his surprised glance without blinking. "Number two, it's not easy being on the receiving end, is it?"

Peter frowned, still processing her number one. "What are you talking about?"

"Hardly a day goes by where I don't have to watch some lovesick freshman knocking on your door for one reason or another," she replied.

"Well, I *am* their professor," Peter said smoothly, rolling back to his earlier position and folding his hands behind his head. "That's my job."

"Oh, *please*." It was Natalie's turn to roll and face him. "They don't need any advice. They just want your attention. It couldn't be any more obvious."

Peter grinned. "They're harmless."

"They're annoying," Natalie shot back. "Especially Kelly Martin. She's had her eyes on you since last year."

"Miss Martin…" Peter knew her—she was a bit hard to miss, to be honest. Still, he repeated the name, eyebrows furrowed in thought. "Isn't she the one that sits in the front row in PSY 300?"

Natalie wasn't fooled. "You know exactly who she is. She's the big-chested blonde that never takes her eyes off you."

Peter laughed out loud. Natalie's display of jealousy was charming. He playfully tweaked her nose. "Don't worry. I've been at this awhile. I can handle myself."

Natalie looked far from convinced.

"Besides," he pulled her close. "You're the one I want, not her." His kiss was long and deep, erasing the lines of irritation from her forehead. In time, the kiss progressed, the sheet was discarded alongside the blankets, and Miss Martin was completely forgotten.

Chapter 7

The ensuing weeks took on a pleasant, predictable rhythm. Mondays signaled the start of their public life together—Peter continuing to teach and work on his manuscript, and Natalie providing research, editing, and classroom help. Rarely a day went by when they were not together, yet their outward behavior never veered from what was expected of professor and assistant.

Natalie had little difficulty with the pretense. In fact, she found it oddly liberating. Gone was any hesitation in expressing her opinions to Peter, whether he agreed with her or not, especially when editing his manuscript. Natalie would simply shrug and stand her ground, to which Peter would grumble and, more often than not, make the suggested changes. Natalie's growing confidence was evident in her teaching, too, which she found herself looking forward to more and more.

One early morning, as Natalie stood at the blackboard diagramming a particularly confusing theory, she heard murmuring among the students. Natalie paused in her explanation and turned around. Peter stood in the doorway.

The students, mostly freshmen and sophomore girls, were thrilled by the surprise visit. Peter smiled ever so slightly, but his raised eyebrows gave him away. His presence was causing a distraction. Natalie could tell he was enjoying the moment immensely.

She tilted her head questioningly at him. His own classes were later in the morning, and he rarely came to the office before 9:00.

Peter answered her unspoken question. "Just thought I would stop by and see how the class is coming along." Peter stepped in and found an empty seat near the back of the room. He smiled at her and straightened in his chair, his full attention on Natalie. "Please, don't let me interrupt you."

Natalie gave a polite smile and turned back toward the blackboard, finishing her explanation.

"Any other questions?" she asked. She scanned the classroom, avoiding eye contact with Peter. She was surprised by the absence of comments and questions.

"Really?" she continued. "Well, considering there's a test on Friday, let's review the main points that might be covered. Stop me if anything doesn't make sense."

Still no response. She glanced out into the seats and saw a sea of faces peering back at her with awkward smiles and occasional glances at Professor Spencer. Natalie turned to the board and shook her head in irritation.

She continued until 8:30, when the bell rang. The room erupted into noisy chatter as students gathered their books and coats and said their goodbyes to Professor Spencer. As the room emptied, Peter remained behind, engaged in a lively conversation with Kelly Martin, striking as ever in a bright red sweater and knee-high leather boots.

Natalie gathered her things and walked down a separate row of seats, hoping to avoid interaction with the pair. Besides, her next class was across campus, and she had little time to spare.

Seeing her pass, Peter ended his conversation with Miss Martin. He managed to catch up with Natalie by the time she had reached the door leading outside.

"Informative class today," he said, holding the door for her as they left the building. "Thanks for letting me sit in."

"Of course," she said. "You're always welcome, although the students were a bit distracted with you there."

"I noticed that, too," Peter agreed. "Your classes are usually much livelier than that."

Natalie looked over at him. "You've been by before?"

Peter gave a half smile. "I make it a habit to visit my assistants' classes now and then. You know, *quality control.* I've looked in on your class a few times now. I just haven't sat in on them."

"That was probably a good idea," Natalie observed.

Peter chuckled. "They did seem a bit like deer in the headlights, didn't they?"

"Except for Miss Martin," Natalie let slip. Peter's eyes crinkled in amusement, though he said nothing. "I hope I wasn't that bad in your freshman class."

"No, as I recall, you weren't intimidated by me at all, at least not enough to stop asking questions."

Natalie stopped walking. "Wait—I thought you didn't remember me from your undergrad classes."

"Not true," he corrected her. "Let's see…." Peter glanced up at the sky, as if reconstructing an old memory. "Your hair was shorter, right? You always sat toward the front and, if I'm not mistaken, you've lost a little weight since then."

Natalie stared at him in surprise. "How did you remember that?"

Peter laughed. "I didn't at first. A few weeks ago, I went back through my old course notes and found a few relating to questions you had raised. I remembered you right away. You were pretty inquisitive."

Natalie shook her head. "I'll bet I was a real pain in the neck."

"No," he smiled. "You were excited to be there. I wish all my students were."

They reached the Cromley Building and began to climb the steps to the second floor. "Do you like teaching?" Natalie asked. It had never occurred to her to ask before now.

"Not as much as I used to," Peter confessed. "It's getting harder to muster up the same enthusiasm I used to have." They approached the door to her classroom. "I can tell you do, though," he said. "I think you're good at it."

Natalie warmed at his compliment. "As long as you don't sit in on any more of my classes," she quipped. Then she stopped, a puzzled expression forming on her face. It dawned on her that they were on the opposite end of campus from the Psychology Building. "Hey, this is where I go. You don't teach a class here, do you?"

"No," he said, giving a good-natured shrug. "See you at 2:00." Without another word, he turned back toward the stairs and was gone. Natalie shook her head in surprise, realizing at that moment that she had just been walked to class.

***

Friday finally arrived, and with it, the best part of Natalie's week. She loaded up her backpack, wished Professor Spencer a good weekend, and made her way to the courtyard of the Psychology building. Breathing in the deliciously frigid air, Natalie felt a surge of energy with each step. The trees had a skeletal appearance now, the cold autumn gusts denuding them of their leaves weeks before. A light dusting of snow in the morning, hard packed by a full day's traffic, would prove the only obstacle to Natalie's ride home. Still, the sky was a deep, bright blue, and she felt ridiculously alive.

As she crossed the mall to where her bicycle was locked, her cell phone rang. Smiling, she answered the call, knowing it was him even before seeing the generic 'Work' pop up on the phone screen. "Hi. How was your day?" she answered brightly. "Sure, how about 6:00? Should I bring anything? Okay, see you soon."

Passersby noticed nothing out of the ordinary, except perhaps a spring of eagerness in her step. Occasionally, on these days, Natalie would pass classmates on their way home, stopping to ask about an assignment or simply chat about upcoming weekend plans. Invariably, invitations to parties or happy hours were issued, but Natalie always declined.

"Hot date, huh?" a friend would ask.

"Something like that," Natalie would reply, a mysterious smile playing on her lips.

"Must be some guy."

Natalie would wave and ride off on her bike without elaborating.

This day, upon reaching home, Natalie bounded up the stairs calling, "Hey Gina, you home?"

"I'm in here." Gina's voice radiated down the hall from the bedroom.

Natalie dropped her bag and keys on the kitchen counter, then went into Gina's room, flopping down on the bed.

"Whew, I'm bushed," Natalie said.

"You really should stop riding your bike, Nat," Gina said. "The roads are getting slippery. How much can a parking pass cost anyway?"

"It's not the cost," Natalie answered. "I like the exercise. After being cooped up all day, it's nice to bike home."

"Three seasons out of the year, that's fine," Gina countered. "But it's winter. It's cold and snowy, and there are a lot of drivers out there who have no business driving in the snow."

"Don't worry." Natalie dismissed her friend's concerns. "Hey, where are you headed anyway—date?"

"As a matter of fact…" Gina grinned and held up a new black skirt and a pair of black boots that looked a lot like Kelly Martin's. "Nice," Natalie replied. "Who's the lucky guy?"

"Joey." Gina's voice barely contained her excitement.

"He's not new," Natalie protested. "You two have been hanging out forever."

Gina took out several tops and held them up to the skirt, appraising each combination in the mirror.

"That one," Natalie pointed. Gina nodded and began to dress.

"So why all the excitement?" Natalie prodded.

Gina leaned against the dresser, skirt in hand. "I ran into him at the end of my shift. Instead of meeting up with everyone at the Oaks, he asked if we could just hang out alone, 'like a date', he said."

Natalie giggled, "That's how he said it?"

"Okay, I know he's not the most romantic guy in the world, but his heart is in the right place."

Natalie nodded with approval. She had always liked Joey. In fact, she wondered why he and Gina had never gotten together before this.

"Where are you two going?"

"Dinner and a movie. Isn't that perfect? It's an actual *date*."

Natalie laughed at her friend's excitement. Gina had known Joey for the last three years, since the two found themselves in the same nursing class together. They had both gone on to find jobs at the University Hospital in town, Gina as a unit nurse and Joey in the rehab wing.

Natalie watched Gina pull on the sweater and examine herself critically in the mirror.

"Well?"

"Beautiful." Natalie smiled. "Hey—one more thing." She trotted across the hall and grabbed a largely unused bottle of perfume on her dresser.

She took it in to Gina. "Here," she said. "See if he likes this."

Gina uncapped the bottle. "Mmm, it's nice. But I don't usually wear perfume."

"Neither do I," Natalie admitted. "But maybe it's time to shake things up a bit."

Natalie opened the bottle and inhaled. It *did* smell nice. "Let's both try some tonight and see what kind of reactions we get."

Gina grinned and held out her wrists. Natalie dabbed each with a drop, and then placed a few on her own. For good measure, they repeated the procedure behind the ears.

Gina gasped at the sound of the doorbell. "Oh, that's him." She rose to answer the door, but Natalie stopped her.

"No, you stay here. I'll get it. There's nothing wrong with making an entrance."

Gina hugged her. "I almost forgot to ask about your plans. Are you seeing him again?"

Natalie got up and stood in the doorway. She called out, "Be right there, Joey," before turning back to Gina.

"Yes, I'll be at Peter's."

Gina became serious for a moment. "Be careful, Nat."

"Don't worry, the roads are fine."

"No," Gina corrected. "I mean *you*. Don't get in too deep, okay?"

Natalie shrugged. "Too late." Leaving her friend to complete the finishing touches, she unlocked the door and invited Joey inside. In spite of his usual rumpled appearance, Joey carried himself differently tonight. There was a restless energy about him that kept him on his feet, despite her invitation to sit down.

Not wanting to add to his nervousness, Natalie busied herself in the kitchen, occasionally stealing glances at him from around the cabinets. There she noticed the smiles that appeared on his lips spontaneously, only to disappear again with a self-conscious drop of the head. When Gina eventually emerged from down the hallway, Joey beamed. Yes, Natalie thought, this could be the beginning of something promising.

After wishing the pair a good night, Natalie hurried into the bedroom to change clothes and freshen up. She smelled her wrists again, looking forward to his reaction. It was true, she was already more attached to Peter than she wanted to admit—certainly more than she would admit to him. But she wouldn't back out now, even if it were possible. She would continue seeing him until the end and only hoped that the eventual fall would be worth it.

***

Natalie parked the car and strode toward the front porch. After getting no answer to her knock, she tried the doorbell.

"Door's open," a voice called out.

She opened the door and scanned the room before her. From the kitchen, she heard the sounds of dinner being prepared even before she saw him bent over the counter, preoccupied with a cookbook. "Hello."

"Hey." Peter's smile was warm. "Put your things down and come kiss the chef."

Natalie laughed. "You cook, too? Boy, I really lucked out."

"Well, sort of…" He smiled self-consciously and followed up with a wink. "The cooking part, that is. We already know you lucked out."

Natalie shook her head and gave him a kiss on his cheek as he abandoned the cookbook and resumed chopping a plate of onions and peppers. "Modest, aren't you?"

"No. Do that one over," he ordered, turning his head to face her. She laughed and gave him a longer kiss on the lips.

"Better. Now, how about pouring us some wine?" He motioned with oniony fingers toward the dining area, where a bottle of red wine had been set out amid two glasses, unlit candles, and a fully set table.

"Wow, what's the occasion?" she said. Uncorking the wine, she poured a glass for herself and then another for him.

Peter glanced up from the pan. "Nothing special. Just felt like something other than spaghetti or pizza for a change."

Natalie took a long, satisfying sip of wine before returning to the kitchen. There she brought a glass up to his lips, letting him take a drink. "Not bad," Peter remarked. Taking the glass from Natalie's hand, he poured the rest of its contents into the pan and stirred it.

Natalie watched his improvisational cooking techniques with amusement as she hopped up onto the counter. "What are you making?"

"Chicken cacciatore." He picked up the pan of simmering red sauce, poured it over a baking dish containing the chicken, and then placed the dish into the oven. He let the door slam shut with a flourish. "Dinner's in an hour."

He made his way over to the counter where Natalie sat sipping her wine. Leaning up against her legs, he began to kiss her neck. Natalie closed her eyes and savored the heady combination of wine and kisses.

Peter's head drew back. "Perfume?"

Natalie gave a sheepish grin. "I guess I wanted to try something a little different, too. Like it?"

Peter resumed his earlier explorations. "I like it," he said thickly. "But I like you with nothing on at all, too."

Natalie groaned and rolled her eyes.

"Any trouble getting home tonight?" Like Gina, he had been urging her to put the bike away for the winter.

"None," Natalie reassured him. "I told you, I'm perfectly safe as long as I'm careful."

"Maybe I can get Gordon to issue a staff permit for you to use the Psychology parking lot. God knows you're there enough."

"I'm fine, Peter." Natalie repeated. "Don't bother with Gordon."

Gordon McMann was the Chair of the Psychology Department. He was generally disliked for the same reasons that made him such an efficient manager, primarily his dogmatic refusal to bend the rules or play favorites and perpetual eye on the bottom line. Under his reign, the department was operating well within its budget for the first time in years. However, he rarely considered staff requests for flextime, unscheduled field trips, or additional classroom equipment unless specified months in advance.

Peter disliked him precisely for his inflexibility, especially since his own teaching style had always been much more spontaneous. It wasn't unusual for him to take his lecture classes outside on nice days, or on impromptu field trips to the zoo to study primate behavior. But with Gordon at the helm, there was little room for spontaneity. The fact that Peter was willing to take up with Gordon for the sake of a parking pass said a lot to Natalie. Still, she wouldn't hear of it.

"Between you and Gina, I've had about as much nagging on this subject as I can take."

"She doesn't like you riding, either?"

Natalie shook her head. "On Monday I'm applying for a permit in Lot 59. It's cheap and has plenty of spots. Of course, it's so far away, I'll need my bike just to get from the lot to my classes."

Peter appeared satisfied. "So, does she know about us?"

"Gina? Yes," Natalie admitted, "but she won't say anything."

Peter walked over and refilled his glass with wine. "What does she think?"

Natalie's answer was honest. "She doesn't approve."

Peter nodded, unsurprised.

"You can't blame her," Natalie began. "Besides the fact that I could get thrown out for it, you've also built quite a reputation for yourself over the years."

Peter leaned against the counter opposite Natalie. "Idle gossip," he said dismissively.

"Maybe," Natalie countered. "But my guess is that there's some truth in there somewhere."

Peter shrugged his shoulders—a tacit acknowledgement, if not a full confession. It was true that he had hardly been a monk during his years at UW. He was an attractive man who enjoyed female companionship but had little interest in long-term entanglements. Unfortunately, in a university community, exploits inevitably became public knowledge, earning him a reputation for being everything from an eligible bachelor to a player, depending on one's viewpoint.

"So, I've had an active social life. No one's been hurt."

Natalie raised an eyebrow. "Least of all you, right?"

Peter paused, then tilted his head. "Do you think I'm going to hurt you?"

Natalie's smile was warm, almost understanding. "My eyes are wide open, Peter. I know what I'm in for with you."

Peter watched her in silence, his face forming some unspoken question. Natalie hopped down from the counter and took his hand. "Come with me," she said. "There's something I've been meaning to ask you about."

Peter set down his glass and let her lead him into the entryway, where she stopped before the photographs mounted there. "Tell me about these."

"This was the summer I drove cross-country to Los Angeles, right after I graduated from UW."

Natalie studied the pictures as she had the first night she had been here. She pointed to various snapshots, asking where they had been taken. Peter laughed and shook his head. "That was a long time ago, Nat. I don't remember."

Then, Natalie reached her favorite, the one of a youthful Peter with his arms thrown across the shoulders of two older men. "This was you," she said, grinning, more a statement than a question.

"Yes," Peter smiled back.

"Who took the picture?" Natalie asked.

"A friend." Peter replied. His tone, more than his answer, made her look up. For a fleeting moment, his expression was wistful.

Natalie took his hand and squeezed it, hoping to chase the shadows from his face. "It must have been an amazing trip."

Peter left the sentence unanswered. With Natalie's hand still clasping his, she led them to the couch.

"Was it hard to move so far away?" Natalie asked.

"In some ways. I had always been pretty content here. I half expected to take over the farm when my father got older."

"Seriously?" Natalie laughed, then stopped herself. "I'm sorry. It's still hard to imagine you in that way of life."

"Oh, you'd be surprised. I did it all—planting, harvesting, milking. I even helped with birthing the calves. I probably would have been there to this day if my father hadn't given me a hard kick and told me to get out into the real world."

"He didn't actually kick you out, did he?" Natalie's eyes crinkled in amusement.

"Not quite," Peter admitted. "But he made it clear that there would be no future for me here unless I got an education first." Peter wrapped his arm around Natalie, prompting her to move closer into his embrace. "He was right, now that I think back. Farming is a hard way of life—well, you know—you have to really want it, or you'll end up miserable."

Natalie did know. She had seen the many worries and setbacks her parents had endured over the years. It was a good life, though. There were days when she missed it, too.

"So, you ended up doing something completely different," Natalie summed up for him. "And then you came back. Your parents must have been thrilled."

Peter shrugged. "My mother was. My father died the year before I returned."

"I'm sorry. Were you two close?"

"We were at one time," Peter replied. He paused as if considering whether to continue, but the thought went unspoken. "My little sister, Dawn, and her husband run the farm now. I help out when I can."

Natalie hesitated. He was such a mystery to her. She felt the familiar tension of wanting to know more, while knowing that to press too far would shut the conversation down completely.

Peter continued along a safer path. "Dawn and Tim, that's her husband, have a little girl, Amanda. She's five years old and sharp as a whip. She makes Sunday dinners a real experience."

Natalie noticed the pride in his face as he mentioned his niece. "I'll bet you spoil her rotten."

"Guilty," Peter admitted. "But pretty soon she'll have to share the spotlight. Dawn's expecting a baby boy in early January. Amanda's not sure what to think. She's torn between excitement at having a little brother and concern that her days of being the star of the show are numbered."

"They are," Natalie laughed. "That's how I felt when my sister was born. I was four. And we still haven't resolved it."

"Where's your sister now?"

"She's in her last year at UW-Milwaukee, majoring in performing arts. It's the perfect profession for her," she said, rolling her eyes. "She was always a drama queen."

Peter smiled. "How about your parents? Where is their farm?"

"White Falls—about three hours north of here. They're beginning to scale down a bit, but it's still a pretty big operation—soybeans, corn, dairy."

"Your father runs it all on his own?" Peter asked, impressed.

"With my mother. They have a hired hand who helps with the milking and assorted chores, but Mom manages the dairy operation, and Dad does all the planting and harvesting," Natalie replied. "They're pretty amazing. I think you would like my dad. You two have a lot in common."

"Yeah? What's he like?"

"Oh, he's stubborn, proud, a perfectionist…"

"And I should be flattered by this?" Peter interrupted.

"You didn't let me finish," Natalie laughed. "He's also hard-working, loyal, and charming in a grumpy sort of way. It wasn't always easy growing up with him, but I hope I find someone like him when I settle down someday."

Peter raised his eyebrows at her.

"Hey, don't get the wrong idea—I'm not proposing to you or anything," she said, coloring. "You just remind me of him sometimes."

"Freud would have a field day with this," Peter said. "And here I am, almost old enough to be your father…."

"Hardly, unless you were having sex at ten," Natalie remarked dryly.

Peter folded his arms behind his head and closed his eyes, a slow smile spreading across his face.

Natalie laughed in shock. "Ten? That's impossible."

"Does playing doctor count?"

"It does not."

"Okay, I guess I don't qualify," he conceded. "You'll have to find your father figure elsewhere."

Natalie's eyes sparkled wickedly as she straddled his legs. "Fine, but before I ditch you, can we play doctor first?"

***

After the dinner dishes were cleared, the candles burned down, and the conversation had reached its inevitable end, Peter took Natalie by the hand, and together they walked to his room. Each undressed the other, their discarded layers forming a growing pile on the floor before Natalie released him and slid between the cool sheets. Lifting the covers, she beckoned him with a smile, further words unnecessary. He was at her side in a heartbeat, lending warmth where the cool fabric had caused tiny goose bumps to form on her skin. Their lovemaking was slow and languorous, punctuated by whispers and faint laughter. Sleep came quickly to the pair; their bodies nested together like spoons, their limbs loosely entangled.

CHAPTER 8

Peter glanced up at the darkening sky. A familiar dread crept into his limbs as he recognized his surroundings, understood the stakes at hand. He quickened his pace to a full-out run, but no matter how fast he moved, his surroundings barely changed, like moving through a tunnel. After what felt like hours, he scrambled unsteadily to the ridge where she was parked. Door open, arms resting in her lap, waiting.

Peter surged forward, determined to reach the car in time. But she turned at that moment, spotted him and pulled the door shut.

She stared at him through the window as the car shot into the abyss, breaking through the rope barrier draped uselessly along the outer edges of the lot. She stared even as the car hung in mid-air, before beginning its downward arc into the rocky waters below. Stared—and smiled.

"Eve!" Peter ran after her, barely stopping when his feet reached the gravel ledge, his screams continuing long after the twisted impact could be heard below.

Peter sat up in bed, his heart pounding in panic, his lungs straining for air.

He turned and glanced at Natalie, undisturbed by his night terrors. He stood up and walked into the living room, where he looked out the window vacantly. It had begun to snow. White feathery flakes dusted the trees and yard, giving them a clean, untouched look. Peter saw its beauty, even mused whether he should wake Natalie so she could see it.

Instead, he remained frozen in place, his thoughts cold and hopeless.

Chapter 9

Wednesday afternoon was bright and clear, the sky overhead a brilliant blue. Natalie pulled the collar of her coat tightly around her, belatedly wishing that she had grabbed the scarf her mother had just sent her. Across the courtyard she shuffled, moving as rapidly as her cumbersome backpack would allow. It was time to work with Peter, so, even as her frame sagged with afternoon fatigue, she felt a predictable lift of spirits.

The office door was pulled shut when she arrived. She slipped her key into the lock and found his chair empty, an explanatory note on her desk. She knew his handwriting by heart—tall, slanted letters applied hurriedly to legal paper, a blend of efficiency and authority.

"Gordon called a faculty meeting. God knows when we'll be finished. Need Chapter Six articles by tomorrow."

Natalie had begun to remove her coat, but then stopped mid-sleeve and slipped it back on. Better to get the articles out of the way first, she decided. It would only get harder to go back out in this weather. She added a message to the bottom of his note. "At the library." She re-adjusted her backpack and turned to go.

As she passed the coat rack, she spied Peter's leather jacket and a brown, woolen scarf thrown loosely over it. On impulse, she pulled the length of scarf off the rack, looping it around her neck. As she made her way across campus, Natalie buried her face in the fabric, enjoying its scratchy warmth as well as the scent he had left behind—an earthy mix of aftershave, books, and the outdoors. When she reached the library, she was amazed at how quickly the walk had passed.

It took some time to locate the articles Peter had requested. Natalie pulled the hardbound volumes in which they were contained from the shelves and photocopied the specific pages for him to read that night. However, the last article proved elusive. After speaking with one of the librarians, who assured her it had not been checked out, Natalie returned to the bookcase to see if it had been misshelved.

The section of the library where Natalie spent most of her time was in an older part of the building. Bookcases rose from floor to ceiling in one continuous row after another. While impressive to the eye, their design made it difficult to obtain books that were out of reach on the topmost rows. For this, a rolling wooden ladder, attached to the front of the shelves by a sliding metal bracket, was needed.

Natalie slid the ladder to the section she wished to explore. Climbing to the sixth row, she scanned the volumes with no success, so she climbed up to the next. Just then, she heard someone call her name in a loud whisper. Looking down, she was surprised to see Peter, standing beneath the ladder, his arms outstretched as if to catch her.

Natalie gave him a puzzled smile. "What's the matter?"

"Get down from there—you're going to break your neck," he whispered loudly, all the while waving her down with his hand.

Natalie gripped the ladder and climbed down, stopping when she reached the bottom rung.

"I've only got one more article to find," she explained. "I'll be down in a few minutes."

Peter stopped her. "No—a library worker should go up there, not you. I'll go find someone to get the book."

Natalie laughed. "In the time it takes you to get someone, I'll have found it." She turned back toward the ladder.

Peter glared at her. "Stay put."

Natalie shook her head in irritation. Satisfied that she wasn't going anywhere, Peter went in search of assistance. Natalie watched him disappear around the corner, and then scaled the ladder to renew her search. It was worth the effort. A few minutes later, she pulled the missing volume, paging through it for the article she sought.

When Peter returned, a library worker following close behind, Natalie was perched high above his head, her head bent in concentration. It wasn't until Peter cleared his throat, that Natalie noticed the two men watching her.

"Hi, Mike," Natalie smiled, choosing to ignore Peter's look of annoyance, and focus instead on the young man beside him. She gave a half wave, book in hand. "I found it. Thanks anyway."

The young man smiled and waved back. "Okay, Natalie. See you later."

"*Mike?*" he inquired with an uplifted brow.

"Do you have any idea how much time I spend here? I'm on a first name basis with all these guys."

Peter gave an unintelligible response and strode up to the ladder, motioning her down.

As she reached the bottom rung, she turned and waved the volume at him innocently. "Here it is."

He gave the book a cursory glance. "Do you ever listen?"

Natalie hopped off the last rung and faced him. "Sure, when the request makes sense." She put the book down on a nearby table and bookmarked the article she wanted. "Did you need anything else?" she asked over her shoulder. "Otherwise, I'm going to the copy room."

"No, nothing else," he replied. "I have to stop by the reference desk."

Natalie copied the final article and was soon packing up her papers and heading for the library exit. Along the way, she spotted Peter, speaking with a young woman seated in the study area. Natalie didn't recognize her, but the flirty, lilting tone she used was familiar enough. It was the same inflection Natalie heard in the voices of all of Peter's young admirers.

Peter appeared to be enjoying their conversation so much that he didn't notice Natalie as she walked past. *Fine with me*, Natalie grumbled to herself. She had experienced enough of these encounters in Peter's office to know how it would play out. Typically, it began with some arbitrary question regarding his last lecture, progressed to a flirtatious compliment, and then ended with a lengthy pause to offer Peter a chance to steer the conversation in a more desirable direction.

Natalie pushed through the heavy doors leading outside before taking the time to fasten her coat. The frigid air hit her, and she felt the immediate shock of her first inhalation. She buried her face inside the woolen scarf, attempting to warm the air before taking any additional breaths into her lungs. Holding her backpack close to her body, she began the long, cold trek across campus.

She hadn't gotten very far when Peter caught up with her. She shot him a sideways glance, completely disregarding his smile. "Why didn't you wait for me?" he asked, rubbing his hands together for warmth.

"You looked a little busy," she said tersely.

Peter thrust his hands into his pockets, his long strides enabling him to keep up despite her brisk pace. "Nice scarf."

Natalie's hand went to her neck, suddenly remembering the borrowed item. "Sorry, I should have asked." She began to unwind it from her neck.

"You don't have to…."

"It's fine," she cut him off. "I don't need it."

Peter grasped the scarf, and her hand with it, forcing her to slow her pace or be strangled.

"Don't take it off," he said. "I like it on you."

Natalie stood as he rewound the loose end around her neck. She kept her gaze aimed at the sidewalk, her lips pressed tightly in irritation.

"Nat, I know that part of my job bothers you. But, like it or not, that *is* a part of my job."

"Chatting up coeds?" Natalie asked. "I didn't realize that flirting was in your job description."

"It's not." His voice had an edge to it that wasn't there a moment before. "But being available and approachable to my students is."

Natalie saw some truth in his words but was in no mood to admit it.

"You don't have to enjoy it so much," she muttered.

Peter smirked but said nothing.

"It's no wonder you're still single," Natalie scolded. "There aren't too many women who would put up with that."

Peter gave her an imperious look. "Maybe. But just so we're clear—I'm single because I want to be, not for a lack of interested candidates."

Natalie bit her lip in aggravation and changed the subject.

"So, what was the deal in there, anyway? Afraid of heights?"

"What are you talking about?"

"The ladder. You looked like you were about to have a heart attack when you saw me up there."

"Ridiculous," he scoffed. "I was just trying to save your neck."

"Maybe," Natalie countered. "But once I was safe from *harm*, why not just go up and get the book yourself? Why go to all the trouble to find some college kid to do it for you?"

Peter hesitated a moment before conceding the point. "So, I have an issue with ladders."

"Just ladders?" Natalie was suddenly enjoying herself. She had found his Achilles heel.

He glared at her. "Okay, maybe not just ladders. But for the record, it's not heights that bother me—it's the falling part. I have no problem standing at my office window and watching you ride home."

Natalie pulled the scarf tighter, concealing a smile. The idea that he watched her leave at night, and even more surprisingly—admitted to it—warmed her. She felt her icy reserve begin to thaw.

"So how long have you been afraid of…falling?"

"Since I was a kid. One time, Dawn and I were playing hide and seek, and she hid in the hayloft. When I climbed up the ladder to find her, she jumped out and scared the wits out of me. I let go of the ladder and fell onto the barn floor."

Natalie frowned. Her family's hayloft was at least ten feet off the ground. "Were you hurt?"

"I broke my wrist, but it could have been a lot worse. The hay on the floor softened my fall."

Natalie glanced at Peter, his arms swinging by his side as he walked. She wondered which one had been injured so long ago. For a moment, she felt an irrational urge to hold his hand. Instead, she shook it off, pointing her gaze forward. "Well, if you need any help with ladders next time, I'm your girl."

He chuckled. "I'll remember that."

The trip across campus went swiftly, their companionship enough to distract them from the elements. When she saw Gordon McMann approaching them, Natalie realized with surprise that they had almost reached the Psychology building.

As always, Gordon walked with a rapid step and a harried expression on his face. However, seeing Peter, Gordon slowed his pace and changed course so he could head him off at the steps.

"Peter, I've been meaning to speak with you about that request you put in for a class speaker next semester."

Peter appeared puzzled as he tried to remember the request. "Oh, right—Karla Livingston. I ask her every semester to come and speak to my Social Psych class."

"And you're requesting funds for hotel and meals while she's here?" Gordon queried.

"She's traveling here from the University of Chicago for a three o'clock class. We can't expect her to pack up and make the three-hour trip home as soon as she's finished, can we?"

Gordon ignored the sarcasm. "I just need the date that she's coming, Peter. My secretary can arrange her stay more economically if we use the department's travel account."

"I'll e-mail her and let you know."

"That will be fine." Gordon turned to go, only then noticing Natalie standing there. "Hello, Natalie. Are you having a good semester?"

"Yes, Dr. McMann. Thank you," Natalie replied.

"That's good. Well, good night to you both." He nodded his head in dismissal.

Peter returned the nod and resumed walking, Natalie rushing to keep up with his quickened pace. She saw his face, tight-lipped with irritation and wondered why he let Gordon get to him this way. Without thinking, she touched his arm and said softly, "Don't let him bother you."

"I detest that man," he snarled. "I don't care how efficient he is, the sooner his chairmanship is over, the better."

She gave his arm a slight squeeze, not realizing that her simple act of support had been noticed. Gordon, remembering one more question, turned to call Peter's name. Instead, the words remained unspoken as he saw the familiar manner in which Natalie and Peter behaved. Given Peter's reputation with women, he would need to keep a closer eye on this pair.

***

The Thanksgiving meal was finished, dishes stacked, leftovers stored away. Tim and Dawn sat on the couch watching the bowl games while their mother, never a fan of football, finished up in the kitchen. Amanda was out in the yard teaching her dog to jump over obstacles, with little success. Peter watched through the window with amusement as the five-year-old repeatedly jumped over the bales of hay, encouraging her aging dog to do the same. The dog simply gave her a bored look and lay down, much to the girl's frustration.

There wasn't a place in that house that didn't brim with memories. For Peter, it felt comforting and confining all at once—a warm, woolen blanket that must be kicked aside in order to breathe freely.

Dawn and Tim had made their home in the same place where he'd grown up, matured, broken free. Family photographs lined the walls, containing images of Peter and his sister, parents, grandparents, and the like. To those, new ones had been added—Tim and Dawn's early years together, Amanda's arrival, pictures of the three as a family. But at its core, it was his home too, heavy with history, successes, and regrets.

Peter walked down the hall to join the others when a framed picture stopped him. It had hung there for years, yet only now did it catch his attention. There he stood in cap and gown, smiling with a confidence and anticipation that no one could have understood at the time. College diploma in one hand, his life was about to take an exciting turn. He still remembered the unspoken energy.

"That was quite a day." Dawn appeared by his side, glancing at the photo.

Peter gave a short laugh. "Until all hell broke loose."

"You certainly made a memorable departure."

He shook his head. "I'm surprised they kept this up."

Dawn straightened the frame. "They were proud of you, Pete. We all were."

"You and Mom were."

"Dad was, too. He just…." she faltered for words. "He just had a hard time with you two leaving the way you did. And then, the way it ended…."

"He could have believed me, Dawn," Peter said, his tone still bitter after all these years. "That would have been a start."

Dawn nodded, her expression sad. "You're right. He should have."

The two were quiet, the picture a convenient distraction from all that remained unsaid.

"Do you ever visit her?" she asked quietly.

Peter looked at her in surprise.

"I was there a few weeks ago," she continued. "There was a bouquet of yellow roses on her grave. I thought maybe you had left them."

Peter shook his head. Yellow roses had been her favorite. "No, I haven't been there for years."

Dawn wrapped an arm around his middle and pulled him close. "I'm worried about you, Pete. I don't think you ever moved on from it."

Pete put his arm around her waist. "It's all good, Sis. You have nothing to worry about."

She looked unconvinced. "You might be fooling everyone else, but I know how much that took out of you. You need to make a life for yourself. A *real* life." She placed a hand on her growing belly, caressed it absently.

The sound of pounding footsteps filled the house. Amanda spotted the two in the hall and ran headlong into Peter, who scooped her up into his arms.

"Uncle Pete, will you play circus with me?"

"Not if it means I have to jump over hay bales."

Her secret revealed, Amanda gave a pout.

"But," he continued, "I will come out and play."

"Hide and seek!" she announced.

"No way," Dawn said. "That's how you get out of bedtime." She reached up and gently pinched the little girl's nose. "I learned that the hard way. This little squirt is way too good at hiding."

"Let's practice soccer," Peter suggested. "You can work on your penalty kicks." He walked down the hall, Amanda still in his arms. "I hear they're starting up a kindergarten team. You want to be ready for that, right?"

Chapter 10

Returning to school after Thanksgiving, Natalie felt the predictable sense of overwhelm—too much to do, not nearly enough time. She knew she should be spending the weekend in the library working on final papers and studying for exams. Yet, after being deprived of Peter for the long weekend, all she could think about was lying in his arms and letting the world go by without her. At least for a few hours.

Unfortunately, when she woke Friday morning, she felt the familiar monthly twinge of pain. *Damn, why today?* She dragged herself out of bed and got ready for classes, her earlier excitement for the weekend fading away.

Riding to school through the cold revived her but did little to improve her mood. Natalie managed to sit through her classes, taking notes and listening to the incessant reminders about upcoming projects, but she found it difficult to concentrate. Already she was feeling the discomfort and fatigue that would likely follow her for the rest of the weekend. Trudging heavily into the office, she offered only a terse greeting.

"Good afternoon," Peter greeted her automatically, looking up from his papers.

Natalie plopped down at her desk.

Peter turned around in his chair. "Something wrong?"

"No, nothing." Natalie answered. She opened her backpack and pulled out files, more in an effort to appear busy than to actually accomplish anything.

Peter watched her for a few moments, then turned in his chair and resumed his work, which managed to both relieve and aggravate Natalie at the same time. She shuffled her papers noisily and dropped her folders on the desk a bit harder than necessary, but in the end, settled down to work.

They remained that way for hours, each absorbed in their own tasks, until Natalie glanced at the clock. 4:53. *Close enough.* Natalie rose from her chair and stuffed her backpack with the files she had yet to complete. Peter looked up as she put on her coat. She returned his glance with little expression.

"Good night, professor," she said. "I'll finish these summaries by Monday, if that's okay." She lifted her backpack in illustration.

"That's fine," Peter replied, a perplexed look on his face.

Natalie nodded but said nothing as she closed the office door behind her.

She had barely gotten down the stairs of the Psychology building when her cell phone rang. She knew it would be him and was not looking forward to the conversation.

"Hello?"

"Would you mind telling me what that was all about?" he said.

Natalie could feel him watching from his office window. "Forget it."

"I'm not going to forget it and if you don't want to tell me now, you can tell me later," he replied. "What time are you coming over?"

"I'm not coming over."

There was a pause. "Why not?" Peter asked, a hint of concern in his voice.

She hesitated. "Because it's not a good time."

"What's that supposed to mean?"

Natalie gritted her teeth. "I'm having my period."

"So?"

Natalie exhaled impatiently. "So, I can't…." She couldn't bring herself to say the words.

There was silence, and then Peter began to chuckle. "*That's* what this is about?"

Natalie said nothing, his obvious amusement not helping her mood at all. Now, besides feeling tired, disappointed, and uncomfortable, she was beginning to feel like a fool.

"Come on, you don't really think that makes any difference, do you?" When there was no answer, he ordered, "Turn around and look up here."

She was halfway across the courtyard but stopped and turned around. There stood Peter, three floors up, framed by the office window.

"Do you want to come over?"

Natalie gave a reluctant nod.

"Good. Then, get in your car and come over. We'll order a pizza and watch a movie. I have a couple of westerns my sister gave me last Christmas. You like Clint Eastwood?"

She frowned. "You're kidding, right?"

"I guess not. Well, we can stream one when you get here. Something you like."

"All right."

"Do you feel too tired to bike home? Would you like a ride?"

"No, I'll be fine. The fresh air might help. I'll be over in a while."

Natalie saw him shake his head as he turned away from the window. Even from where she stood, she could see his bemused smile.

***

Natalie came home to an empty house. A note was taped to her bedroom door, *"I'll be at Joey's. Have a good weekend, G."* Natalie pulled the note from the door and tucked it into her pocket. Things seemed to be working out between those two, she thought with satisfaction. After a long string of heartbreaks and romances that went nowhere, it was good to see Gina so happy. Maybe the perfume had done the trick.

Natalie selected a soft cotton sweater and roomy, well-worn jeans from her dresser—her go-to outfit for those days when she felt particularly fat, uncomfortable, or out-of-sorts. Unfortunately, today encompassed all three, and she gratefully slipped on the forgiving garments. Next, she removed the clip from her hair, brushing the long strands until they were silky to the touch and her body more relaxed from the effort. With what little energy she had left, Natalie assembled her bags and plodded out to her car. She only hoped that she didn't look as tired and drawn as the rest of her body felt.

***

Natalie trudged up the porch steps, her overnight bag slung over one shoulder, her purse over the other. Reaching his door, she rapped twice before leaning against the door frame.

Peter opened the door and studied her briefly. "Come on in, Sunshine." He took her bags and motioned her inside.

Natalie ignored the greeting and made her way into the kitchen, sitting down on one of the stools that ran the length of the counter. Peter followed a safe distance behind and helped her off with her coat. Tossing it on an adjacent table, he stood there for a moment, wearing the same bemused smile he had earlier. Then he sat down on the stool next to hers and pulled her close. Peter kissed her lightly, tracing his lips along the side of her neck before returning to her lips again. By the third time, his kiss was deep and lingering.

Despite her exhaustion, Natalie could feel herself respond in that predictable way. Her body began to relax, her mood began to soften. *That's all it takes,* she marveled to herself. Just like magic.

Peter pulled away a final time and whispered into her ear. "You know, for someone who's relatively intelligent, you're pretty clueless sometimes."

Natalie lifted her head in irritation, but Peter just laughed. "So, you thought I'd have no use for you tonight? Or wait—

maybe it was the other way around," he said with a grin. "Maybe you had no use for *me*?"

"I'm not that shallow," Natalie replied, mildly annoyed.

"I see." Peter sat back on his stool, still smiling, eyes never leaving her face. "But I am?"

"I didn't say that."

"You didn't have to. Your assumption that I wouldn't want you here made it clear."

"I made no assumptions. I was simply being considerate," Natalie retorted, suddenly feeling wide-awake and more than a little provoked.

Peter, on the other hand, seemed to be enjoying himself. "I'm fully aware of the dangers of living with a woman during her time of the month," he responded matter-of-factly. "A sister, a mother, a few girlfriends—I've managed to survive them all in one piece. I think I can handle you."

Natalie opened her mouth to respond but was at a loss for words. *Handle* her? Her eyes narrowed. She felt a sudden urge to punch him in the mouth, her hands unconsciously clenching into fists.

Peter saw her expression and looked down at her hands with surprise. Wrapping his hands protectively around hers, he gave a rueful smile. "Maybe this isn't the time for teasing," he conceded, kissing her on the forehead. "Truce? Come on, the pizza is on its way. Sit down and relax."

He coaxed her off her stool and led her by the hand over to the sofa, where he began to rub her neck and shoulders. She closed her eyes and let her body relax, enjoying the massage in spite of herself.

Several minutes passed before Natalie broke the silence. "Can I ask you something?"

"Sure." His hands continued to knead her tired muscles.

"What are we doing here? I thought I knew, but now I'm not so sure."

Peter turned the question back to her. "What do you think?"

She shook her head. "When we started this, I knew it was mostly physical. But...." She faltered. "Lately, it feels like there's more to it than that. I'm just not sure where this is going."

Peter continued his rhythmic movements as he considered her question, eventually letting his hands slide down her shoulders until they rested at her sides. She could still feel the lingering effects of his touch when he began to speak.

"Nat," he began finally, "I knew a long time ago that I wasn't meant for anything long term. I don't like making promises I can't keep. And I don't believe in making commitments, because sooner or later, most relationships stop working."

Natalie said nothing.

"But you're right. This isn't just physical. I might not be able to do anything but hold you tonight, but I can't think of anyone else I'd rather be holding."

Natalie gave a faint smile as Peter continued. "You're beautiful, intelligent, and *generally*," as he kissed her neck, "a pleasure to be around. As things are right now, I'm exactly where I want to be."

As things are right now. "But things change, Peter," Natalie persisted. "What then?"

Peter wrapped his arms around her from behind. "That's my point. Things will either stay as they are, and we'll continue enjoying each other's company. Or they'll change for the worse, and we'll let each other go." He turned to face her and kissed her softly. "But either way, I won't regret this. I hope you won't either."

Natalie gave herself up to his embrace. In Peter's eyes, she was beautiful, desirable and the object of his affection, at least for now. Irrationally, she felt a breathless, hopeful feeling. Yet, he hadn't promised anything, *wouldn't* promise anything— only that he didn't want it to end at this moment.

***

Peter paid the delivery man and brought the pizza over to the coffee table with a stack of paper plates, napkins, and drinks. Exhausted but content, Natalie put her feet up on the ottoman and let him wait on her. Pulling out the TV remote wedged between the sofa cushions, she studied the movies available for streaming. Comedies, action, suspense—nothing grabbed her attention until she spied a favorite stand-by. She pressed *"Select"* with a smirk. He *did* tell her to choose something that she would like.

On his way back to the sofa, Peter glanced at the TV and did a double take.

"Sense and Sensibility?"

Natalie gave him an innocent shrug. "It's a classic."

Peter's gaze narrowed. "You could have been a bit more sympathetic to my side of the aisle."

Natalie patted the cushion beside her. "Have an open mind. You might even like it," she said encouragingly.

Peter sat beside her and watched the opening credits scroll by, grumbling all the while. "…there sure as hell must be something about you if I'm willing to watch Jane Austen, when there is a perfectly good Clint Eastwood movie that I could be watching instead."

Natalie laughed and handed him a plate with pizza. "You're a good man. I'll remember this."

They finished their dinner and left the remains to be cleaned up later. Natalie curled up and laid her head on his lap. He covered her with a blanket that lay folded on top of the couch and stroked her hair.

The next thing Natalie remembered was Peter gently placing her on the bed. As he unbuttoned her sweater, she stirred and protested weakly, "No, Peter, I can't."

"Shh, I know that," he whispered, freeing her arms from the garment and covering her with the comforter. "Just go to sleep."

Natalie closed her eyes. "Did you like the movie?"

"It was great."

"Told you," she said, smiling into her pillow. With a contented sigh, Natalie curled up under the comforter. Moments later, the bed shifted under Peter's weight as he wrapped his arm around her and pulled her close.

Chapter 11

Peter opened his eyes, a slow recognition of his surroundings sinking in. The night-black sky of his wakeful life was replaced now by a bluish grey glow. It was a colorful reminder of the dwindling time he had left before daylight ran out.

This was their spot. He knew it by heart. Long, idyllic hours spent on the hood of his car watching the sun set and then counting the stars as they popped into view. The only way up—and down—was a serpentine road that climbed up the mountain until it leveled off at the top. The view was millions of years in the making--towering cliffs of striated rock falling away to a deep ravine of fast-moving water.

Peter would make it this time. He had to. Abandoning the road, he went up and over the rocky walls that abutted it, struggling through razor-edged brush along the way. But the shortcut proved successful and Peter reached the plateau. The little Dodge, its dull white paint even more faded in the waning light, sat alone at the lookout, its front wheels perched perilously close to the sheer drop below.

She sensed him and looked up. "Go away," she said, her voice devoid of emotion.

"Come out of the car, baby."

She shook her head, an ugly smile of contempt on her face.

"Eve, let me help you," he stretched out his hand, determined to yank her to safety. As he neared the car—only a few feet more—she shrank from him, her hand already reaching for the door handle.

"It's too late," she said.

He watched the car lurch forward. Watched it hover in mid-air, then descend, then fall. Running after her, he stopped just short of the edge and dropped to his knees, shouting her name over and over.

CHAPTER 12

Natalie woke with a start, sensing something amiss. She sat up and studied the room, holding her breath as she listened for any unusual sounds.

She turned to Peter, sleeping soundly next to her, one arm thrown across his chest. Satisfied it was nothing, she began to lie back down when Peter's body jerked, his face twitching in fear. He murmured something unintelligible, followed by the same word over and over again. *What was he saying?* Suddenly, his whole body stiffened with panic. Natalie watched him with horror, afraid to wake him, yet loathe to see him in such distress.

"It's okay, Peter," she whispered, gently stroking his hair. "It's just a dream."

Peter went silent for a moment, and then jerked his head off the pillow sharply. He sat upright in bed, breathing hard, a dazed expression on his face.

Natalie touched his arm. "You were having a bad dream. It's over now."

Peter gave her a vague stare as his breathing returned to normal. Natalie continued to stroke his arm soothingly. The tension had not left his body.

"I'm sorry I woke you," he said finally, his eyes staring into blank space.

"Are you okay?"

"Fine," he said, his voice distant. "Just go back to sleep." He rolled over onto his side, his body facing away from her. Natalie moved next to him and draped her arm across his chest. To her surprise, he clasped her hand, tightening her hold around him. Silence fell over the pair, though sleep eluded them for some time. Her hand pressed flat against his chest, Natalie felt the rhythm of his heartbeats as they gradually slowed to normal.

***

The next morning, Natalie awoke to an empty bed and the smell of coffee drifting in from the kitchen. She stretched her achy body, her mind still groggy. As she often did in the mornings, she replayed in her mind the events of the night before. She remembered their talk, dinner, the movie (*did they watch the movie?),* Peter's nightmare. Her thoughts then strayed to the load of papers and assignments to be completed that weekend. A feeling of fatigue hit her, and she swung her legs out of bed with a sigh.

A shower was essential, Natalie decided. She undressed as the water heated up, and then searched for her toiletry bag, remembering too late that it was probably still in the living room where she had dropped it the night before.

Undeterred, she scoured the bathroom for a spare toothbrush, finding a new one in one of the drawers. After brushing her teeth, she stepped into the shower, exhaling with pleasure as the hot water ran down her hair and back. It took little time to wash up, but she remained under the spray for several minutes more before finally stepping out. She was just grabbing a towel when Peter knocked on the door.

Natalie hastily pulled the towel around herself as he proceeded to walk in uninvited.

"Hey, I'm not dressed!"

"I can see that," Peter answered with a wry smile. "Perfect timing, if you ask me."

"So, get out of here so I can *get* dressed, will you?"

Peter leaned up against the door frame, in no hurry to leave. He crossed his arms.

"You know, I think I've seen just about everything that's under there," he said, pointing to the towel. "Don't you think it's a little late to be modest?"

Natalie held the towel tightly against her. "It's *never* too late to be modest," she said primly. "Go." She waved him off with her free hand.

He grinned. "Fine. I just came in to tell you there's coffee if you want some."

"Thanks. I'll be out soon." As he shut the door after him, she remembered her toiletry bag. "Hey, wait!" she called out. "Can you bring me my overnight bag?"

He was halfway to the kitchen when he answered. "On one condition—skip the makeup. I want to see you without it for once."

"I look awful without makeup."

"Then get your own bag."

"Oh, all right, you win," she said in exasperation.

Seconds later, Peter returned with the bag and handed it through the open door. He kissed her lightly.

"Good morning."

She returned his smile and his kiss.

Natalie towel-dried her hair and then brushed it out into long, damp strands. She found an elastic band and tied her hair into a ponytail down her back. Without the need for makeup, her morning routine was considerably shortened. She dressed and applied some lotion to her face before joining Peter in the kitchen where he was reading the paper. Given the demands of her weekend, she had enough time for a quick cup of coffee and then it would be time to leave.

He gave an appreciative nod. "I like."

Natalie concealed her self-consciousness with a dramatic bow. "Thank you, Professor."

She moved past him to the coffee mug waiting on the counter, but an outstretched arm intercepted her.

"You should go without makeup more often."

Natalie shook her head. "It makes me look too young."

Peter pulled her onto his lap, managing to place his coffee cup down safely in the process. "It makes you look irresistible."

This time his kiss was deep. His newly freed hand entangled itself in the wispy strands that hadn't made it into the ponytail.

Natalie lifted her head from his, opening her eyes with difficulty. She smiled with regret. "You're making it awfully hard to leave."

"I'm good at that," he murmured, his attention now focused on a particularly sensitive part of her neck.

Natalie groaned, torn between the hours of schoolwork waiting for her at home and the immediate contentment of where she sat—clearly not much of a choice.

"Peter," she warned through half-closed eyes, "if I flunk my courses, you'll have to find a new assistant."

Peter wasn't swayed. "You worry too much." He returned to her mouth but was unable to linger there long before she sat up and pushed him away.

"I'm serious. I have too much to do." She held out her hand and began listing the first of many tasks still unfinished, one outstretched finger for each. "I've got a paper to finish for Dr. Henry's class and a Neuro exam on Tuesday, and there are those articles that you need me to summarize by Monday...."

Peter watched the little lines of worry gather on her forehead. He took her hand and gently pressed one of the fingers back down. "At least I can cut you some slack on the articles. I probably won't need them before Wednesday."

"Oh, no—no special favors." Natalie held up her hands in mock protest. "I don't want to think I'm getting away with anything just because..." She chose not to finish the sentence.

"...you're my Girl Friday?" he teased, ignoring the glare she shot at him. "Actually, you've accomplished more in the space of one year than all of my other assistants combined. Maybe I should have started sleeping with the help years ago. I might have finished this book by now."

Natalie slapped him hard on the shoulder. Peter laughed out loud and tried to dodge as she swung at him a second time.

"Bastard," she said, unable to conceal a smile for long. "You're lucky to have me, you know. I'm too good for you."

"Yes, you are," Peter conceded. He paused, his expression becoming more serious. "Hey, why don't you stay and get your work done here this weekend?"

Natalie was surprised by the invitation. He had never asked her to stay the entire weekend before.

"I'd…love to," she admitted, "but I don't have any of my books with me."

"Check my office. I might have some of the books you need right here."

"Okay," Natalie answered cautiously, already considering the books she would need. "But first, coffee." She slid off his lap and headed to the counter, where she poured herself a cup. Then, with an appreciative nod at Peter, she strode toward the office in search of the priceless books which might afford her one more day and night with him.

Peter's office was taken up almost entirely by a large desk and swivel chair, with built-in bookcases flanking the adjacent wall. Natalie circled the desk, glancing at the papers and books that covered almost every available inch of space. Most were chapter drafts for his book, long since reviewed and edited. *Did he ever throw anything away?*

Reaching across the desk to grab a stray paper, she uncovered a nameplate, burnished gold against a solid block of cherry. *F. Peterson Spencer.* Natalie narrowed her eyes in momentary surprise. "Peter" obviously was a nickname. Strange that she never knew that.

"Hey, who is this Peterson character?" she called out.

Natalie heard Peter's footsteps as they moved leisurely down the hall. He appeared in the doorway, coffee cup in hand, a laconic smile on his face.

"That would be me."

"Why didn't I know that?" she scolded, though not very convincingly. "To think I've been calling you by the wrong name all this time."

Peter took a sip of his coffee before replying. "Have I ever not come when you've called me?"

She ignored that. "Still, you could have told me. I like it, by the way. It sounds very…" She searched for the right word. "Distinguished."

"It's my mother's maiden name," he supplied. "She was the last of her line, so I guess she wanted her family's name continued on in some form."

Natalie picked up the nameplate and showed it to him. "What does the 'F' stand for?"

"Frank. My father's name." Had Natalie imagined it? Peter's smile seemed to fade a little with those words.

She replaced the nameplate on the desk. "So, maybe I should call you Frank?"

"Not if you expect me to answer," he replied. "I stopped going by that name in my teens."

"Or maybe 'Frankie'?" Natalie stood up on her toes and kissed him playfully, enjoying the scratchy feel of his beard against her skin before dropping back down onto her heels.

Peter returned the kiss and ignored the suggestion. "Now, stop snooping around and find those books." He turned her in the direction of the bookshelves and left the room.

By the time Natalie returned from the office with an armful of books, Peter was stacking the last piece of wood in the fireplace.

"You made a fire!" Natalie exclaimed. She laid the books down, headed back to the office to retrieve what was left of her coffee, and returned to the floor where he sat. Flopping down on her stomach, she stretched her legs behind her and propped herself up on her elbows. "I love fires," she said, closing her eyes and delighting in its warmth.

Peter, still kneeling before the hearth, watched her show of contentment with a placid smile. "You are easy to please."

Natalie opened her eyes, unsure how to take his remark. Yet, there was nothing unkind in his expression. "Is that so bad?" she asked.

"Not at all," Peter replied. "Those who can be content with the ordinary things in life are undoubtedly the happiest."

Natalie cocked her head. "And are you?"

"Content? I guess," he shrugged. "It depends on how you define it. Things aren't always that simple."

A momentary sadness touched his expression, a wistful air of something lost along the way. Natalie moved over to him and kissed his forehead. "It doesn't go away," she whispered. "You can get it back."

Peter looked into her eyes, his gaze almost searching. He nodded and kissed her back.

For the next few hours, Peter and Natalie sat beside the fire, each absorbed in their own worlds. Despite the relative silence, they enjoyed an easy companionship, similar to the one that Natalie often felt in the presence of her parents. Theirs was a relationship she admired, one that had weathered its share of ups and downs but remained strong. Natalie hoped that she would one day find a love like that.

In some ways, she already had. At least for a few hours each week.

***

Her steps brisk and light, Natalie left the Psychology building, tipped her head back at the cloudless sky and breathed the first easy breath she could remember taking in over a week. Her last exam of the semester was over. The frigid air pierced her lungs, but she delighted in the sensation. The worst was behind her, and anything was possible at that moment.

Natalie waited at the crosswalk for the light to turn green. She stared out at the sea of cars parked across the street in Lot 59, nicknamed "Egypt" because it stood on the far, outer fringes of campus. Despite its remote location, it was popular among students because it was the cheapest place to park. Natalie boarded a tram that took her to the last row in the lot. There, her compact car awaited her, a light dusting of snow on its roof. Ironically, the drive to her house took less time than her trip to the car. Reaching her porch, Natalie flung open the door and shouted Gina's name.

"I'm right here," Gina's head popped up from under the kitchen counter. "What are you so happy about?"

"I'm done!" Natalie dropped her bags on the couch and sat on one of the bar stools. She placed both hands on the counter dramatically and took a deep breath. "God, I feel good."

"Congratulations. Do you want some coffee? Wait—cancel that. You're hyper enough as it is."

"Give me the coffee. I'm going to do some housecleaning." Natalie motioned for a cup with her hand.

Gina groaned. Natalie was notorious for her housecleaning binges—all-day events that concluded only when the house was absolutely spotless. While Gina appreciated the final result, she had learned to steer clear while cleaning was in progress.

"I can't believe I'm saying this, but I'm actually grateful that my shift starts early today."

"Coward." Natalie watched her roommate's retreating figure. "Okay, have it your way. I'll have the place looking brand new when you get home."

"Deal."

Minutes later, Natalie had changed into her cleaning clothes, fastened her iPod onto her waistband, and assembled the arsenal of cleaning supplies she would need for the day.

There was something therapeutic about cleaning, especially after a long semester of school. Just focusing on the simple acts of sorting, discarding, vacuuming, and dusting, Natalie felt herself disconnect from the tensions of the previous weeks and slip into mental autopilot. Not unlike yoga, she liked to think, but with the added benefit of a clean house when she was done.

***

As she worked, Natalie's mind inevitably strayed to Peter and their last weekend together. Though just days before the start of finals week, Natalie had found it impossible to refuse when Peter invited her to stay with him.

It had been a full day of studying and, in Peter's case, writing by the time the pair called it a day. Their evening was spent on the most pleasant and ordinary of tasks—making dinner, washing dishes, and finally, settling on the couch to watch the evening news. These were the things Natalie would miss most during her time away from him.

She tucked her legs beneath her and leaned against him on the couch. Eyes still on the newscaster, Peter draped his arm around her and pulled her close. Natalie rested her head on his shoulder.

God, how she loved him. Natalie had known for some time, although she wasn't sure when it had actually happened. Loving Peter Spencer was no small undertaking. She knew she took a huge risk in becoming so deeply invested in him. And that was what made it so painful. Not the love itself—what hurt was trying to hide it, the fear of how he might react if he knew. The intensity of what she held inside was so palpable that it felt like another living organ to her. To conceal it meant continually pushing it out of view, causing a physical pain akin to a heavy weight resting on her chest.

Natalie knew she couldn't hide her feelings indefinitely. At some point, they would be detected—or worse—erupt on their own with an embarrassing messiness. So, faced with an impossible situation, she continued on the best way she knew, monitoring her words and actions around him for fear of destroying the fragile bond they had formed.

Peter did care for Natalie. This she knew, though nothing was ever said. They shared an unspoken agreement to avoid any declarations or promises to each other. Natalie accepted this arrangement, not only because she had little choice, but also because Peter conveyed his feelings for her in a myriad of unspoken ways. The way he stroked her hair as they sat on the couch; how he held her in his arms at night; the contented gazes cast her way when he thought she wasn't looking. These actions spoke as loudly to her as any of his words could have.

Yes, she knew Peter cared for her. What she didn't understand was his fear of acknowledging it.

Natalie recalled the frequent nightmares he had at night, convinced they held the answer. Several times she awoke to find Peter struggling in his sleep, repeating the same name over and over again: *Eve*. She asked him about it once, but was shut down by his sudden, almost defensive, change of the subject.

Who was this Eve, and what had she done to him to make him so afraid? Why did he call her name so frantically in his dreams? An unexpected wave of anger shot through Natalie as she imagined the pain this woman must have put him through. She tightened her grip around Peter, pulling his body closer. Peter glanced at her, surprised at the fierce expression on her face.

"Whoa, what's going on in there?"

Natalie shook herself from her thoughts. She gave a self-conscious smile. "Don't worry, you're not in danger."

"Good thing," he replied. "I'd rather not get on your bad side again if I can help it."

Natalie gave him a puzzled frown and then laughed under her breath as she remembered. "Your run-in with Andrew," she said. "You're right, I was mad as hell at you that night."

"I got that impression. But, if I recall, you were pretty forgiving, too." He elbowed her with a grin.

But Natalie's expression remained serious. "I thought you deserved a second chance."

Peter paused, abandoning his playful tone. "I'm glad."

The two gazed into each other's faces, recalling memories of that night and the days and nights that followed.

A commercial appeared on the TV, drowning the room with loud music and distracting images. Natalie peered at the TV, her face frowning in irritation.

"Enough of this," she murmured, more to herself than him. She reached for the remote control that he held in his hand and turned off the set, bathing the room in a peaceful stillness.

Peter watched her, his eyes still adjusting to the newly darkened room. "Now what?" he said, lifting his eyebrows.

Natalie laid the remote control on the table beside them, meeting his gaze.

"Starting tomorrow, I'll be doing nothing but eating, sleeping, and dreaming finals. And then, I'll be heading home. Let's make the most of the time I have left."

As she said this, Natalie reached out and touched his face, gently pulling him toward her. Peter needed little encouragement. He stretched his long frame across the couch, Natalie's body moving in tandem until it nestled snugly beside his, her arms wrapped around him tightly.

"You're something else, you know that?" Peter said, his voice low and affected. His face was only inches from hers.

"Is that a good thing?" Natalie whispered.

For a split second, Peter's face was transparent, the emotion in his eyes unmistakable.

"Yes."

"Good," she responded, her eyes never leaving his. "Don't forget that while I'm gone."

***

As she prepared to leave Peter's house, Natalie reached into her backpack and pulled out a package wrapped in red paper.

"Merry Christmas," she said, handing it to him.

Peter glanced at the book-shaped package, a frown beginning to spread across his face. "I thought we agreed not to give each other any presents."

"You agreed. I didn't," Natalie replied. "Open it."

Peter pulled off the paper to reveal an early edition of *Cannery Row.* He opened the cover with care, reading the copyright date and the original foreword. He gently slid his hand down the page, feeling its smooth, cottony texture. He said nothing at first, and then looked up at her with obvious appreciation.

She smiled. "Do you like it? I noticed you had all of Steinbeck's books in your office except this one. Have you ever read it? It's a great story."

Peter nodded his head, returning his gaze to the book. "Many times. It was one of my favorites. I lent it to someone once and never got it back. Thank you," he said, his voice tinged with an emotion that Natalie couldn't quite identify. "This was an excellent choice."

Natalie was gratified by his reaction. She stood watching a moment longer, and then went back to packing up her things.

Peter helped her with the remaining books and then picked up her backpack and hung it over her shoulder.

"It will be strange not seeing you these next few weeks," Peter admitted as they walked to the door together.

"Oh, you'll hardly notice I'm gone," Natalie replied with a light-heartedness she didn't feel. "Have a good Christmas with your family."

"You, too."

Unsure of what else to say, Natalie was reaching for the doorknob when Peter took her hand and stopped her. As she turned around, he bent down and kissed her. "Thank you," he said. "For everything."

Natalie nodded and smiled. With all the strength she could muster, she opened the door and left, praying for the time to pass swiftly so she could return to him. And that when she did, he would still be there waiting for her.

Chapter 13

Peter unfastened the car seat and waited for Amanda, clad in a pink down parka, to hop out onto the driveway. She looked around in curiosity at the small brick house and then looked up at Peter. "Where are we?"

Peter held out his hand. His decision to come here was impulsive. Not only was he not sure if Natalie had finished her final exams, but there was no guarantee that she'd be able to join them. Still, the familiar sight of Natalie's car in the driveway was a positive sign. He squeezed the five-year old's hand.

"We're going to see if my friend Natalie would like to spend the day with us."

"Your friend's a girl?"

"Yep, she's a girl," Peter confirmed.

Together they walked up to the front porch, Amanda skipping the entire way.

"Do you want to ring the doorbell?"

Amanda ran over to the bell, pressing it twice in quick succession. She hopped excitedly as she waited for a response.

A young woman in a ponytail and hospital scrubs answered the door. She looked at the pair vaguely at first before a flicker of recognition sparked in her eyes.

"Professor Spencer?"

Peter smiled. "You must be Gina. I feel like I already know you." He held out his hand in greeting. "Please, call me Peter."

"Okay…Peter." Gina almost stumbled on the name. She gazed at the young girl by his side and then back at him. "Is Natalie expecting you?"

"No. Is she here? I saw her car out front."

"Oh, she's here all right," Gina responded. She glanced down the hall where Peter could hear the faint sound of singing. "Come on in. She's in the throes of a cleaning binge right now." Gina backed away from the door and let the two enter.

Peter took the girl's hand and stepped inside, glancing around the living room as he did so. He had been in this house once before, the night he brought Natalie home.

"Gina, this is my niece, Amanda. Amanda, this is Gina, my friend Natalie's roommate."

The bouncing suddenly stopped, and Amanda gave Gina a shy smile, never letting go of Peter's hand. "Hi."

"Hi, Amanda," Gina responded, kneeling down in front of the girl. "Hey, do you want to see something funny? Go down this hall and open the last door on the left." Gina pointed toward the end of the hall and then stood up and grinned at Peter. "Go ahead. I'm pretty sure she's decent."

Peter led the way down the hall with Amanda following close behind. He knocked on the door, but there was no answer. That she was in there was beyond dispute. They could hear her singing at the top of her lungs. Amanda looked back at Gina and giggled. Gina nodded and urged them on.

Peter pushed the door open slowly. At first they saw nothing, but as the space widened, there was Natalie, dusting cloth in one hand, can of furniture polish in the other, singing and dancing in place as she wiped off one of her shelves. She was dressed in a white tank top, baggy sweatpants, and a brightly colored scarf tied around her hair. Peter and Amanda stood motionless as she continued her song. Suddenly, Natalie whirled around to grab a book off her desk and saw the pair standing in her doorway. She shrieked, yanking the earbuds from her ears.

"What...?" she stammered.

"I hope we weren't interrupting anything," Peter said, unable to hide his amusement. Amanda giggled again.

Natalie struggled to turn off the music still blaring from the attached ear buds.

"Peter, what are you doing here?" she demanded, still out of breath. "How did you get in?"

In answer, Gina's howl of laughter radiated down the hall. Natalie slowly nodded her head in understanding. "Thanks, Gina," she called out. "I'll remember this." She was met by more laughter.

"I hope you don't mind," Peter began, his eyes twinkling. "I brought my niece, Amanda, with me."

Natalie looked down and saw the little girl that Peter had spoken about so often. Placing a hand on her chest, she took a deep breath to calm herself, then held out her hand in greeting. "So, you're Amanda. Your uncle has told me a lot about you."

Amanda smiled and shook her hand.

Natalie continued. "I hear that you are five years old and very smart, and you're about to be a big sister, is that right?" Amanda nodded, clearly enjoying the interest that this young woman was paying her.

"Which is the reason we're here," Peter interjected. "Amanda's mom and dad are at the hospital right now having the baby, so I'm taking care of Amanda while they're busy."

Natalie shot Peter a look. He nodded soberly.

"Wow, that's exciting news," she continued. "So you get to spend the whole day with your Uncle Peter? That *is* a treat. What are you two planning to do?"

Amanda peered up at Peter in anticipation, who then looked at Natalie. "Well, I thought we might go to the Children's Museum and then maybe for a bite to eat somewhere. Beyond that, I'm not sure."

"Sounds like fun," Natalie said with approval.

"I know it's last minute, but would you like to join us?"

She faltered for an answer. "Is…that a good idea?"

Peter understood Natalie's hesitation. Months of careful attempts to keep their relationship undercover had become second nature for them both. He threw out a suggestion in the hopes of convincing her.

"You've done some babysitting for Professor Osgood's kids. I don't see the harm in helping me with my niece for the day."

She brightened. "Well, since you put it that way, I'd love to."

Natalie glanced around the room and then down to her clothing. "I should change. Why don't you two go into the living room and watch some TV while I get ready."

Peter gave her a grateful smile as he ushered Amanda out the door. "Thanks," he said.

"Don't mention it."

"Oh, by the way, I like the *babushka*," he said, pointing to the peasant-like scarf tied around her hair. "Maybe you can wear that again sometime." His voice had just a trace of suggestion to it.

Natalie's hand moved to her head and blushed. She slammed the door behind her as Peter retreated down the hall with a grin.

***

Gina was putting on her coat when Peter and Amanda returned to the living room.

"Was she decent?"

Peter nodded and laughed. "Does she do this often?"

"Often enough," Gina replied. "She's a real force of nature. If you hadn't come by when you did, she would have had the entire house cleaned by the time I got home from my shift."

Peter gave a wry smile. "Sorry." He motioned for Amanda to sit down on the couch while he found a program on TV for her to watch.

Gina shrugged good naturedly. "Well, I'm off to work. There's still some coffee in the kitchen. You're welcome to what's left."

"Thanks, I might have some," he replied. "It was good to finally meet you, Gina."

"You too, Profess…I mean, Peter."

Gina grabbed her purse and left, leaving Peter and Amanda watching "Curious George." She smiled to herself as she unlocked the car. After all this time, she finally got to see the infamous Peter Spencer. As handsome as she had remembered and personable, too. It was easy to understand why Natalie was so attached to him. She just hoped for her friend's sake that he felt the same about her.

***

Peter and Amanda were on the couch when Natalie emerged from her room, freshly attired in jeans and a sweater. She laid her hand on his shoulder.

"Two more minutes and 'Curious George' will be over," he whispered, pointing to Amanda's rapt expression as she watched the cartoon. A bomb could have exploded in the room and the preschooler wouldn't have noticed. Peter placed his hand atop hers, giving it a slight squeeze.

"When are you leaving?" he asked.

"Tomorrow morning."

"Are we keeping you from your packing?"

Natalie shook her head. "I don't have any big plans while I'm there. I can pack a bag in ten minutes. I'd much rather be out having some fun on my last day."

"Well, I'm not sure if this is everyone's idea of fun," Peter countered, "but I appreciate your being a good sport about it."

"Is your sister all right?"

Peter shrugged. "I don't know too much. Tim gave me a call before they headed for the hospital. He sounded worried, to say the least. Dawn's not due for four more weeks. Our mother stayed with Amanda until I could get to the house, and then she headed off to the hospital, too. They'll give me a call when they hear anything."

"I'm sure they'll be fine, Peter," Natalie assured him. "Let's just focus on keeping Amanda busy."

The sound of the closing credits turned their attention to the TV. Amanda's head popped up, an instant smile forming at the two adults watching her. "Natalie's ready. Let's go, Uncle Pete!" She launched herself off the couch and ran to the door.

"Hold on," Peter's stern voice stopped her. "Get back here. You need to put on your coat." Amanda retraced her steps to where her uncle stood, pink parka in hand.

By the time Natalie pulled on her own coat and locked the front door, Peter was finishing up with the straps and buckles of Amanda's car seat. Natalie watched as his hands moved deftly from one fastener to the other.

"Wow, you're a pro at this," she marveled.

Peter laughed and held open Natalie's door, closing it behind her. As she slid inside, a slight smile touched her face, her eyes closing briefly. For a moment, he watched her through the window, intrigued by the change and what was behind it. Yet, by the time he circled around to his side, her expression had returned to normal and she gave him an excited smile.

The children's museum took up an entire downtown block. Pedestrians walked along State Street, many of them students who were either celebrating the end of finals or heading to the coffee shop for another caffeine-fueled day of study. Peter waited for a group to pass by, then pulled into the covered parking lot adjacent to the museum. Finding a spot, he switched off the motor and turned to his passengers, "Ready?"

"Yes!" Amanda responded. "Let's go!"

Peter took a deep breath and gave Natalie his best "*it's now or never*" look. Once Amanda was released from her straps, Peter took her one hand and Natalie the other as they made their way down the sidewalk, no different from any other young family that day.

In the museum, Amanda was unstoppable. Room after room of bright, colorful, and often noisy displays opened up before them. With Peter and Natalie doing their best to keep up,

Amanda sampled each exhibit before excitedly moving on to the next.

They spent hours there, racing miniature boats through water-filled tubes, playing customer and cashier in a fully stocked grocery store, sampling musical instruments, and creating life-sized silhouettes in the Shadow Room. Peter participated in all the activities, laughing and hamming it up for his niece as they proceeded through each of the rooms.

The last exhibit was clearly the most popular, given the numbers of raucous, laughing children running in all directions. Three stories tall and spanning half a city block, the space resembled a tropical jungle with palm trees, hanging vines, and stuffed animals suspended from the ceiling. But it was the giant tree houses, springing up in three corners of the room, that attracted the most activity.

Peter watched with apprehension as children scurried up and down the ladders that led to the structures. Once inside, there was a pulley system that conveyed messages from one tree house to another. They watched as children wrote messages on small slips of paper, hung them on a cord with clothespins, and took turns pulling the cord across the expanse until it reached the intended recipient in one of the other houses. The system reminded Peter of the way women in the cities once hung their wash out to dry, pulling on the clothesline to retrieve the articles once they were ready.

Amanda was eager to join the other children.

"No, Amanda," Peter said. "Those are for bigger kids. You're not old enough yet."

"But, Uncle Pete, look," she grabbed his hand and pointed to a particularly small child that was halfway up the ladder. "She's younger than me! Please?"

Peter looked to Natalie for reinforcement but received little more than an amused smile in response. He was well aware of being reduced to a meek pushover in the presence of this little girl. Still, in the end, he merely dropped his shoulders and nodded.

"But be careful," he ordered. "And take Natalie with you," he added as an afterthought.

Natalie's head came up at the sound of her name. "What?"

Peter stared back. "You once said I could count on your help with ladder emergencies," he answered. "Here's your chance."

Amanda wasted little time. She clasped Natalie's hand and half-dragged her to the nearest tree house. Peter watched as the two climbed carefully up the ladder and entered the enclosure, Natalie ducking her head to clear the child-sized roof.

Amanda's head peered out from the window. "Hey, Uncle Pete, I'm up here!"

Peter waved back, keeping a close eye on the girls.

Once inside, the pair jockeyed for space among the other children and adults. Baskets of scrap paper and clothes pins were passed around, Amanda taking a piece for herself. Natalie knelt as her young companion wrote something and showed it to her. She read it and laughed, prompting Amanda to join in. Then Natalie took the pencil and wrote something herself. Amanda nodded with enthusiasm and ran to the clothesline, fastening her message to it with a clothespin.

"Uncle Pete," she called to him from the window. "Go over to the other tree house—I'm sending you a letter!"

Peter glanced at the structure beside them, its slender connecting line transmitting messages to and from Amanda's house. Towering twenty feet in the air, it made him uncomfortable just looking at it.

"Sorry, sweetheart. I'm not going up there. Just bring down your message."

"But you *have* to!" she pleaded. "See? I'm sending it over right now!" She rushed back to the clothesline and began pulling it toward her, propelling the pinned note across the expanse.

Peter shook his head again. "No, Amanda. I'm not going up. You come down if you're finished." He waved the two down.

The little girl's face fell, and she began to whine. Natalie bent down and appeared to be reasoning with her. Eventually, the pair moved to the doorway, Natalie turning and inching down the ladder backwards. Peter stepped closer to the tree-house, waiting for them to descend.

"Wait!" Amanda shouted, a ring of panic in her voice. She stretched her arm toward Natalie. "Don't leave me!"

Natalie stopped and took Amanda's hand, her words inaudible, but her tone and manner clearly intended to calm the little girl.

Amanda just stared down the length of the tree house, frozen in place.

"I can't," she whimpered.

Natalie paused, as if considering her next step, then climbed back up the ladder and enfolded the little girl in her arms. She pointed to the ladder as she spoke, but Amanda kept shaking her head and closing her eyes.

"Is everything all right?" Peter called from below.

Natalie looked out the doorway at Peter, her expression a mix of exasperation and concern.

"Peter, we're going to need your help."

He watched the two expectantly.

"Amanda needs me up here with her. Can you climb up and help her down?"

Peter searched for Amanda's face, still buried against Natalie's chest.

"Baby, are you okay?" he called up to her.

Amanda peeked out from Natalie's embrace. "Uncle Pete, it's so high up." As if to reinforce the statement, she peeked down and recoiled back to her original position.

"We'll get you down, honey," he said, moving to the ladder without hesitation, a grim frown of determination his only indication of fear. Natalie watched in concern.

Rung by rung, Peter climbed, ignoring the quickening of his heart. Keeping his face trained on the two girls waiting at the top, he reached their level in no time.

Amanda left the protection of Natalie's arms to watch Peter's progress. When his head popped into view, she gave a weak smile.

Peter smiled back. "Come on, Mandy," he said, reaching out and squeezing her hand. With Natalie's help, Amanda turned around and placed her foot on the ladder, while Peter stood below her and calmly talked her down one step at a time. Natalie followed behind, positioning herself so she could maintain eye contact with Amanda. The whole process took less than a minute.

Once again on solid ground, Amanda turned and wrapped her arms around Peter's legs, hugging him tightly. He was visibly pale, a sheen of sweat on his face.

"You did good," Natalie whispered, meeting his eyes.

Peter bent slightly at the waist as he returned his niece's embrace, staring at Natalie with an expression of unmistakable relief.

"Come on, you two," he said. "I think we've had enough excitement for one day. Let's get out of here."

There was little complaint from Amanda. Holding on to Peter's hand, she skipped down the hallway, glancing only briefly at the playrooms that she had previously visited. That is, until they emerged into the sunlit plaza.

"Uncle Pete, we forgot my note!"

He groaned. "Well, we're not going back for it."

"*Please....*"

"No, Amanda. Just tell me what it said."

She pouted. "You tell him, Natalie."

Natalie repeated the message, willing herself to keep a straight face.

"'I love you'."

Peter looked up sharply, for a moment forgetting that she was merely the messenger and not the composer. He couldn't seem to find any words to reply.

Amanda looked on in frustration at the two adults before interjecting, "'*From Amanda!*' Natalie, you forgot the *Amanda* part!"

"Sorry," she said, smiling at the little girl and reaching out to tousle her hair. "'From Amanda'," Natalie corrected herself. She glanced at Peter with an unreadable expression. Peter straightened up and cleared his throat.

"I wrote it all by myself, too," Amanda said proudly. "With just a little help from Natalie."

Peter gathered his niece up in his arms. "A very nice note," he said, kissing her on the forehead. "I love you, too."

Chapter 14

It was close to five o'clock when they pulled open the doors to the indoor mall down the street from the museum. Choosing one of the more kid-friendly restaurants inside, they found a table and Amanda immediately got to work on the children's placemat with the box of crayons she was offered.

As they waited for their meals to arrive, Natalie drew pictures on her placemat, which Amanda tried to identify.

"A cat?" Amanda guessed.

"No …."

"A dog?"

"No, one more guess."

"A gorilla, definitely," Peter interjected.

Natalie scowled. "How is that a gorilla?"

"Well, it's kind of hairy," he laughed, pointing out features from her drawing.

"It's a *cow*! Can't you see that?" Natalie protested. "Come on, I'm not that bad of an artist, am I?"

"Well, I didn't want to say anything but…" Peter began, elbowing Amanda with a grin.

Amanda giggled, clearly enjoying the friendly banter between the two adults. She turned to Peter and asked, "Uncle Pete, are you going to marry Natalie?"

Natalie looked up in surprise, then at Peter, who was equally at a loss for words.

"No, Amanda, we're just friends." His matter-of-fact tone left little room for discussion.

Amanda persisted. "But can't friends get married?"

Peter hesitated and looked to Natalie, who smiled and waited for his response. It wasn't often that Peter found himself at a disadvantage in a debate. The fact that his inquisitor was five years old made the moment all the more enjoyable. Natalie had no intention of rescuing him.

"Sure, sometimes. But sometimes friends just stay friends."

"Well, I think you should be the kind that gets married," Amanda persisted.

Peter lifted his eyebrows in curiosity. "And why is that?"

Amanda gave a patient smile, as if the answer was obvious. "Because then I could be the flower girl and wear a poofy dress and walk down the aisle with a basket of flowers."

Natalie laughed at the logic of her answer. "You would make a beautiful flower girl."

"I know! And Uncle Pete could wear a black suit and you could wear a long white dress. And at the end you would have to kiss and then we could have a big party with a cake."

Even Peter chuckled at her well-conceived plans. "It sounds like you've put a lot of thought into this, but I'm afraid you'll have to find someone else to wear that black suit."

Not hearing the response she was expecting, Amanda began to pout again. This time, Natalie stepped in.

"So, Amanda, what color would your dress be?"

The little girl perked up and began to describe in great detail the standard uniform for flower girls. With Natalie's help, a prototype was drawn in crayon of a pink dress with yellow ribbons and a basket filled with purple and red flowers.

Before long, dinner was served and the three settled down to eat. Conversation was lighthearted and touched on Natalie's home and family.

"You live on a farm?" Amanda said in between bites of her grilled cheese. "I do, too!"

"Well, I used to. Now I live here while I finish school."

"Is Uncle Pete your teacher?"

"He was. Now he's my boss."

"And your friend," Amanda interjected.

"Yes, my friend, too." Natalie nodded and caught Peter's eye. He had described Amanda well. Sharp as a whip.

As the conversation waned, Natalie absently scanned the restaurant and the other diners. She froze when she noticed Leslie Osgood, the wife of Professor Osgood from the Psychology Department, two tables away.

Natalie babysat for Leslie and Neil's two school-aged children from time to time. She enjoyed the family and was happy to help out when they needed a night away. Leslie was reserved, but very friendly when one got to know her. Neil was anything but quiet. At the department, he was known for his practical jokes and loud, booming laughter that could be heard clear down the hall from his office. He often stopped by Peter's office in the morning to chat over coffee, and never missed an opportunity to tease her about working for such a bore.

On any other day, Natalie would have waved hello. But today, she looked down, hoping that Leslie wouldn't notice her. Too late—Leslie glanced over at that moment and gave a warm smile mixed with surprise. Excusing herself to the other woman at the table, Leslie strode over.

"Well, hello, Natalie. And Peter! What are you two doing here? Are finals over, Natalie?"

"Hi, Mrs. Osgood. Yes, I finished my last one this morning," Natalie said with a polite smile.

Leslie's attention shifted to Peter. "I hope this is your treat, Peter. Neil says you work this poor girl day and night." She winked at Natalie.

Natalie swallowed.

"Actually," Peter jumped in, "Natalie is offering some last-minute help with my niece. Neil told me that Natalie was a great babysitter for your kids. I hope you don't mind."

"Not at all. You're lucky to have her."

"Oh, by the way, this is my niece, Amanda."

"It's a pleasure to meet you, Amanda," Leslie nodded toward the little girl.

Amanda smiled back. "My mom's having a baby right now," she explained in great seriousness.

"Oh my. That is important news," Leslie remarked. "Are you having a good time today?"

Amanda sat up on her knees, temporarily abandoning her grilled cheese. "We went to the kids' museum, and I got stuck in the tree house, but Uncle Pete rescued me, and then we came here for dinner. I got to have a grilled cheese!"

Leslie laughed at her enthusiastic reply. "That's wonderful. It's so nice that Natalie could come with you today."

"She's fun," Amanda nodded. "Uncle Pete and Natalie are friends, but they're not getting married."

Natalie blushed bright red and Peter concealed a nervous laugh by coughing into his napkin. "Okay, Amanda, I think you've had the spotlight long enough," he replied.

Leslie took note of their embarrassed reactions. "Well, I'd better get back to my table. Merry Christmas. Peter, I know Neil is planning to call you to watch the bowl games, so maybe I'll see you this weekend. Natalie, have a lovely break. We'll be sure to call you for more help next semester. That is, if you have time." For some reason, she glanced over at Peter when she said that.

Natalie smiled, relieved the conversation was nearing its end. "Sounds good. Merry Christmas."

They watched Leslie Osgood return to her table but, before Natalie could say anything, Peter's phone rang. He answered it on the second ring.

"Hi…how is she?" There was a lengthy pause as he listened to his brother-in-law. "And the baby? Good. No, that's great. Thanks for calling. Do you want to talk to Amanda? Okay—before I hand you over, when do you want me to bring her home? Will Mom be there? Well, give Dawn my love. I'll see you when you get home."

Peter handed the phone to Amanda. "You are officially a big sister. Here's your dad." Amanda squealed with delight and took the phone.

"Is she all right?" Natalie asked, safely out of earshot of the excited preschooler.

Peter nodded. "Tim said she'll be fine. They had to do an emergency C-section, but she and the baby came through it well. Dawn's resting now, and they have the baby in NICU for observation. As long as his lungs and color check out, Tim's hoping that Dawn and the baby can come home together by the weekend."

"That's good news. So, it was a boy?"

Peter nodded, then gave an ironic shake of the head. "They named him Andrew."

Natalie laughed out loud. "Well, you'd better start learning to like it. You're going to be hearing that name a lot."

"I don't have much choice, it seems." Peter conceded.

Natalie glanced at Amanda, who appeared to be losing interest in her conversation and attempting to put what was left of her grilled cheese sandwich in her mouth as her father continued speaking into the receiver.

"So, what's the plan?" Natalie asked. "Are you going to visit them in the hospital?"

"God, no. I hate hospitals," he answered. "I'll see everyone when they get home. Our mother is on her way back to the house. I can drop Amanda off with her as soon as we're through here."

Amanda handed the phone back to Peter. "Natalie—I'm a big sister! His name is Andrew, but Daddy says I can call him Andy."

Natalie reached over and gave her hand a squeeze. "Mandy and Andy! You're going to be such a good big sister. Remember to study hard so you can teach Andy to read, okay?"

Amanda gave an emphatic nod as she chewed the remaining crusts of her sandwich.

Peter stood up from the table. "Okay, you two, let's get going. Grandma will be waiting for you at home, Panda-Bear."

While Peter paid the bill, Natalie and Amanda strolled around the mall atrium, which had a large fountain as its focal point. Amanda ran to the fountain and asked Natalie for a coin to throw in and make a wish. Natalie obliged her, reaching into her purse and extracting a penny and a quarter from her wallet. By the time Peter reached the pair, both had made a wish and thrown their coins into the water.

"What did you wish for?" his voice, hushed and low, startled her.

"If she tells, it won't come true—right, Natalie?" Amanda announced. Natalie nodded, grateful for the distraction.

In the lobby, several artisans had set up booths to market their hand-made crafts. As the trio made their way out of the building, Amanda stopped at one to look at the jewelry on display.

Not one to buy jewelry for herself, Natalie glanced at the designs on the chance of finding something that her mother or sister might like for Christmas. As she scanned the rows of earrings and bracelets, Amanda pointed to a pendant that caught her eye.

"What is that?"

Natalie examined the item more closely. "It's a locket," she answered. She glanced at the artist, who invited her to take it off the display.

Natalie held the locket in her hands. It was a small, silver, oval-shaped piece with a delicate rose engraved on the front. Natalie opened the clasp and showed it to Amanda. "See? You put a picture of someone you love inside so you can carry them close to your heart."

Amanda was charmed by the idea. "Get it, Natalie."

Natalie held it in her hands, admiring the craftsmanship. However, one glance at the price tag made her put the locket back.

"No, honey. I want to buy presents for my family. Not spend it on myself." She thanked the vendor and walked away.

The wind had picked up, making the trek back to the parking garage long and cold. Peter scooped Amanda into his arms, sheltering her with his arm as she rested her head drowsily on his shoulder. When they finally reached the car, Peter belted in Amanda as Natalie hurriedly slipped into the front seat, rubbing her arms for warmth.

Peter felt in his pocket and cursed.

"What's wrong?"

"I think I left my wallet at the restaurant. Can you wait here with Amanda while I run and get it?"

"Of course."

Peter started the engine and turned the heat on high before taking off at a brisk jog. To help pass the time, Natalie entertained Amanda with a story that she remembered her own mother telling her as a child. Wrapped snugly in her favorite blanket, her long, auburn hair spilled across the pillow, a much younger Natalie would drift to sleep with the images of Pooh bear, Piglet, and Eeyore keeping her company. Now, as she neared the end of the story, Natalie found the same dreamy expression on Amanda's face as her mother must have seen in hers so many years ago. By the time Peter returned, Amanda was fast asleep, still clutching the stuffed rabbit she had brought with her.

"Did you find it?" Natalie whispered as Peter put the car into reverse.

"What?"

"Your wallet, silly."

"Oh. Yeah, I found it."

***

Amanda remained fast asleep when they reached Natalie's house. With care, she pushed the car door closed, listening for its telltale click. Amanda did not stir. Natalie exhaled in relief, her reaction prompting a gentle smile from Peter.

Peter followed her up the steps and waited as she unlocked the front door. For an awkward moment, he just stood on the stoop, then reached into his pocket and pulled out a small white rectangular box.

"This is for you. Merry Christmas."

Natalie took the box and lifted the lid, glancing at Peter as she did so. Peeling away the protective layer of cotton, a flash of silver caught her eye. Natalie let out a tiny gasp as the locket was revealed. She shook her head, the words already forming in her mouth.

"Peter, this is too much. I can't…"

"I want you to have it," he said, pressing the box back into her hands.

Natalie took the piece out of the box and held it up. Fragments of silver glinted in the waning twilight. "It's just beautiful—thank you." She leaned up and kissed him.

Peter gently gripped her coat, drawing her closer. Their kiss was soft and lingering, and he pulled away reluctantly.

"I'd better go." He glanced out at the sleeping child in the car. "Thanks again for helping with Amanda."

"I had a nice time."

"So did I."

Natalie smiled. "Merry Christmas, Peter."

"Merry Christmas."

Peter turned around at the bottom of the steps. "Drive safely, all right? Don't go too fast. Have you checked your oil and brakes lately?"

"They're fine. I had them checked last month. I'll drive carefully."

"Okay," he spoke with hesitation, and then cleared his throat. "See you next month."

"See you then."

Natalie held the locket as she waved goodbye to him. The weight of the piece felt good in her hands. Substantial. Something that would last for a long time.

***

His niece safely delivered into the arms of her grandmother, his sister and nephew resting comfortably across town, Peter pulled his car into the garage and switched off the ignition.

He closed his eyes, letting the silence envelop him. It had been a good day. A faint smile touched his lips as he replayed the events and conversations in his head. He tried to imagine what she was doing that moment, wondered if she was thinking about him, too.

Spurred on by the cold, he reluctantly exited the car and pulled the garage door shut. The house was warm but felt oddly empty to him and he looked around for an indication of something lost or missing. Nothing. Sitting down on the sofa, he spotted the book lying loosely in its red wrapping paper from where he had left it the afternoon before. *Cannery Row.*

Memories of lazy, long-ago mornings flooded his mind. Limbs entangled, bedsheets and blankets kicked aside, they took turns reading aloud—she, more haltingly, he with the ease of one who had read the words many times before. She liked it most when she could listen, when he read the characters with different voices, occasionally mixing the voices up just to make her laugh.

Peter flipped through the book, its pages producing a gentle breeze as they flew by. It was one of his favorites and he had so wanted her to feel the same way, though he knew she hadn't. There was so much he had wanted to show her, to teach her, but in the end it hadn't been enough. He hadn't been enough.

He closed his eyes and pictured her face. "You would have liked her, you know," he whispered to the empty room.

Chapter 15

For Natalie and her sister, returning to White Falls during winter and summer breaks was an accepted family obligation, a way of giving back all that the farm had given to them. This winter was no different.

From the moment she woke and shared a light breakfast with her family, to dinner time when she slumped in her chair from exhaustion, Natalie worked. She ran the milking machines, fed and watered the livestock, mended fences, and helped her father make repairs on the machinery.

Monica arrived home from Milwaukee a week later. Natalie anticipated these visits with a certain unease. She loved her sister, but Monica's need to be the center of attention could be exhausting at times. This, along with Monica's tendency to compare her accomplishments with those of her big sister, made Natalie feel as if they were in constant competition. No matter how self-assured she felt about herself at work and at school, Natalie's self-confidence took a predictable nose-dive after listening to her sister's successes on stage and in class.

But this time was different. Perhaps it was simple maturity. Or perhaps the difference lay in the small touchstone that rested beneath her turtleneck, out of sight, but well within comforting touch. Inside lay a reminder of Peter—a reddish-gold petal, the texture of straw, gently torn from the blanket flower she had kept since their first night together.

Natalie was emerging from the shower one morning when Monica burst in unannounced, exclaiming something about a lost hairbrush. Natalie wrapped herself in a towel and pointed with annoyance toward the counter, where the presumed lost item had been resting since the night before.

"Oh, thanks," Monica mumbled, the drama in her voice evaporating as quickly as it had surfaced. As she turned to leave, she spotted the silver glint of the locket, now clearly visible against Natalie's bare, wet skin.

"Hey, where did you get that?" Monica moved closer and touched the pendant, holding it in her fingers for a better look.

This was the last thing Natalie wished to discuss with her sister, but with the locket still in Monica's grasp, she couldn't pull away either. She stood there uncomfortably as her sister continued to examine the piece.

"It's just a necklace."

"It's a locket and…hey, what's in here?" Monica opened the latch and eyed the dried, darkened contents with suspicion.

"Just a flower petal. Are you finished?" Natalie regained hold of the locket, severing its connection with her sister. She stepped away to the corner of the bathroom and began dressing.

Monica remained by the counter, eyeing her sister. "So, who gave it to you?"

"A friend."

Monica grinned. "No way. You're being way too secretive for it to be just a friend. Who is he? Is he *married*?" Monica was enjoying this exchange, thinking up scenarios in which Natalie was honor-bound to conceal the identity of her lover.

Natalie ignored her sister's barrage of questions and once dressed, returned to her bedroom across the hall and closed the door behind her. Monica followed her out, opening the bedroom door and continuing her interrogation.

"Come on, Nat. You know I'm not going to leave you alone until you tell me *something*—his name, how you met him—*anything*." She gave a good-natured laugh and flopped on the bed.

Natalie shook her head at the girl before her. No matter how aggravating Monica could be, there was a certain charm about her that could not be ignored.

"His name is Peter," she said. "And he's not married. And that's all you're going to get. Now get out of my room. I need to find my shoes and get to town for supplies."

Monica stood up and gave her sister a final victorious grin. In a child's voice, she sashayed through the door, chanting an old rhyme from their youth. *"Natalie and Peter sitting in a tree, k-i-s-s-i-n-g. First comes love, then comes marriage...."* Monica's singsong delivery was interrupted by the sound of Natalie's shoe as it landed with a hard thud against the wall. The younger sister dodged the projectile, giggling as she ran down the hall.

***

"Incoming—nine o'clock." Neil said as he lifted his beer, his eyes deliberately avoiding the young women walking past their table.

Peter shot him an irritated look and went back to watching college football.

A twenty-something brunette and her two friends shot purposeful glances their way before ending up at the bar just beyond. Their laughter could be heard over the TV announcers' voices and, as hard as Peter tried to ignore them, they didn't seem to be in any hurry to abandon their bar stools. Reaching for the pitcher on the table only to discover it almost empty, Peter turned toward the bar, where the brunette caught his eye and gave him an inviting smile. He nodded and swiveled back in his chair.

"Your turn to get the beer," was all he said.

Neil watched the TV until the play was over and then shifted his attention to Peter. He smirked, suddenly understanding. "Coward. Since when were you afraid of a few coeds?"

"I'm here for the game and the stimulating company," Peter retorted, pointing his mug at Neil. "Coeds aren't on the agenda."

"I don't know, man," Neil said, giving a solemn shake of the head. "I think you're off your game. In all the years I've known you, there hasn't been a night you didn't walk out with at least one phone number in your pocket."

Peter set down his empty mug, more in need of a refill than ever. "It's an off night. Are you getting the beer, or what?"

Neil shot him a grin and made his way to the bar, pitcher in hand. There, he greeted the girls and said something that started them laughing again. Peter confined his gaze to the TV straight ahead.

***

An hour later, Peter was back home, dropping his car keys on the kitchen table and looking through the refrigerator for something to drink. Remembering he'd finished the last of the beer the night before, he turned to the cabinet and found a half bottle of red wine. He poured himself a glass and walked to the couch, sitting down heavily.

The dark liquid warmed on the way down, calming in part the restlessness he'd been feeling all week. Loathe to put a name to it, Peter knew the reason behind his changeable moods. Looking for a distraction, he searched for the remote control, digging into the cushions when it didn't immediately turn up.

He spotted something white and pulled out a piece of fabric wedged in the back of the couch. Natalie's t-shirt. He had no trouble recalling their last evening together, the hours spent in this very spot. Peter touched the t-shirt to his face, breathing in the scent that still remained.

He wondered what she was doing tonight. Christmas was two days away. Perhaps she was shopping or spending an evening with friends. He wondered if she was wearing his locket; hoped she was. Reaching into his back pocket for his cell phone, he began dialing the familiar number, then changed his mind and hung up.

After more searching, Peter located the remote and turned on a late bowl game being played on the west coast. He had little interest in the outcome, but it was better than a blank screen yawning back at him. With Natalie's t-shirt balled up in his lap, he eventually fell asleep to the distant sound of cheering fans.

***

Christmas came and went. The Brooks family celebrated the morning quietly in front of the Christmas tree in the living room. In contrast to years past when the girls would race downstairs at the crack of dawn to view their holiday windfall, these days the family calmly gathered and took their turns handing out, opening, and admiring each other's presents. It had all happened gradually; yet another reminder that the girls were girls no more.

Later that night, Natalie sat on the bed and surveyed her gifts before placing them in her suitcase. Good woolen socks because, well, her parents were above all practical. And a warm and remarkably stylish sweater for the same reasons. Monica had given her a silver bracelet, its cast and accents coincidentally similar to her locket, making them a perfect set. *Her locket.* Natalie's fingers found the piece, as they did a hundred times a day and gently pressed the weight against her neck. She closed her eyes, counting down the days.

On Tuesday morning, as her family ate breakfast, Natalie announced that she would be leaving early.

Her mother turned to her with surprise. "Tomorrow? But school doesn't start until next Monday, does it? Why do you need to go back so soon?"

Monica, paging through a magazine as she ate her breakfast, glanced up and saw the guarded expression on Natalie's face.

"Mom, she probably needs to get settled in before classes start. Right, Nat?" Natalie returned her sister's look with a grateful nod. "And I'll bet that slave-driver of a professor wants her back to work. In fact, now that I think about it, I should be heading back soon, too."

Natalie's mother poured her coffee and sat down with a disappointed sigh. "That's too bad. Margerie's son was planning to come home this weekend. I was hoping you two could get together while he was home."

Natalie gaped at her mother. "Kenneth?" she asked. "You aren't still trying to fix me up with him, are you?"

"What's wrong with Kenneth?" Mrs. Brooks asked in all earnestness.

Mr. Brooks interrupted from behind his newspaper. "He's fat, bald, and boring."

Monica snorted. Natalie smiled at her father, but her mother was not amused.

"He is *not* fat."

Mr. Brooks put down the newspaper. "That still leaves bald and boring. Natalie can do a hell of a lot better than him."

"Watch your language, Henry," Natalie's mother scolded. "He's a nice boy, with a good job in Eau Claire. And I don't think it would hurt for Natalie to meet him, seeing as how she's not involved with anyone else right now."

Natalie's cheeks reddened.

Monica jumped in again. "Natalie's doing just fine on her own, Mom. No telling what she's been up to in Madison. Right, Sis?" She stood up and motioned to Natalie, who, despite having a full bowl of cereal in front of her, accepted her sister's offer of escape.

"Come on, let's get to work." The two grabbed their coats and boots and tramped out the door, enjoying their new-found solidarity.

***

Natalie began her drive back to Madison with a heady sense of excitement. She kissed her mother and father goodbye and gave her sister a warm hug, smiling at her in silent thanks for the unexpected support she had offered in their last days together. Then, waving them back into the comforting warmth of the kitchen, she headed to the place she now considered home.

Natalie settled back into her seat and turned on her favorite radio station. She let her mind wander from lesson plans to term papers to midterm exams, but each time her thoughts returned to Peter. She wondered where he was, what he had done in her absence, and if she had entered his mind as often as he had hers.

Her cell phone sat on the seat beside her, charged and ready for the phone call that Natalie eagerly planned to make during her drive. Yet every time she reached for the phone, her hand drew back, leaving it undisturbed. She couldn't explain it. This was what she had been looking forward to ever since she had announced her departure the day before—four days and nights with Peter before the work and responsibilities of spring semester began.

As she neared her destination, though, a strange uneasiness began to settle into her thoughts. He might already have plans. He might have gone out of town. Perhaps he wanted to spend his final days with his family. By the time she crossed the county line, Natalie had made a complete about-face. She would not contact Peter at all.

In the wake of her silent decision, Natalie's earlier excitement evaporated, replaced by a growing fatigue that surprised her with its suddenness.

***

An hour later, Natalie trudged into the house and dropped her bags on the floor with a heavy thud. It was only mid-afternoon, the sun reflecting brightly off the snow outside, but Natalie felt more tired than she had been in ages.

Gina found her fast asleep when she returned from her shift at the hospital.

"Hey, lazybones," Gina called from the doorway. "I didn't know you were coming back today." When Natalie didn't stir, Gina sat down on the edge of her bed, nudging her awake. Natalie's eyes opened with effort, her body still heavy with sleep.

"Wow, you were out," Gina smiled, shifting back on the bed as Natalie struggled to sit up. "What are you doing back today? I thought you were staying until the end of the week."

"I guess I got homesick," Natalie replied with a drowsy smile.

"Wouldn't have anything to do with a certain professor, would it?" Gina teased. "Does he know you're back?"

"No," Natalie answered. There was no point in troubling Gina with her reasons for not contacting him. Besides, she wasn't sure she could offer up a rational explanation. "I'll see him on Monday."

Gina said nothing.

"Anyway," Natalie pressed on, "I thought it would be good to get back early and get organized before the semester starts. Clean up a little, you know."

"And here I was going to surprise you by cleaning the house before you got back," Gina grinned. "But you've spoiled it. Now you'll have to help."

"No problem," Natalie agreed, smoothing her hair out of her face. "If I could just get myself up and moving. I'm so tired."

"Take it easy," Gina patted her arm and got up off the bed. "The cleaning can wait for another day. Hey, Joey's working tonight—how about we order a pizza and kick back with an old movie?"

"The movie sounds good," Natalie answered. "But I think I'll pass on the pizza." She hadn't eaten since breakfast, but the mere thought of food made her stomach lurch.

"You're turning down *pizza*?" Gina frowned at her. "Are you sure you're not coming down with something?"

Natalie curled back into bed, her eyes already closing. "I'm fine," she said. "I'll be out in a few minutes. Don't start the movie without me."

***

The sun was shining through her bedroom window when Natalie woke up next. Peering at the alarm clock, she was startled to see the time, 8:37. *In the morning? How could that be?*

Still groggy, Natalie rose and stretched. She was famished. Thinking back, she realized it had been close to 24 hours since her last meal.

She padded down the hall to the kitchen, where a note from Gina awaited her on the counter. In her large, flowing script, it said simply, *"Sorry—had to start the movie without you. I'll check in with you this afternoon. Sweet dreams...G."*

Natalie smiled and turned her attention to the cabinets in search of something filling that could be prepared with a minimum of fuss. As she waited for the bread to pop out of the toaster, she pulled out the coffee maker and set a new pot to brew. It wasn't long before the familiar sounds and smells of brewing coffee filled the small kitchen. Typically a welcome sensation, today she was surprised to find the smell almost aversive.

"First pizza, now coffee?" Natalie said out loud. "Those are my two favorite things in the world."

Abandoning the coffee and sitting back down at the table, Natalie made a half-hearted attempt at her toast, but her appetite seemed to vanish. Turning off the coffee maker, its contents still hot and untouched, she grabbed a bottle of water and headed back to her room, determined to make a more productive use of her day.

The next few days passed for Natalie in an almost routine manner, predictable except for the ever-increasing list of symptoms that began to hit her each day like clockwork.

The fatigue that hit her so hard on her arrival now returned every evening and bore little connection to what her activities had been that day. Most nights she turned in early, cutting short the projects she had hoped to finish before the semester began. Still, Natalie remained unconcerned, attributing it to some strange virus that would run its course in time.

Chapter 16

Natalie crossed campus with a mixture of excitement and uneasiness. The Psychology building loomed ahead. She gazed up at the third-floor window, almost expecting to see him standing there, but only empty space stared back. She shrugged, smiling at the romantic absurdity that he would somehow be awaiting her arrival. Still, it didn't stop her from taking the stairs two at a time to get to his office.

At the top and out of breath, she shook her head and reminded herself for the hundredth time of their unspoken arrangement at the office. He was Dr. Spencer, and she was his assistant. And they would remain so until the weekend when she looked forward to a long overdue reunion.

Natalie slowed her pace as she neared Peter's office. From the doorway she could hear a student inside, the sounds of conversation commingling with laughter. Natalie sighed.

Of all people, it was Kelly Martin who stood by his desk while Peter leaned back in his chair and spoke to her with an easy familiarity. A twinge of jealousy hit her as it often did when she witnessed this scene. Natalie rapped lightly on the half-open door, her presence alone not enough to get their attention.

Peter's chair snapped back to an upright position. For a moment he seemed flustered by her arrival.

"Natalie–wow, is it two o'clock already?" Peter glanced down at his watch. Kelly shifted position but was in no hurry to relinquish the spotlight, even for Dr. Spencer's assistant.

"Hi, Natalie," she said at last, her smile saccharine. "How was your break?"

Natalie gave her a placid look. "Nice. Yours?"

"Great! My family rented a house down on Marco Island. It was gorgeous there." Kelly began repacking her backpack. As always, she wore a perfectly coordinated sweater and skirt combination accented by those same knee-length leather boots from the day Peter visited Natalie's class.

Kelly stood and gave Peter a final, winning smile. "Thanks for your advice, Dr. Spencer. I'll check out that internship."

"Glad I could help. See you in class."

Natalie watched Kelly sweep out of the room, noting the golden tan on her hands and face, the highlights in her long blonde hair. In contrast to her own pale exhaustion, Kelly seemed to exude energy. Natalie turned and saw Peter watching her, an odd expression on his face.

"Welcome back, Natalie. Did you have a nice break with your family?" he asked.

There was something different in the way he spoke to her, a visible discomfort bordering on coldness that surprised her. Natalie gave him a puzzled look.

"Yes," she answered. "A lot of work, but it was nice to spend time with everyone."

"That's good."

Natalie plunged ahead with questions of her own. "How was your break? How are Dawn and the baby? And Amanda? Did you get to spend a lot of time with them these past few weeks?" Natalie could feel herself run on, but his behavior made her nervous and her impulse was to fill in the uncomfortable gaps any way she could.

"Dawn and Andy are fine," Peter replied. "They came home from the hospital a few days after you left. Amanda is fine, too. I think she enjoys being a big sister, at least for now."

More silence. This time Peter turned toward his desk and scooped up some files that were sitting there. He handed them to Natalie, who still hadn't moved.

"I hope you're ready to hit the ground running," he said. "I'll need summaries of these articles, and the last folder contains a list of titles I need from the library. Try to get everything to me by the end of Wednesday, okay?" Not waiting for her reply, Peter spun around in his chair and began to work.

"Okay, professor," she mumbled, retreating to the safety of her own desk. She removed her coat and backpack and settled into her chair, but not before giving one last glance to Peter, who, by this time, was bent over his desk.

Natalie spilled out photocopied articles from a file onto the desk. Choosing one, she leaned forward and forced herself to read. But she barely made it through the first sentence when her own thoughts began interrupting her. *What happened?*

Staring at the words before her, Natalie might as well have been studying a blank sheet of paper. She replayed their last days together, trying to recall anything that might have caused such a shift in his behavior. Natalie's hand swept across her neck, resting on the locket that lay beneath her sweater. She remembered the self-conscious way he had given it to her, almost shy, except for the intensity in his eyes. No, their last days together had been their closest. Whatever was affecting him had happened while she was away. *But what?*

Natalie and Peter worked in virtual silence until five o'clock, when Natalie finally pushed out from her desk and prepared for the long, cold trek back to her car. The fatigue that had clung to her for days showed no signs of easing up. More than anything she wanted to sink into a warm tub and let the water loosen up the knots of worry that had formed in her neck.

The sound of her chair caused Peter to glance up. He seemed startled, as if he had forgotten she was there. Watching her as she packed up her backpack, Peter seemed at a loss for words. Gone was the easy familiarity the two usually shared at the office. Instead, he fell back on work-related questions to fill the silence.

"Do you have a classroom yet for your Statistics lab?"

Natalie pulled on her coat. "Yes. I'll be in room 203."

"Good." Peter's eyes darted around the room without ever stopping at her face. "And you remember my Intro class tomorrow at 10:30?"

"I'll be there." Natalie gave a final glance at Peter, who had already begun to turn his chair away from her. The knot in her throat migrated into the pit of her stomach, accompanied by a growing feeling of dread.

"Good night, professor." Natalie stood by his desk, resolving not to move until he looked up at her. He did so, grudgingly, his eyes uneasy as they met hers.

"Good night, Natalie."

She began to leave, and then stopped and turned back. "Is anything wrong, Peter?" she said quietly, all too aware of the breach in using his name at the office.

Peter hesitated before replying. When he did, his voice was smooth and controlled. "Nothing at all. I'll see you tomorrow in class." He nodded to her a final time and turned away.

***

It was a hard week. The hectic schedule came as a shock after the sluggish days Natalie had spent at home leading up to the semester. In her quest to graduate early, Natalie registered for a full load of classes each semester. This, plus leading study sessions for two of Peter's undergrad classes and research every afternoon made Natalie's schedule non-stop. Up until now, she had kept up with the demanding schedule; in fact, she thrived on it. However, this semester, with the fatigue that had settled into her body, Natalie began each day with a growing fear that she had taken on too much.

She managed to get through her classes, including Peter's Intro and Beginning Statistics classes. In each one, she sat in the back row, subjected to the excited chatter and adolescent giggles of the freshmen girls who were seeing Peter for the first time. Toward the end of each class, Peter scanned the auditorium for Natalie's face and asked her to stand. Reluctantly, she did so, lifting her hand to the students when he introduced her as his teaching assistant. Repeating the speech she had given so many times before, Natalie reminded the students of the time and location of her weekly tutorial sessions, her phone number, and office hours before sitting back down.

Each afternoon Natalie entered his office hoping for some sign that his icy demeanor had thawed, but it never did. Nor did she ever come any closer to understanding why he'd changed. They spent their hours separated by only a few feet, but miles apart from the comfortable working relationship they shared just a month before.

Distressed and confused, Natalie shut down in Peter's presence, saying little except in response to his questions. If Peter felt the difference, he didn't acknowledge it. Instead, he acted as if she wasn't even there.

Despite this, Natalie clung to the hope that everything would be explained on Friday. Friday—the night when they could be alone, shed the roles they played all week, and be themselves. Perhaps then she could find out what was troubling him.

***

As it turned out, Natalie never got the chance. Descending the steps from the Psychology building on Friday afternoon and emerging into the bright expanse of the courtyard, her steps were slow and deliberate. She wondered if he was watching her from his office window.

As if she had willed it, her phone rang. Reaching into her pocket, she fumbled to answer the call. It was him. Natalie answered with a palpable sense of relief, her voice suddenly light and out of breath.

"Hi," she said. "I was hoping I'd hear from you."

There was a slight pause on the line before Peter responded. "Hi. I…just wanted to let you know that you shouldn't count on me for tonight. Actually, for the foreseeable future. It's turning out to be a pretty hectic semester."

Natalie's momentary elation evaporated. "Oh."

"Well, I…" Peter faltered. "I just wanted to let you know so that you could make other plans."

Natalie was stunned. "Okay," she replied haltingly. "Thanks for letting me know."

"Sure. Have a good weekend."

"You too," she whispered, although the phone went dead even as the words stumbled out of her mouth. Natalie stared dumbly at the phone in her hand. Despite the noise of students around her, she heard nothing but the sound of her own breathing, which had grown shallower. The full effect of what just happened washed over her.

It's over. He's letting go, just like he once said he would. Yet in all the time they had been together, she didn't expect it to end like this—with no warning, no explanation. He didn't even have the courage to tell her in person.

Natalie replaced the cell phone in her pocket, feeling the soft give of the fabric as she released the phone from her grasp. She turned around, her gaze rising to the third floor. There stood Peter, watching her from his office window. As she knew he would be.

***

Peter felt her accusing stare, seemed unable to turn from it. He understood the impact of his words, and from the expression on Natalie's face, so did she. All he could do now was stand and face the pain he had caused. If nothing else, he would at least give her the grim satisfaction of being the first to turn and walk away.

***

Natalie was lying on her bed when Gina came home from work. Although surprised, she accepted her friend's explanation that Peter had out-of-town guests and would be unavailable all weekend.

"That's perfect—now you can come out with us!" Gina excitedly outlined the plans for a girl's night out that evening.

Natalie was less than enthusiastic.

"Come on," Gina urged. "This is Sharon's first night out since the baby was born. We're going to McHenry's, no boys allowed. Sharon would be hurt if you didn't come."

"I'm really tired, Gina. It's been a long week."

"Precisely why you need to get out," Gina pulled her up until she was sitting on the edge of the bed. "You need to get out and put it all out of your mind for a while. Have a little fun."

Natalie began to make another excuse, but Gina interrupted her. "I'm not taking no for an answer. Get dressed and be ready to go in an hour. I promise we won't stay out long."

The hot shower helped to ease the tension in her neck but did little for the grief spreading throughout her chest. *A broken heart*—such a cliché. Natalie had been hurt and disappointed in love before, but never like this. The mere act of turning away from Peter that afternoon had triggered a pain so real she'd had to sit down on the first bench she passed to catch her breath.

After pulling on their heavy coats and gloves, the two roommates drove to McHenry's where they were greeted by the rest of their friends. In many ways it resembled her 25th birthday a year ago. *When it all started.* This year, her celebration had been quiet, a bowl of cereal and a movie, Gina her only company.

Sharon, a close friend from their undergraduate years at UW, was now married and working as a second-grade teacher. At least she had been until her daughter was born six months ago. And while Sharon was crazy about her husband, and even crazier about the baby, a night out with the girls was something she had needed for quite some time.

"God, I need a beer!" she practically sang as the others sat down around her. "Who's buying the first round?"

A waiter appeared a few moments later and took their drink order before disappearing into the growing throng of patrons. It was Friday night, so there would be a live band later on. Natalie had spent many evenings here dancing with friends and strangers alike, but tonight she would have given anything to be home. Besides the gnawing ache in her chest, Natalie could feel the nausea and fatigue returning.

Still, catching up with her friends, some of whom she hadn't seen for months, was a welcome distraction. Sharon regaled them with stories of motherhood, some good, some positively ugly, but with a sense of humor that had them laughing at even the most unappetizing of details.

For much of the night, Natalie managed to hide her untouched beer in full view of the others while nursing a diet coke instead. There was no way she could stomach the smell of alcohol, much less the taste. Still, she preferred not having to explain this to her friends who were becoming increasingly tipsy as the night wore on.

Natalie began to glance at her watch when a noisy group of students entered the bar and sat at the table next to theirs. Boisterous laughter and the cloying smell of cigarettes hit Natalie, pushing her senses into overload. Overwhelmed, Natalie excused herself from the table and rushed into the ladies' room. She barely made it into the stall before the retching began.

Natalie lost track of how long she knelt in the stall, her chin resting on her chest between spasms. The sound of Gina's voice, heavy with concern, was sweet relief to her ears.

"Natalie? Are you in here?"

"I'm here."

"Honey, are you all right?" Gina tried to open the stall door, but Natalie's body was in the way.

Natalie flushed the toilet and began the difficult process of getting back on her feet. Her legs were unsteady and weak—she grasped the top of the stall to steady herself.

"I'll be all right," she said as she emerged from the stall, although her words were less than convincing.

Gina's face clouded with alarm. Natalie looked into the mirror and hardly recognized herself. Hair strewn across her forehead, her eyes were red and watery, and her face a waxy pale. Gina asked no questions, instead positioning her friend near the sink. Hurrying out to the bar, she returned a few minutes later with a glass of water, which Natalie gratefully sipped.

"Come on," she said, wetting a paper towel under the faucet and pressing it against Natalie's forehead. "Let's get you home."

Natalie allowed herself to be led out of the bar, giving a weak wave to her friends as they passed by the table. Shocked at Natalie's changed appearance, they began to stand, but Gina motioned them back with the promise that she would call later.

The drive home was silent. Natalie put her head on the seat and watched the streetlights swim by, her eyes open but unfocused. Once home, she dragged herself to her room, pulling off her clothes and falling into bed.

Gina sat down on the bed beside her. "God, how much did you drink tonight?" She smoothed Natalie's hair away from her face.

"I didn't," Natalie gave a wretched shake of the head. "I drank soda all night."

Gina stopped and studied her with narrowed eyes. She slipped her hand over Natalie's forehead and felt for a fever. There was none.

"Natalie, could you be pregnant?"

Despite her exhaustion, Natalie turned sharply to her friend. "Of course not. I just had my period last…"

Natalie's color became paler, if that was possible. They had always been careful.

"Hey, I'm sure there's nothing to worry about." Gina's voice was reassuring. "Right now, just get some sleep, okay? I'll pick up a test in the morning so you can put it out of your mind for good. You probably just caught a virus."

But Natalie could see the concern on her friend's face. She watched as Gina adjusted the covers and switched off the light before finally leaving her room.

Chapter 17

Natalie forced down half a salad and a Sprite for lunch and re-copied her notes from the morning. This was her one break in the day, and it never seemed to be enough anymore. Before she knew it, the time had come to leave for Peter's office, as she had every day last semester and the two semesters before that. Only, instead of walking there with eagerness, her gait was slow and plodding, her heart beating fast in her chest.

Things would have to change, of course. She couldn't continue working for him. Besides the obvious awkwardness, it hurt too much to see him every day. Still, quitting was not an option. To keep her graduate scholarship, Natalie was required to work twenty hours per week for the department. She also depended on the weekly paycheck for rent, food and other essentials. She might have transferred to a different professor, but the semester had already started, and all the graduate positions were filled. For now, she had little choice but to continue as Peter's assistant.

For a brief moment, she wondered if he'd had second thoughts over the weekend, perhaps even a change of heart. Then again, it didn't matter. Too much was changed now. Even if he felt differently about their relationship, he would never welcome the child she was carrying. Natalie's only decision now was how to salvage her life from the costly decisions she had made. And whether to keep what they had created together.

Peter looked up as she entered the office, a mumbled "Hello, Professor" her only acknowledgement of his presence. He replied something in return, although she gave no indication of hearing him.

A folder of articles lay waiting on her desk, along with an accompanying note of instructions. Without taking off her coat, Natalie read his note. Then, opening her backpack, she slipped the note and folder inside and began to leave. Peter glanced at her with surprise.

"I will be in the library if you need me," Natalie announced. Within moments she was gone, the sound of her footsteps fading as she trudged down the hall.

***

How she managed to get through the next two weeks, Natalie could not begin to explain. To a large degree, she found herself shutting down from all conscious thought—breaking down each task, each assignment, into its smallest parts and then performing them as automatically as a robot might be programmed to do. Her work suffered, there was no doubt. A lab report from her Experimental Psychology class had been returned to her with a B minus and a note from the professor admonishing her to put more thought into future reports. A group report due by the end of the week would likely have produced the same results had her partners not covered for her inattention.

Natalie's work for Peter was no better. More than once, he returned the same file to her desk with a clarification of the instructions given to her the day before. Unable to concentrate, even the most mundane of tasks became difficult. So, day after day, she sat at her desk in the library, accomplishing little, but at least grateful for her few hours of sanctuary.

***

Natalie made her way across campus, heading for the building where she taught her study session. Normally one of her favorite activities, she now found each step an effort. It had begun to snow again, the light flakes resting on rooftops, overhangs, upturned leaves and branches, making everything seem bright and fresh. Occasionally the wind would pick up, sweeping the weightless flakes into a mini cyclone of flurries before they found a new resting place. Natalie watched the snow with an almost hypnotic stare, glancing up in surprise when she finally reached the door of the building.

Struggling with the door, Natalie was again struck at how much heavier it seemed to her than just a few weeks before. Then again, she thought sadly, everything required more effort these days. Not for the first time, she wondered how she would have the strength for what was yet to come.

Natalie unlocked the classroom door and turned on the light. She deposited her heavy backpack on the desk and began to unpack her files when a wave of nausea hit her. Almost like clockwork, her morning sickness typically arrived early, just after she rose and dressed. Cold comfort, but at least she was able to retch in the comparative privacy of her own bathroom. However, on the mornings when she taught a study session, there was no such guarantee. Grabbing her purse, Natalie raced for the hallway, already having memorized the location of the nearest bathroom.

****

Twenty minutes later, Peter stood in the same hall, scanning the room numbers for the classroom where Natalie was to be teaching. He had not observed this class yet; in fact, he had been putting off the task for the last week.

He located the classroom and peeked inside, expecting to see Natalie at the chalkboard answering questions from her class. Instead, students were sitting and chatting with each other, the front of the room empty of Natalie's presence.

Annoyed, Peter glanced at his watch. The class should have started ten minutes ago. Natalie had never been late for a class in the past. *When was she going to get over this?* Of course she was upset by their breakup. He understood this and had tried to make every allowance for her feelings. If anything, he had been more than tolerant with her drop in productivity and quality of work. But now being late for classes?

Peter heard footsteps in the hallway behind him. He hurried past the classroom and down the next hallway to remain out of sight. The footsteps eventually stopped in front of the classroom where he had stood. Peering out from behind the wall, Peter caught a glimpse of Natalie as she paused briefly to collect herself.

Not for the first time, he was struck by her appearance. These days, Natalie appeared to wear a permanent mask of fatigue and pallor, symptoms he had dismissed as a simple lack of sleep or overwork. However, today she looked positively sick. Her face was wet with a sheen of perspiration, her movements shaky. As she entered the classroom, she calmly apologized to the classroom for her tardiness and began the session with little of her normal enthusiasm.

Peter looked on in concern. *Something was wrong with Natalie*, he thought. Something besides him.

***

It turned out to be a productive day. Natalie avoided Peter's office altogether, spending the afternoon in the library in an attempt to finish off all the projects he had assigned to her throughout the week. She would not be going into the office tomorrow. Her appointment was at 3:30.

She worked with unusual clarity and attention, barely glancing up until her work was finished. She closed the last file with a sense of relief and stood up to stretch. Now all that remained was to deliver her work to Peter, along with a note that he should not expect her the next day. One day without seeing his face. It seemed unfathomable that this had become a relief to her when only weeks ago she couldn't imagine a day without him.

Today as she approached his office, file folders already in hand, she heard voices. For once, the sound was welcome. The presence of one of his many cloying undergraduates was just the distraction she needed to get in and out of his office without delay. However, as Natalie approached the door, she saw that the woman standing across from Peter's desk was no student. Tall and slender, with short, cropped black hair and an olive complexion, this woman was the antithesis of the young, affected females who typically paraded in and out of his office. She appeared to be in the middle of telling a story, something amusing about Chicago politics given Peter's reaction, when he spotted Natalie waiting by the door. His change in expression caused the woman to turn around.

"Oh, hello," the woman said.

Natalie looked at the woman and back at Peter. "I'm sorry to interrupt, Dr. Spencer. Here are the rest of the files you requested." Natalie reached past the woman and laid the files on his desk. As she turned to go, Peter found his voice.

"Natalie, let me introduce you." He lifted his hand in the direction of the woman. "This is Karla Livingston, professor of Psychology at the University of Chicago. She spoke to my Social Psych class this afternoon. Karla, this is Natalie Brooks, my research and teaching assistant."

Natalie regained her composure long enough to offer her hand to the woman. Karla Livingston had been a guest of Peter's in the past, giving lectures to his classes in the fall and spring for the last three years. Natalie had never met her personally, although from the comments of undergraduates who had, it appeared that Ms. Livingston's intelligence and striking appearance had made quite an impression. Seeing her in person, Natalie had to agree. She was a beautiful woman.

"How do you do, Natalie." Turning to Peter, she commented, "She looks like a sharp one, Peter. She must keep you on your toes."

Natalie turned away in embarrassment, not so much from the comment as from the familiar way in which she spoke to him. Peter seemed to sense her discomfort. Clearing his throat, he motioned Natalie over to the other side of the office where her largely unused desk stood.

"Natalie, before you go, I need to speak with you about this morning's class."

Natalie stared at him, puzzled. Karla turned and pulled out her cell phone.

"I'll leave you two to finish up. I have to make a call anyway." She stepped out of the office, the phone already pressed to her ear.

Natalie walked over to the desk, where he stood waiting. "Yes?" she said.

"I came to observe your class this morning, but you were running late, it seemed."

Natalie shifted in place. "I'm sorry. It won't happen again."

Peter gave a dismissive wave. "You seemed sick when you came into the classroom. Are you all right?" His expression of concern, after so many weeks of cold disinterest, caught Natalie off guard. For just a moment, she was gazing into the face she remembered. Still, she knew all too well how easily Peter could switch from one emotion to the other—affection to disinterest, concern to disdain. He did it so effortlessly that Natalie wondered if the emotions he expressed were genuinely felt at all.

No, she couldn't trust him, not with such a painful secret. His reaction, his *rejection* would tear apart what little strength she had left. Natalie hesitated before responding. "Late night out with the girls. I guess I had too much to drink."

Peter's eyes narrowed. He wasn't convinced, but she returned his gaze with such unflinching composure, he had no choice but to drop the subject.

The sound of Karla's heels echoed down the hallway. "Peter, are you ready?" she peered inside the office, cell phone still in hand. "I need to get back to the hotel to freshen up if we're going to make our 6:30 reservation."

Peter gave a final glance at Natalie before pulling on his coat and heading out the door, where Karla was waiting. Natalie glanced up just in time to see the woman drape her arm possessively over his. Peter didn't object to the intimate gesture. Swallowing hard, Natalie turned away.

Crossing to the desk, she busied herself with the papers still lying there, all the while waiting for the sounds of their footsteps to fade away. Only then did she trust herself to turn around. Natalie gathered up her backpack and began to leave the office when she remembered the note she had composed in the library. It was carefully written on a sheet of notebook paper, the third of three attempts to excuse herself from work the next day. She had discarded the first two for sounding too awkward or too wordy. Pulling it from her bag, she gently laid it on his chair, where he was sure to see it the next morning.

"I will not be able to work on Friday afternoon due to a prior appointment. Natalie."

For all he knew it could be a dentist appointment. Unconsciously, Natalie brought her hand to rest on her abdomen. She felt little but the bulkiness of her winter jacket, but she knew that something rested deep inside her, beyond her touch. And tomorrow it would be gone.

* * *

Peter and Karla were halfway through dinner when a couple entered, following the hostess past their table to another against the wall. They were strangers to Peter, but something about the woman made him stop and stare. Her hair, worn long with a simple clasp at the nape of her neck, looked strikingly similar to the way Natalie wore hers. From behind he could almost swear it was her. Yet, he had seen the woman's face; it wasn't Natalie. Right now, Natalie could be anywhere, with anyone, a thought that Peter found unsettling. He watched the woman sit down, stopping himself only after she and her partner began reading their menus.

Late night out with the girls. Peter couldn't get her explanation out of his mind. It was possible. As sick as she looked that morning, she seemed fine when he saw her again that afternoon. And yet, what concern was it of his? He had given up any say in her plans when he had ended their affair weeks ago.

Peter glanced at the couple again. The woman's hand rested lightly on the arm of the man beside her. She was laughing at something he was saying. Peter turned away, piercing his steak with greater force than necessary before bringing the bite to his mouth. *Had she met someone last night? Did she let him bring her home? Did she invite him into her bed as she had once done with him?* Peter raised his glass of wine and drained the last of it in one gulp. Images of another man touching her flashed through his mind. Feeling the anger well up inside of him, Peter reached for the wine bottle, only to find that it had already been emptied.

"Peter, did you hear a word I just said?" Karla's voice startled him from his thoughts.

He looked up and saw Karla sitting back in her seat, her eyes squarely on him. He paused to recall her question. "Of course, I did. You were talking about your plans for the summer."

Karla glared at him in annoyance. "That was ten minutes ago. Like to try again?"

"Not particularly," he answered. In his present mood, he wasn't interested in a sparring session. "I just got distracted. Go on." He motioned with his hand for her to continue her monologue, but Karla probed further.

"You're more than distracted. You've been acting this way all night. What's going on?"

"I just have some things on my mind," Peter answered, wishing she would just let the matter drop.

No luck.

"It wouldn't have anything to do with that assistant back at the office, would it?" Karla continued.

Peter's look of surprise conveyed more than anything he could have answered. "Of course not."

Karla nodded, unconvinced. "Have it your way. But something, or *someone,* is clearly bothering you. And judging by the stolen glances you were giving little Nancy at the office today…"

"Natalie," Peter corrected.

"Mm hmm," she smiled at his instinctive response. "My guess is she has something to do with it."

Peter began to deny her assertion but stopped himself. She had him, and they both knew it. He shrugged, sitting back in his chair. "Another bottle of wine?"

Karla laughed, shaking her head. This was as close to an acknowledgement as she was going to get. "I don't think so, my dear," she replied. "In fact, I think it might be best for all involved if we called it an early night."

***

With little interest in the usual small talk, it wasn't long before they finished their meals, and the plates were cleared from the table. Peter signaled for the check, grateful that the evening would soon be coming to an end. At least he could be spared the awkwardness of feigning interest in one woman while his thoughts were monopolized by another.

Strange, he thought. Karla's occasional visits had always been immensely enjoyable for them both. In fact, ever since he and Karla met at a conference in Chicago three years ago, they had made a point of reuniting at least a couple of times each year, "for old time's sake." For Peter, Karla was the perfect match—intelligent, sexy, and as disinterested in commitment as he was. Under the guise of Visiting Professor, Karla would give a lecture to one of Peter's classes, and then spend the rest of her weekend in Peter's bed. At the end of their tryst, Karla packed up and returned to her life in Chicago, with hardly a backward glance. Yes, these weekends suited him just fine. Until this year.

Peter pulled into the parking lot of her hotel, letting the car idle while Karla searched her purse for her room key. Finding it, she turned and gave him a light kiss on the lips. Peter gave a guilty smile.

"Thanks for coming."

Karla smiled back, accepting his unspoken apology. "Be careful, Peter. Getting involved with a student is dangerous. You know that as well as I do."

Peter nodded. "I'll be careful. Have a safe trip back, okay?" He took her hand and gave it a squeeze.

"I'll be fine. You just worry about yourself." Karla climbed out of the car. Before shutting the door, she turned and added, "See you next semester, sweetheart. You should be through with her by then."

Peter had no time to respond. Karla shut the car door and, with a wicked grin, turned and sauntered toward the hotel lobby.

***

Despite arriving ten minutes early, Natalie reached the clinic five minutes late. Giving the door a tentative tug, she peered inside, unsure of what she would find. Yet, the waiting room appeared no different than any other doctor's office she had visited over the years: off-white walls with blinds pulled tight against the street-facing windows, several couches and chairs and a large coffee table covered with magazines.

Natalie approached the front desk. A receptionist sat behind the closed partition, busy with a phone call, although she opened the window long enough for Natalie to announce her name. Without a word, she reached down and selected a manila folder with "Brooks" written along the side edge. Inside were several forms, which the receptionist slid out and attached to a clipboard. "Fill these out," she whispered, turning her attention back to the caller.

Natalie selected a seat by the window and scanned the first of several papers she was to complete: name, address, date of first period, previous pregnancies, previous live births, and previous abortions. She tried to answer each question in the same unaffected manner that she would have used on a job application. The second form was not as easy. It requested specific information on her pregnancy, how many weeks along she was, if there had been any complications thus far. It also asked if a person was available to drive her home afterward. Natalie answered *no*.

The last form was a description of the procedure she was about to receive. A signature was required to acknowledge the risks inherent in the procedure, as well as another signature granting permission for it to be performed. Natalie signed both lines, her handwriting unrecognizable from the trembling in her hands. Gone was the calm detachment she promised she'd maintain while she was here. Instead, she felt a growing panic, beginning in the pit of her stomach and migrating upward until it closed off her throat, making it suddenly hard to swallow.

Scanning the room, Natalie tried to distract herself with the pictures that lined the walls. She was struck by how generic they all appeared—muted pictures of flowers, trees, and landscapes. Nothing with people in them, certainly not families or children. She peered at the magazines. They could have been found in any doctor's office—*Time, Reader's Digest, Glamour.* However, others were noticeably absent—*Parents Magazine* and *Ladies Home Journal.* It was logical really; how many women in this room wanted to read about taking care of a home and family? Most of the women in the room were college students, though not all. And they could have been there for a myriad of reasons, although she suspected that most were there to prevent a pregnancy. Or end one.

Natalie shook her head, her brows tightly knitted together. Family had always meant so much to her. Even with all her professional hopes, she never once doubted that she would have children of her own someday. The constriction in her chest and throat coiled more tightly. *What was she doing here?*

Natalie stood up and began to gather her things together. Forgetting the clipboard balanced on her lap, she was startled as it landed on the floor with a loud clatter. She grabbed it hurriedly and took it back to the reception window. The receptionist, off the phone now, held out her hand expectantly for the completed forms.

"I, uh, didn't finish them," Natalie mumbled. "I don't… I'm not…." She closed her eyes and tried one last time. "I have to go."

The receptionist nodded. "Give us a call if you want to reschedule." Then, as if this sort of thing happened all the time, she took Natalie's partially finished forms, slid them cleanly into the slender folder with her name typed on the side and went back to work.

Natalie headed for the door, her heart beating hard and fast, as if she had just made a narrow escape. She walked down the street until she reached her car. There, she climbed in and closed the door with more force than was needed. Letting the muffled silence wash over her, she waited for her body to stop its uncontrollable shaking.

CHAPTER 18

The clock on the dashboard read 4:19 when she finally looked up. Almost an hour had passed since Natalie had arrived at the clinic, and she was no closer to a solution.

Still, she felt a curious sense of relief. She didn't know what the right answer was yet, but at least she hadn't let fear push her into doing something she might regret later. When the time came to make a decision about this child, she would do it with a clear head.

Natalie leaned forward, turning the key in the ignition and shifting the gear into drive. As she checked her rearview mirror, her phone rang. Startled, she fumbled for it in her purse, intent only on silencing the jarring sound. Then she noticed the caller's name. *Peter.*

Natalie stared at the phone, its incessant ring filling the car. She felt frozen in place—unable to answer it, unable to put it down. The phone was on its last ring before she brought the phone to her ear and answered.

"Hello?"

"Natalie?" Peter's voice was unmistakable.

She willed herself to be calm, despite the trembling which had returned to her limbs.

"Yes?"

Peter hesitated. "How are you?"

"I'm fine. Is there something you needed?"

He was tentative. "No, nothing like that. I, uh… just wanted to…see if you'd like to come over." Stumbling at first, his final words were delivered in a rush, as if he were anxious to be rid of them.

Natalie frowned into the windshield. Several moments passed before she answered.

"Why?"

"I'd like to see you," he said simply, adding, "It's been a long time."

***

Gina was home when Natalie returned from the clinic. She sat beside her on the couch, relief spreading across her face when she learned of Natalie's decision to see Peter.

For weeks, Gina had made it clear that Natalie had a responsibility to tell Peter about his child. Not only was it the right thing to do, but Natalie had been shouldering this burden alone for too long. She needed Peter's support to help her decide what was best for her and the baby.

Natalie felt little of her roommate's optimism. She held no illusions about what his reaction would be when she told him. To think that he would gather her into his arms, excitedly making plans for their new lives together was beyond delusional. He would feel blindsided, much as she had when she had first learned the news.

Still, this was her chance to be honest. Natalie might not gain strength from their encounter, but at least it might help her know which direction to turn, which solution to choose.

The drive to Peter's house felt comfortingly familiar. She glanced at landmarks along the way—the university, the children's museum, the restaurant where they had shared lunch with Amanda—each one triggering memories of their months together. Passing the parking structure, she remembered Peter's search for his lost wallet, only to be surprised by the locket instead.

She touched the pendant which still hung from her neck, already so much a part of her she didn't have the heart to take it off. She had meant to, of course; had gone as far as laying it on her nightstand several times, but before the day was over, she would fasten it around her neck yet again, aching for the ever-weakening connection that it gave her to Peter.

Natalie pulled into his driveway and shut off the ignition. Light snowflakes brushed the windshield. Forecasters predicted a large storm system moving in over the weekend. Chances were good that the city might be snowed in by tomorrow night. Of all nights to venture out, this certainly wasn't the one. And yet here she was, facing more than one source of danger.

***

Peter stood in the hallway, waiting, but not enjoying the wait. He glanced at his sweater, flicked off a stray piece of lint before renewing his watch out the windows flanking the front door. Taking a deep breath, he hoped once again that this evening would not turn out to be a colossal mistake.

He spotted headlights as Natalie's car pulled into the driveway, its beams illuminating the snowflakes falling around it. He was already at the door when she rang the bell, welcoming her inside with a slightly affected smile on his face.

Closing the door tightly against the cold winds, Peter moved to take her coat. Natalie hesitated before unfastening it and allowing him to slip it off her arms.

"Did everything go well today?" He asked as he hung her coat in the closet.

Natalie turned, her eyes widening in surprise. "What do you mean?"

"Your note," Peter explained, more than a little curious now by her reaction. "It said something about an appointment?" He regarded her with a puzzled grin. "Hey, you're not secretly interviewing for other jobs, are you?"

Natalie cleared her throat. "No, it was nothing like that."

"Good—I don't know what I'd do if I had to find another research assistant."

Natalie turned and looked at him with an unnerving directness. He could almost see the wheels turning in her mind.

"You would be fine, Peter," she answered dispassionately. "You would land on your feet, like always."

Peter hesitated. The bitterness in Natalie's voice was something he had never heard before. He knew tonight might prove a bit awkward at first, but she was there, right? That fact alone signaled her willingness to continue their affair as before. No questions. No explanations. At least that was how he had seen it.

However, looking at her now—the expression on her face virtually unreadable, her arms held tightly against her body—he wondered if he had misjudged the evening. Not for the first time, Peter scolded himself for picking up the phone and calling her, for going back on what he felt had been a sound decision in the first place. But nothing about Natalie was easy or straightforward. He needed to see her again, despite all rational arguments to the contrary.

"Well." He cleared his throat, disregarding her comment. "Would you like to sit down?"

Natalie nodded and made her way to the couch, Peter following closely behind. Sitting down beside her, he reached up and gently touched her hair, smoothing it down in the places where the wind had caught and swirled it around her head. His voice carried a deeper quality when he finally spoke.

"I've missed this. Have you?"

Natalie sat woodenly, not meeting his eyes.

"Peter, I need to talk to you."

He heard her, but they were just words. He was already feeling the magnetic pull toward her that was impossible to ignore.

"Yes, we have a lot to catch up on," he murmured, his face already bending toward hers to kiss her. Natalie drew back, but he was undaunted. He knew she felt the same way.

"Relax," he whispered, his hand sliding from her hair to touch her face. "We'll take it as slow as you like." His voice was soothing, not unlike the tone a mother might use to pacify an anxious child. His hand moved again, this time to the back of her neck, where he held it for his next attempt. He kissed her firmly.

Natalie accepted his kiss but pulled away at the probing of his tongue. Her hands braced in front of her in a defensive stance, pushing him away. He gave her a surprised frown.

"I'm…" she fumbled. "I… could use something to drink, if you don't mind."

Peter took a moment to process her words and stood up. Perhaps a drink would do them both some good. "Red wine? I just opened a new bottle."

She shook her head. "Just water. Thanks."

Before Peter could reply, his phone rang. Under any other circumstances, he would have let it go to voicemail, but right now he welcomed the distraction. This night was not starting out the way he had intended. Striding into the kitchen, he answered the phone, hearing his brother-in-law's voice. As he poured a glass of water for Natalie and a generous glass of wine for himself, he fielded questions about the best way to fix a milking machine.

"Did you check the pipes?" He returned to the living room and handed Natalie her glass. "They might be clogged. Check the vacuum pumps, too. Oh, and the vacuum control valves. If you're still stuck, I'll come by tomorrow. Come to think of it, I might still have an old manual here somewhere. I'll bring it by if I find it…." With a brief glance in Natalie's direction, Peter turned and headed into the office.

***

Natalie stood up from the couch, relieved by the interruption. While she wasn't sure what to expect from this meeting, she felt shaken by Peter's apparent intention to simply pick up where they had left off.

Natalie took a long drink of water and set the glass down on the table. Peter didn't appear to be in any hurry to end his conversation, so she walked to the foyer, still one of her favorite places in the house. Glancing at the now familiar photographs that lined the wall, she reached out to the one containing Peter's youthful image.

Eve had taken this one, she was sure of it now. Only she could have made him smile like that. Natalie's hand gently moved down the length of the frame, and then fell away in defeat.

You win. He never cared for me the way he did for you.

Natalie was too lost in her thoughts to hear Peter's approach from behind. Wrapping his arms around her, he whispered in her ear, "Now, where were we?" Without waiting for an answer, he buried his face into the soft nape of her neck and began kissing her in earnest.

Natalie felt her body tense, her senses heightened to his every touch. Not long ago, the feeling of Peter's body against hers had made her feel warm and alive. Now, it only magnified the uneasiness she had felt since arriving at his house.

Peter moved to the other side of her neck, his hands reaching under her sweater to the warm skin beneath. Natalie's eyes opened in alarm as she put her own hands in the way to stop their upward movement.

"No, Peter, please. I really need to talk to you."

Peter's voice was husky. "We have all night to talk…"

His hands moved to her breasts, easily slipping past the protection of her bra until he was caressing the swollen and very sensitive tissue beneath. Natalie's uneasiness turned to panic. *He wasn't listening. She didn't want this.* As one hand remained in its present spot, his other hand moved across her belly, igniting a visceral response that surprised them both. Natalie spun around and shoved him away from her. Hard.

"I said, '*no*'!"

Under different circumstances, Peter's breathless, bewildered expression might have seemed almost comical. It was obvious he had never encountered this kind of reaction before.

"What's the *matter* with you?" he breathed. "Why did you do that?"

Natalie, close to tears, struggled to gain her composure. Closing her eyes, she forced herself to take deep breaths until the panic subsided.

"I… I didn't come here for this."

Peter's mood visibly shifted from shock to a cold anger.

"Why *else* would you come here?"

Natalie flinched as if he had struck her. Suddenly, it all made sense. That was all tonight had been about, she realized—satisfying a physical need, nothing more. Peter had never intended to explain or apologize for how he had treated her. There had been no change of heart. He had simply run out of willpower.

Natalie paused before replying, her voice shaky. "I needed to talk to you about something…." She stopped. "But it doesn't matter now. I found out what I needed to know."

Natalie didn't bother to readjust her sweater or the garments beneath it in his presence. She simply retrieved her coat from the closet and began fastening the buttons on it as swiftly as her trembling fingers would allow. Picking up her purse, she gave him one final, heartbroken glance.

"Goodbye, Peter."

He strode toward her, hand outstretched. "Come on, Natalie. There's no reason to leave like this. Nothing's changed." He motioned her back into the room.

At that moment, Peter resembled a child whose day at the park had been cut short. Aggravated, yes. Disappointed, surely. But not so injured that he wouldn't bounce back. As she said before, he would land on his feet, likely finding a replacement for her by next weekend, if not sooner. *How could she have loved him so completely?*

"You're wrong," Natalie replied. "Everything's changed."

Without waiting for a response, she opened the door and made her way to the car, not noticing the falling flakes of snow until she was safely inside. Peter stood in the doorway and watched as she backed out of the driveway.

Natalie remembered little of the drive home. She kept her eyes on the road, wary of the accumulating snow and wind that blew the flakes into drifts along the highway's edge. She wanted desperately to get home, to bury herself beneath the comforting softness of her blankets and pretend her world hadn't just ended…again.

But the car was so hot, so confining. Natalie had trouble drawing a full breath. Struggling with the buttons of her coat, she attempted to part the heavy folds of wool gathered by her neck. She tore at the fabric as she continued to drive, finally exposing the skin beneath. And the locket. With a heavy yank, Natalie tore the offending pendant from its slender chain and rolled down the window beside her until it was fully open. The blast of icy air made her gasp, but it supplied the fresh air she needed. With only a moment's hesitation, she hurled the locket out the window.

Eventually, she found herself in her driveway, watching the steady fall of snowflakes cover the windshield until the outside disappeared from view. For a few minutes, she sat there taking in the hushed stillness around her, gaining a measure of calm from it. With the engine turned off the car became colder, the warmth of her breaths visible and white. It was strange, Natalie thought vacantly—no tears. Everything that mattered to her was lost, or about to be, and yet she couldn't cry. She just felt cold and numb.

***

It was late Sunday evening when Gina returned home, weary from an unexpected double shift at the hospital. She had planned to be home much earlier, eager for news about Natalie's night with Peter. However, Natalie's door was already pulled shut with the lights out. Opening the door, she peeked in and saw her friend curled up on top of the covers.

Gina crept closer and pulled an afghan over her. *Strange.* Natalie was still wearing her clothes. Glancing around the room, she saw several boxes sitting on the floor in front of the closet, some already packed to the top with what looked like textbooks and binders.

Gina frowned, wondering what had happened on Friday night. Natalie had promised to call her with news—good or bad. But Gina received nothing but a brief text the next day, "Everything is fine. See you Sunday."

Gina couldn't shake the feeling that something had gone very wrong. Casting a final worried glance at her friend and the half-filled boxes that surrounded her, Gina stepped out of the room. Her questions would have to go unanswered for one more night.

***

In an ironic twist, it turned out to be one of Natalie's most productive weekends. Desperate to shut off the flow of painful thoughts, she coped in the only way she knew how—continuous, physical work. For once, her body cooperated—the daily bouts of nausea and fatigue abated, allowing her to tackle the many tasks on her list.

Consummate planner that she was, Natalie had even made a list for this one. Under different circumstances, Natalie might have seen the humor in a 'post-apocalyptic to-do list.' Step by step, she outlined the tasks that would dismantle the life she had built for herself in Madison. School, work, home—everything from her years here would be divided up and either packed or thrown away. Bills were paid, letters of resignation written, half-finished research reports pieced together with instructions for the next assistant to take her place. Belongings were boxed up with the plan that whatever didn't fit in her car, Gina could ship back to her in White Falls.

White Falls. Just a few weeks ago, Natalie had been so eager to leave there, so anxious to get back to her new life. How quickly things could change, she thought bitterly. Her new life now obsolete, all she could think of was salvaging her old one.

***

Natalie woke early Monday morning groggy from little sleep and troubled by a vague, disquieting sense of something wrong. She lay in bed, staring at the ceiling as her mind assembled the fragments of the previous days. She closed her eyes again, remembering it all.

She sat up and inspected the fruit of her efforts—four sealed envelopes lay on the desk, and five fully packed boxes sat stacked next to her closet. Natalie rose from bed and walked to the bathroom to clean up. Then, back to her room to retrieve the letters she had written. The sealed envelopes, all addressed in her neat, efficient print, contained requests for withdrawal from the Psychology Department and the Graduate College, along with resignation letters to Peter and Dr. McMann, with immediate effect. On the way down the hall, she pulled her coat from the arm of the sofa, where it had rested all weekend.

The scene was startlingly bright—stark, white snow backlit by the purest blue sky Natalie could ever recall seeing. In total, Madison had received eight inches of precipitation. County snowplows had been running day and night since then. Still, it was impossible to know the condition of the less-traveled roads; those might still be slippery or impassable.

Natalie tucked the letters into her backpack and headed outside, shutting the door behind her softly. The car stood waiting; a mass of undisturbed snow piled atop every exposed surface. She trudged toward the shed, in search of the shovel that was stored there, but instead spotted her bicycle parked against the wall. Without reason, she found herself drawn in its direction.

Running her hands along the handlebars, Natalie remembered the last time she had ridden it. The snows had hit Madison by early December, but there had been one afternoon in the not-too-distant past where the sidewalks and roads were relatively clear. She had been riding home from the Psychology building, Peter watching her from his third-floor window. As she gave a final glance back, she saw him wave, his smile evident even from a distance.

Nothing again would ever compare with that feeling. His desire and affection felt like a rare prize, made more so by the knowledge that it wouldn't last. Natalie always knew it would end. Now it was time to let go.

CHAPTER 19

Peter was nearing the end of his lecture when Mrs. Gibbs, the department secretary, knocked on the open door of his classroom. Seeing her, he stepped away from the lectern and met her at the door, a puzzled look on his face. Mrs. Gibbs had never interrupted one of his classes before.

"Martha?"

"There's a phone call for you, Professor. Gina Chisholm. She says it's urgent."

For a moment, Peter stood there, trying to recollect the name. *Gina…?*

Natalie's roommate. A feeling of panic ran through him as he darted back into the room and began to stuff papers haphazardly into his briefcase. He barely managed to utter "class dismissed" to the bewildered students before rushing out of the classroom, leaving Mrs. Gibbs several paces behind him as he half-ran down the hall to the departmental office.

Stopping at Mrs. Gibbs' desk, he reached for her phone. Line one was blinking. "Is it line one?" he called behind him. Without waiting for her to answer, he picked up. "Peter Spencer."

"Peter, it's Gina." Her voice had a strained quality to it, which only added to his anxiety.

"What's happened?"

"I'm at University Hospital. Natalie was just brought in. She's been in an accident."

Peter sat down on the edge of the desk and began to stroke his beard nervously. "How is she? Is she going to be all right?"

"She's hurt, Peter—broken bones, internal bleeding. A car hit her when she was riding home from school this morning. She was on her bike, for God's sake. She just went into surgery. That's all I know." Her voice began to crack. "I...I just thought you should know."

"I'll be right there. Where are you? Where do I go?" He slid off the desk, oblivious to the curious stares of Mrs. Gibbs and several other faculty members who had entered the office while he was on the phone.

"Second floor surgical waiting room. Turn left when you get to the lobby and take the 'B' elevators up to two. I'll be there."

Peter dropped the phone back into its cradle, grabbed a piece of paper from Mrs. Gibbs's desk and jotted down Gina's location. Despite the looks of anticipation surrounding him, he offered no explanation to his colleagues, only a curt, "Cancel all my classes today," before running to his car.

***

Peter strode down the hospital corridor with grim determination, eyes darting from one side of the hall to the other in search of the elevator that would take him upstairs.

Seven years had passed since he had last been to this hospital. Peter still recalled the frantic call from his mother—massive heart attack, not much time. He swallowed the bitterness and anger and flew home to make his peace, but in the end it wasn't enough. The weak, expressionless man who stared back at him little resembled the larger-than-life figure from his youth. Peter could ask for forgiveness, but his father couldn't. In all those years, he never could.

Sensations bombarded him the moment he stepped through the revolving doors—the smell of antiseptic, the over-air-conditioned chill in the air, the incessant sounds of gurney wheels and beeping monitors. All brought back with nauseating clarity their last hours together. Peter promised himself he would never come back to this place if he could help it. Yet here he was again, and this time he couldn't get here fast enough.

He reached the elevator just as the panel doors were closing. He squeezed in with a throng of other visitors and headed to the second floor, where he found Gina waiting for him in the doorway. Closing the gap between them, he put his arms around her.

Gina accepted the embrace, resting her head on his chest. The irony wasn't lost on either of them. The man she had mistrusted most in Natalie's life turned out to be the first one she called when Natalie was in trouble.

Peter pulled away, resting his hands on her shoulders. "Have you heard anything?"

Gina shook her head. "She's still in surgery."

"Have you gotten in touch with her parents?"

"I've tried three times, but all I get is their answering machine," Gina responded. "I left a message for them to call my cell phone."

Peter exhaled as he studied the room: the empty chairs, the stacks of magazines, the sun shining through the large picture window, piercing the room with the reflected glow off the snow outside. Peter felt a wave of anger at the sight—it was inconceivable that so much brightness could exist on such a dark, frightening day.

"She's been in surgery for at least an hour, hasn't she? How long do these things take?"

"There's no way of knowing. It all depends on the extent of her injuries." She saw him flinch. "Peter, the head nurse on this floor knows me. So does the surgeon. We'll find out more as soon as Natalie comes out. For now, all we can do is wait."

Wait. Peter stepped over to the window and stared out at the cars in the parking lot below. His hands clenched and unclenched. His body was a coiled mass of nerves. *She has to be all right. I can't lose her.*

***

The sun's migration marked their hours of waiting, from its highest point in the sky to its gradual descent toward the horizon. They were joined throughout the day by others waiting for loved ones, though by late afternoon most had received news and gone. Each time a doctor entered the room, Peter looked to Gina, watching for a sign that this was the one they were waiting for. But still no news.

Gina stood up and stretched. She looked exhausted. It occurred to Peter that she had been at the hospital far longer than he had.

"Why don't you take a walk," he suggested. "I'll stay here in case the doctor comes."

Gina hesitated, and then nodded. "Okay. Maybe I'll go to the cafeteria. I'll try Natalie's parents again while I'm down there. Can I get you anything?"

Peter shook his head. His appetite was nonexistent. He watched her leave and then stood up to work out the stiffness in his body, achy from hours of tense waiting.

Returning to the window for probably the fiftieth time that morning, Peter replayed their last night together and her anguished goodbye. It shouldn't have been a surprise that she chose to end the affair. Especially considering how he had treated her since her return. It was exactly what he had wanted, wasn't it?

Yet, from the moment she walked out the door, Peter knew he had made a horrible mistake. All weekend he felt restless, unable to concentrate, and curiously short of breath. He picked up the phone to call her a dozen times, but always hung up before the first ring, uncertain of what he would say even if she did take his call.

In the end, Peter decided to wait until Monday to speak with her, hoping that a little time might soften the pain he had caused. *It was simply a misunderstanding,* he would say. *Of course I still care for you,* and then she would smile and forgive him, and things could go back to the way they had been before she had left.

Horribly naïve, he now realized, but in the end it didn't matter. The Monday he counted on never came. In its place was an endless day spent before a bright picture window, waiting to hear if Natalie would live or die. Peter pressed his head against the glass and closed his eyes, silently forming the words of a prayer he had not uttered since he was a child.

***

Gina moved down the corridor, barely registering the sights and sounds around her, when she glimpsed a doctor in scrubs heading in her direction. Her head snapped up in attention. "Dr. Gibson?" she called.

The surgeon recognized Gina and smiled. "Hello, Gina, how are you?"

"Doctor, were you the one who was working on Natalie Brooks?"

Dr. Gibson stopped, a questioning look on his face. "Yes, why?"

"She's my roommate. Can you please tell me how she is?"

He hesitated. "Gina, I really should speak with family first. You know how these things work."

Gina nodded, turning to match his steps in the opposite direction. "I haven't been able to reach them, Doctor," she began. "They live hours away, and they don't even know what's happened yet. Natalie and I have been roommates for years. She's my best friend. Please, could you tell me?"

Dr. Gibson paused, his expression sober. "I'm afraid she suffered multiple fractures to her ribs and extremities. There was some internal bleeding in the abdomen, but we were able to stop that. She must have been wearing a helmet, because the only evident head trauma seems to be a mild concussion. Unfortunately, we were unable to prevent her from miscarrying."

Gina closed her eyes, feeling a mix of relief that her friend had survived and deep sadness at the emotional toll this would leave behind.

"She'll be okay, though, right, Doctor?"

Dr. Gibson nodded. "She'll recover, but she's going to have a long road ahead of her. The fractures alone will take several months to heal. She'll need full-time help and intensive physical therapy. Will her family be able to care for her?"

"Yes." *If we could just reach them.* Gina shook his hand. "Thank you for everything, Dr. Gibson. When can we see her?"

"We?"

By now, the pair had reached the doors to the surgical waiting room. As they slowed to a stop, Gina spotted Peter standing at the window, his back turned to them.

"That's her friend, Peter," Gina replied, nodding in his direction. "He and Natalie," she hesitated, "were close. I know he would want to see her, too."

"He was the father?"

"Yes."

The doctor nodded. "She hasn't come out of anesthesia yet. I'll ask the nurse to let you know when you can see her. Short visits only, Gina. She needs plenty of rest right now."

"I understand, Doctor. Thank you."

"Good luck." Dr. Gibson patted her shoulder and continued down the hallway. Gina turned back to the waiting room, where Peter had noticed the two talking. He strode toward her.

"How is she?" he asked.

Gina saw the fear in his face. "She's going to be all right."

"Thank God," he breathed. "What did the doctor say?"

Gina repeated the doctor's message, listing Natalie's injuries and the protracted recovery ahead. Peter listened intently, nodding and asking occasional questions. Gina paused before delivering the final piece of news. She was uncertain how to word it—uncertain of what his reaction would be.

"There's one more thing, Peter. She lost the baby."

Of all the possible reactions, Gina was unprepared for the one he finally displayed. Peter's expression went blank, his voice silent. A cloud of confusion spread across his face. Moments passed before he regained the ability to reply.

"Baby?" he said, his voice barely above a whisper. "Natalie was pregnant?" Peter stumbled on the last word.

"She didn't tell you." It was more a statement than a question. Gina shook her head in disappointment. *Natalie, you promised.*

Peter sank into a nearby chair, his arms resting on his knees, his head bowed. "How long has she known?" He spoke without inflection, not looking up.

"A few weeks. She kept putting off telling you. I guess she was afraid of how you would react. I thought she was going to talk to you this weekend."

"No." Peter gave a bitter laugh. "Things ended a little differently."

"What do you mean?"

"She broke it off."

Gina's expression changed to bewilderment. "She broke up with you? But--I don't understand. Why didn't you say something earlier? Why are you *here*?"

Peter dropped his head back into his hands. "It was my fault," he answered, his voice stripped of emotion.

He recalled how pale Natalie had looked the last few weeks, how weak and shaky before teaching her class last week. That he could have mistaken her condition as nothing more than a broken heart was beyond arrogant. And then to behave the way he did that night....

"How could I have been so stupid...?" he whispered.

Gina knelt beside him, watching his silent struggle. "Peter, I don't know what happened between you two, but right now we need to think about Natalie. Maybe it's not a good idea for you to be here."

Peter straightened up and shook his head. "No—I need to be here for her."

"That's how *you* feel," Gina responded. "But is that what's best for Natalie?"

He didn't answer. All of a sudden, nothing made sense.

She placed her hand on his shoulder. "Look, Peter, Natalie loves you—you must know that. But, unless you feel the same way, maybe it's best that you go now and just let us take care of her. It's going to take every bit of strength she has to get through this. She can't be dealing with relationship issues on top of it all."

Peter sat back in his chair, feeling more exhausted than he ever had in his life. Gina was right. This was no time for childish games.

He thought back to the last few months. They had been some of the happiest he could remember. After years of meaningless attractions, Natalie made him feel alive and safe and loved. After years of pushing others away before they got too close, she gave him the courage to open up his heart.

But then she left. And with her went his courage. Peter felt lost without her—glancing at her desk in the office, waiting by his window for her bike to pass, reaching for her in the morning. And he hated it, hated how much he had come to depend on her.

His solution—trying to prove how insignificant she was to him—hurt them both. And in the end, it did nothing to change the truth. Peter loved her. He always had.

Peter's shook his head, his expression resolved. "She means everything to me, Gina," he replied. "I'm not going anywhere."

Gina gave a faint smile. "The nurse will let us see her in a little bit," she said. "Why don't you go first?"

***

Peter followed the nurse into the intensive care unit and paused as she pulled open the curtain. In the bed was a small form covered by hospital sheets and surrounded by machines emitting intermittent flashes and beeps. He moved closer, hesitating as he reached the bedside. This couldn't be Natalie. He turned to the nurse, half expecting her to admit she had made a mistake. However, she squeezed past him, checking the tubes and sensors that seemed to cover Natalie's body. She nodded in the direction of a chair beside the bed.

"Have a seat. I'll be at the nurse's station if you need me."

Peter stood motionless, studying the small, broken body before him, this woman he had fought so hard not to love. Natalie's face was scored with cuts and bruises; her hair matted and tucked behind her on the pillow. One arm, her right, was in a splint up to the elbow, the other bare but limp at her side. Gina said that both legs had been broken in the accident, although the blankets made it difficult for him to see for himself. He sat down to wait for Natalie to wake up, the rhythmic sounds of the machines his only distraction.

***

Natalie's eyes opened, drifted shut, and re-opened, the exertion of focusing almost too much for her. For a moment, Peter remained still, and then snapped to attention as he realized she was waking.

"Hi," he whispered.

Natalie turned her head to the sound of his voice, her expression cloudy. She swallowed with difficulty. "Hi," she said hoarsely. "What…happened?"

"You had an accident. You're in the hospital."

Natalie blinked but said nothing. Peter wasn't sure how much she understood. "You're going to be just fine," he continued. "But you need to rest now."

She nodded her head. "Stay." Her voice was barely a whisper. With great effort, she lifted her hand, but was unable to move it more than a few inches in his direction. Peter took her hand and held it with both of his. "I'm here," he promised.

Natalie closed her eyes and returned to sleep.

***

Gina and Peter took turns sitting with Natalie. She woke intermittently, each time newly unaware of her whereabouts or what had brought her there. Still, the comforting presence of her friends helped her drift back to the sleep that her body so desperately needed.

It was 8:00 p.m. when the unit nurse approached Gina, who sat slumped in a waiting room chair, ready to take over for Peter in a few minutes.

"Gina, you two should call it a night."

Gina began to protest, but the nurse was ready for her excuses.

"You won't be doing her any good if you don't take care of yourself," she reminded her. "You know I'm right. We'll take good care of her until you get back in the morning."

Gina nodded. It was the same advice she had given to families over the years. With great effort she rose from her chair and entered the curtained area where Natalie lay sleeping. There was Peter, leaning against the bed rail, tenderly stroking Natalie's hair.

"Peter," Gina whispered. He jerked up, startled by her voice.

"We should leave. Visiting hours are over."

"You go ahead. I'm staying." He gave her a stubborn glance, his eyes bloodshot.

"Peter, you're not doing her any good like this."

Peter returned his gaze to the motionless figure beside him. He didn't answer.

Gina stepped over to his chair and rested her hand on his shoulder. "Just get a few hours' sleep. You can come back first thing in the morning. That's when she'll need you most."

Peter exhaled in resignation. Reluctantly, he rose from his chair, his body stretching to its full length, his hand rubbing the back of his neck.

Gina led the way out of the room, stopping once for a final glimpse of her best friend. Each, in their own way, said a silent prayer that Natalie would make it through the night without their watchful presence.

CHAPTER 20

Pausing only long enough to peel off his jacket and shoes, Peter collapsed onto the bed, the hospital smells that lingered on his clothes already permeating the room. Although his body was exhausted, his mind refused to rest. Thoughts of Natalie were constant and troubling, waking him in a panic each time he drifted to sleep. Only after countless attempts, did his body finally succumb.

And when it did, Eve was waiting.

She sat at the top of the canyon road, door ajar, wheels perched close to the edge. Running blind with panic, Peter scaled the same uneven ridges, fought his way through the same cutting outcrops and underbrush until he reached the peak. Heart pounding, lungs burning, he began to cross the last few yards that separated them—the ones he could never seem to cross in time.

Eve was smiling when he arrived, which puzzled and frightened him.

Peter held his arms out, ready to embrace her if only she would get out of that damned car. "Please come out of there, Eve. Let me help you. Please."

Eve's smile twisted into an expression of hatred. "I have a friend of yours here." She glanced at the passenger beside her. "Say hello to Peter."

Peter's chest tightened in horror as he saw Natalie's face peer out from the passenger's seat, a smile of recognition brightening her face.

"Hi, Peter!" Natalie greeted him. "Eve and I are going for a ride." Sitting back in her seat, she picked up an object

from her lap and handed it toward him. "I almost forgot. This is yours." Eve took the object and gave it a brief glance before tossing it at him through the open door. The book landed on the ground with a hard smack.

Cannery Row. *Peter stared at it before turning his terrified gaze to the two women in the car. He could see Natalie's face, still smiling, completely oblivious to the certain fate ahead of her.*

"Remember when you'd read that book to me?" Eve snarled. "You were always trying to improve me, trying to make me into someone I could never be." She glanced at Natalie, then back at Peter. "You'll destroy her, too."

The car door swung shut.

Peter lunged at the car, his screams drowned out by the revving engine and wrenching sound of wheels spinning against loose rock. He reached the cliff in time to see the car make its slow-motion descent into the canyon below, Natalie's hand still waving from the passenger window.

Peter lunged upright in bed, his heart pounding, his body shivering despite the thin sheen of sweat that covered him. Ripping at the covers, he stumbled into the hallway and the office a few steps beyond. He reached for the book that lay on his desk, opening it to her simple inscription:

Merry Christmas, Peter… N

Peter tenderly stroked the words with his fingers, tears coursing down his cheeks.

***

The telephone's jarring ring woke him. Peter sat up quickly, but his mind and body felt drugged. He glanced at the alarm clock. *7:14.* He couldn't remember what day it was or why anyone would be calling him at this time of the morning. All at once, the events from the day before came flooding back and he grabbed the phone in a panic.

"Hello?"

"Peter, it's Gina. I know it's early, but I thought you'd want to know. Natalie's condition has been upgraded. She'll stay in ICU for another day and then should be transferred out to a regular room by tomorrow."

Peter exhaled at the news, realizing only then that he must have been holding his breath the entire time she was speaking. "Thanks, Gina," he said. He got out of bed and peered out the window. It was snowing again. "I'll be in as soon as I get dressed."

"Take your time," she said. "The nurse will be with her for a while. Mid-morning would be best."

"Okay. I'll come then." He was about to hang up when he remembered something. "Hey, did you ever get in touch with Natalie's parents?"

"They left a message on my cell phone last night. Turns out they never even got my calls. They're visiting Natalie's aunt in Virginia and got worried when Natalie didn't return their calls. I phoned them back late last night and told them. They are leaving first thing this morning. Hopefully, they'll be here by tomorrow."

Peter voiced his relief. He knew how close Natalie was with her parents. She would need them now more than ever.

Gina continued. "I'll be working the third floor until three o'clock. If you need me, just have the unit nurse page me. I'll visit every chance I get."

"Thanks for everything, Gina."

Peter hung up the phone but remained at the window, watching the falling snow and the occasional car pass by. It occurred to him that he should call the department about what had happened but felt strangely reluctant to do so. Letting them in on the news would open the floodgates of phone calls and visits by classmates and faculty. Natalie wasn't ready for that and, truthfully, neither was he. Selfish as it was, Peter wasn't ready to share her with others yet. He wanted to be there for her and no one else. It was the only way he knew to make up for the pain he had caused her.

Peter headed to the bathroom to shower and shave. He let the water run over him, the heat and steam clearing his mind. He could have stood there for hours, but he forced himself to turn off the water and get dressed. He wanted to get back to the hospital as soon as possible.

On his way to the kitchen, he passed the office. There, lying on the desk where he had left it, was *Cannery Row*. He retrieved the volume, opening it again to see Natalie's simple inscription and touch the cottony pages inside. He gripped the book tightly and headed to the kitchen.

It was after nine o'clock when he picked up the phone and dialed the departmental office. Mrs. Gibbs answered the phone on the second ring. "Department of Psychology, may I help you?"

"Martha, it's Peter Spencer. How are you?"

"Dr. Spencer—how are *you*? You left in such a hurry yesterday, we were all so concerned."

Peter hesitated. "I'm fine, Martha. Natalie Brooks was in a serious accident yesterday. I spent most of the day at the hospital."

"Our Natalie?" Mrs. Gibbs exclaimed. "My goodness, she was just in yesterday morning, dropping off letters for you and Gordon. Is she going to be all right? We should circulate a get-well card for her and send some flowers. What hospital is she in?" Mrs. Gibbs seemed unable to stop herself.

Peter was already regretting the phone call. Wanting nothing more than to tell Mrs. Gibbs to mind her own business, he responded with as much tact as he could. "She's expected to recover, Martha, but she's suffered some serious injuries and needs to rest as much as possible right now. Cards and flowers are fine, but there should be no visitors for the time being."

Mrs. Gibbs paused, obviously surprised by his imperious tone. "Of course, Dr. Spencer."

Peter continued. "I would appreciate it if you could cancel my appointments this morning. If anyone asks, I will be at my 12:30 and 2:30 lectures."

"Yes, Professor. So, *you* will be at the hospital?" There was an unspoken question in her response, but Peter chose to ignore it.

"Yes. Thank you, Martha. Goodbye." He hung up the phone and grabbed his briefcase, taking care to put Natalie's book inside. Then he left for the hospital.

***

Natalie was awake and reclined in bed when Peter entered her room. The nurse was just finishing checking her bandages.

"Should I wait outside?" he asked, feeling acutely uncomfortable in their presence.

"You're fine. I was just leaving," the nurse answered. She turned to Natalie one last time. "Now remember—no straining and no sudden movements. If you need anything, use this." She set the call button beside Natalie's uninjured arm.

Natalie nodded and turned to Peter. Her eyes still had a drowsy quality about them, but she was more alert than the night before. She gave him a pleasant, but quizzical look– pleased to see him, yet somehow surprised that he was there. Peter wondered how much she remembered about their last night together.

"Hi," she said, her voice still hoarse.

"Hi." With care, Peter sat down on the edge of the bed and took Natalie's hand in his. "How are you feeling?"

"I've felt better," she answered.

"I'll bet. You really gave us a scare."

Natalie gave a weak smile. "Sorry."

Peter gave her hand a gentle squeeze. "Looks like you'll be needing a new bike when you get out of here."

"And a new body." Natalie attempted to shift position but winced and closed her eyes. Peter straightened, his hand still gripping hers. "Are you all right?"

Natalie opened her eyes and took a slow, tentative breath. "Need to keep still."

Peter stroked his beard nervously. He hated feeling so useless. "Can I get you anything? Do you need the nurse?"

The spasm began to subside, and Natalie's body relaxed. She shook her head. "No... just keep me company."

The tension in Peter's body seemed tied to hers and he began to relax as well. "I can do that, at least. Here," he began, pulling the book out of his briefcase. "I brought *Cannery Row*. Maybe we can read it together."

Natalie reached for the book with her unaffected arm but was seized by another painful spasm. She gazed at him helplessly.

Peter gently took her hand and repositioned it by her side. Then he held the book up for her to see. "Let me read to you for a while. Just close your eyes and listen."

Natalie nodded as he opened the book and turned to the first page. She closed her eyes and let his deep voice flow over her.

Peter read to her for an hour. When he closed the cover, she was sound asleep. He sat by her bedside as she dozed in relative peace, her face finally free of the pain. He found a pad of paper nearby and tore off a piece as a bookmark, slipping it inside the book and laying it on her bedside table. Glancing around the room, he noticed how cold and sterile it looked. This afternoon he would bring some flowers to brighten it up.

***

Peter spent the rest of the day in class and staff meetings. It was a torturous day. His thoughts repeatedly drifted to Natalie, and, on more than one occasion, he was startled back to reality by a student or colleague calling his name. With relief, he dismissed his last class and was the first one out of the classroom, oblivious to the questions being called out about the upcoming midterm exam. His only thought was returning to Natalie.

Peter was halfway past the office when he took a detour to collect his mail. The mail slot was overflowing from days of inattention. Thankfully, Mrs. Gibbs was not at her desk, so he took a few moments to flip through the papers for anything pressing. Natalie's envelope was near the bottom of the pile.

His throat constricted as he tore through the flap. Mrs. Gibbs said she had been here the morning of her accident.

> *Dear Dr. Spencer,*
>
> *I regret to inform you that, due to personal reasons, I will be unable to continue working as your graduate assistant. All academic notes and materials pertaining to our work together will be returned to you as soon as possible.*
>
> *Thank you for giving me the opportunity to assist you in your work.*
>
> *Sincerely,*
>
> *Natalie Brooks*

Peter stared at the paper in his hand long after its message had been absorbed. He shook his head, silently rejecting her resignation, condemning himself yet again for pushing her so close to the edge. Sliding the remaining letters back in the slot, he stalked out of the office, crumbling up the letter and stuffing it into his pocket.

As if on cue, Gordon intercepted him as he approached the stairwell. "Peter, I'm glad I caught you. Do you have a minute?" Gordon stepped in front of him to prevent any further momentum.

"Not now, Gordon," Peter replied with impatience, beginning to circle around the obstacle he presented. "I'm on my way out."

"Going to the hospital?" Gordon asked pointedly. The set expression on his face made Peter stop his attempts at escape.

"I don't see how that's any of your business."

"Peter, it's obvious what's going on here," Gordon began. "And I was willing to turn a blind eye as long as you managed to keep the affair discreet. However, now…" Gordon waved his hand toward the stairwell, and presumably the building as a whole, "it has become a source of public speculation. I'm afraid that's unacceptable."

Peter regarded him evenly. "What's your point, Gordon?"

"My point is that you've crossed the line, and it has to stop."

Peter continued to watch him, almost enjoying the agitated way Gordon shifted his gaze despite all attempts to present a hard, unyielding stance.

"If you do not," Gordon continued, "I'm afraid the department will have to consider disciplinary action."

Peter shook his head in disgust. "Do what you have to, Gordon. Fire me if that's what you want—I honestly don't give a damn. Just get out of my way. I've got more important things to do."

And with that, he circled around the stunned figure and continued down the stairwell.

***

Peter arrived at Natalie's room just as Gina was leaving, her expression grim. His heart began to race as his mind replayed every possible complication that might have struck since that morning. "What is it?"

Gina held up her hand. "Her condition hasn't changed." Then she sighed. "The doctor was in a while ago. He told her about the miscarriage."

An odd mix of emotions ran through him. Peter still hadn't come to terms with the news that she had been pregnant. With his child.

"How is she handling it?" he asked.

"Not well. I'm not sure this is the best time for a visit."

Peter nodded but was undeterred. "Maybe, but I'll let her be the judge."

"Good luck," Gina said, her expression sad. She watched him enter the room before heading back to her rounds.

The lights were dimmed. Natalie lay semi-reclined in bed, her head turned toward the window.

"How's the patient?" Peter said, stepping over to the side where she lay staring.

Natalie looked up but gave no sign whether his presence was welcome or not. She seemed to stare right through him, her face empty and inconsolable at the same time. On closer examination, he could see faint streaks down her cheeks from tears recently shed. He sat down in the chair next to her bed.

"What time is it?" she asked.

"4:30."

"Why aren't you at school?" Natalie questioned, her voice cold.

"I was. I came over after my last class."

"You go to the gym after your last class."

"Well, today I didn't."

Natalie glanced back out the window. She trembled slightly and drew her one arm around herself. Peter stood up and pulled a blanket over her.

Natalie shrugged off the blanket with irritation. "Why are you here?"

In the space of a few seconds, her expression had turned hard with undisguised anger. Peter could only imagine what she had gone through these past few weeks, how the doctor's news had affected her. He owed it to her to be as patient as possible.

"This is where I belong."

"You don't have to be here." Natalie shot back. "I'll be *fine*. At least that's what everyone keeps telling me."

"I want to be here, Natalie."

"Well, I *don't* want you here," Natalie countered, her voice heavy with emotion. "Just go away and leave me alone." She turned sharply toward the window, wincing in pain with the movement.

For a few moments, he sat in silence, gathering his thoughts before speaking. "Natalie, if you want me to go, I will. But you need to hear some things first."

Natalie didn't move. She continued to stare out the window, but her breathing became even. He could tell she was listening.

"My place is here." He paused. "I love you, Natalie. I have for a long time. I guess I was just too stupid to realize it before this."

It took a few moments for his words to sink in. When they did, her only reaction was to close her eyes, rubbing them tiredly with her good hand. "Why are you saying this?" she asked, her voice sad.

"It's true."

Natalie shot him an accusing stare, her eyes filling with tears. "It's *not*. You couldn't possibly love me. You've been shutting me out ever since I came back. Don't lie to me. Not now."

Peter got up and sat next to her on the bed, taking care not to hurt her any more than she was already. "You're right. I was shutting you out. I felt like I was getting in over my head, and it scared the hell out of me. It was the only way I knew to slow things down."

The anger in her face faded, replaced in time by a painful weariness. He took her hand and gazed into her eyes. "Please believe me. I am so sorry I hurt you."

Natalie lowered her head. "It doesn't matter. It's too late."

Peter squeezed her hand, his voice persistent. "Why is it too late?"

"I can't make things right."

"What things?"

Natalie shook her head. "I can't fix it now. It's too late. You wouldn't understand."

"I think I do," he confessed. "The baby?" Peter hesitated. "I wish you could have told me."

Natalie shuddered, her eyes shutting tightly. He put his arms around her and gently embraced her, feeling her body shake with emotion.

The baby. With those two words, the floodgates opened, releasing weeks of raw emotions held in check. All the fear, ambivalence, and overwhelming grief that Natalie had concealed for so long found its way out with a force that she was unable to stop.

Peter didn't know how long he held her; he didn't care. Long, painful sobs wracked her body, made all the more painful by her fragile condition. Peter did not try to stop her. He knew that to hold the pain inside any longer would cripple her. Natalie had to let go of the grief.

Peter rocked her in his arms until her tears began to subside, her body becoming limp with exhaustion. When only her ragged breaths were audible, he laid her back on the pillows and covered her with a blanket. He kissed her battered face and stroked her hair, whispering over and over, "Everything will be all right. I promise. Everything will be all right."

Peter stayed until she fell asleep. Only when a nurse's aide entered the room to check her vital signs did he stand up and go, stealing a final glimpse before he did so.

As he trudged through the dark parking lot, avoiding the thick remnants of slush left by passing cars, Peter's thoughts returned to the weeks before Natalie's accident. In hindsight, there had been so many signs that something was wrong, but Peter had misread or dismissed them all. The constant look of fatigue about her, the deep lines of worry etched on her face, the disquieting way she avoided his eyes whenever he glanced at her. The night he had invited her over—he realized now that she had intended to tell him about her pregnancy, but in the end had abandoned the idea.

The hardest truth for Peter to admit was that she had been right to conceal it from him. Peter knew how he would have reacted that night—disbelief, blame, and finally, rejection. As ashamed as he was of his behavior that night, the realization of how much worse he might have behaved caused him no end of pain.

Peter reached his car and fumbled with the keys, his hands already numb with cold. The winds blew the dusty snow in swirls around his feet as he climbed in. Closing the door behind him, he sat motionless, letting the full effect of what had happened wash over him. He stared into the illuminated hospital windows, knowing Natalie lay behind one of them. Struck with a wave of protectiveness, he promised himself that this time he would be the kind of man she deserved, the kind she needed to get through this ordeal.

Chapter 21

Peter awoke and went about his morning routine with considerably more energy. Intent on visiting Natalie before his morning class, he rushed through his shower and shave and skipped breakfast altogether.

On the way to the hospital, he stopped by a nearby café for coffee and a blueberry scone, Natalie's favorite. Standing at the counter, he added extra ingredients to her cup, remembering how she liked her coffee. It seemed like a lifetime ago when they had shared lazy Saturday mornings together. Peter would watch her fill half the cup with milk and sugar and remark that it wasn't even coffee by the time she was through with it. Natalie would just laugh off his disapproval and sit down, picking through the newspaper for her favorite sections.

Coffee and bakery bag in hand, Peter strode through the parking lot and hospital corridors, taking the elevator to the fourth floor where she had been transferred from ICU.

Natalie's door was partially closed. He knocked lightly, looking again at the number he had written down to be sure he had the right one when he heard her voice. He swept through the door before coming to a halt. Natalie was lying in bed, but she wasn't alone. Beside her were two other visitors, who, after his initial surprise, he concluded must be her parents. They stared at him, and back at Natalie.

Natalie's face brightened when she saw him, and then grew more reserved. With a shy smile, she beckoned him into the room. "Come in, Peter. Come meet my parents."

Peter approached the older man and began to extend his hand out in greeting when he found he was still holding Natalie's coffee. Self-consciously, he raised the cup and placed it on the tray over Natalie's bed. "I thought you might appreciate the good stuff. I fixed it up the way you like it."

Natalie gave him a thankful smile. She reached slowly for the cup, aided by her mother, who stood closest to her bedside. One hand now freed, Peter resumed his earlier handshake with Natalie's father. "Mr. Brooks, Peter Spencer. It's good to meet you. How was your trip?"

Henry Brooks accepted his handshake. "Long. We just got to Virginia when we got word from Natalie's roommate. Would have gotten here sooner, but the weather got in the way."

"I heard there were storms. I'm glad you made it here safely."

"We're fine," he countered. "All that matters is our girl here," Mr. Brooks glanced tenderly at his daughter and lightly tousled her hair.

"We are so thankful that she'll be all right," Mrs. Brooks added, a worried smile on her face. "That was the longest drive of my life."

Peter nodded and extended his hand to the woman. She returned his greeting.

"Please, call me Laura. It's a pleasure to meet you, Mr. Spencer. Natalie's told us a lot about you."

"Peter," he corrected. "She has?" Peter gave a quick glance in Natalie's direction, wondering how much she had actually told them.

"Yes, it sounds like she's learned a great deal working with you."

"Well, I'm lucky to have such a good assistant," he responded. "Natalie's become pretty indispensable."

The conversation stalled, and Peter turned to Natalie, his manner changing from mild civility to genuine concern. Had it just been last night that he held her, promising her that everything would be all right? How he wished he had one more morning with her alone—to talk, to listen, whatever she needed. It was ironic—the words he had avoided for months were now on his lips begging for release, but he had lost his chance. Once again, he felt the walls rise up between them, their secret forcing him onto the sidelines, as if he were just another visitor.

"How are you feeling?" he managed.

Natalie shrugged. "I was up a lot last night, but I feel a little better now." She reached for her mother's hand and gave it a weak squeeze. Her mother cradled it in both of her own hands.

Peter stared awkwardly at the floor as he watched Natalie's mother assume the role of caregiver. Glancing at his hands, he noticed with surprise the bag that he still held.

"I almost forgot. I brought you a scone. Blueberry, right?"

Natalie laughed. "Thank you. How did you remember?"

Peter smiled as he placed the bag on the table. "You eat those things at least three times a week at the office. How could I forget?"

Natalie rewarded him with a warm smile of gratitude, her eyes conveying emotions she felt unable to express in front of her parents.

"Well, I guess I should be getting to the office," Peter replied. "I'm sure you have a lot to catch up on." He began to back his way out of the room. "It was good to meet you both."

Natalie's voice stopped him. "Will you come back later? After class?"

"I'll see you tonight," he promised and gave a parting wave to Natalie's parents, feeling their gazes on his back as he left.

***

Laura Brooks straightened up the blankets on Natalie's bed and refilled her cup with ice water. Her voice was polite and unaffected, but Natalie knew what was coming. "It was very nice of Mr. Spencer...uh, Peter to visit you this morning. Does he come often?"

Natalie prepared herself for the inevitable flurry of questions.

Mrs. Brooks glanced over at her husband. "Henry, do you suppose you could find the cafeteria in this place? I could do with a cup of coffee myself."

"But you just had one at the hotel this morning…."

"I could use another one, dear. Do you mind?"

***

Peter was gazing absently out of a waiting room window when he heard his name. He turned to see Natalie's father approaching.

"Oh—hello, Mr. Brooks. Is there something you need?"

"Just going on a fool's errand," he muttered. "And call me Henry. The ladies needed an excuse to get me out of the room so they could talk about you. I know what they're up to, but it's easier to just go along with it sometimes. Besides, since you're still here, I suppose I can get it straight from the horse's mouth."

Peter wasn't sure how to respond.

"Where do you get coffee around here, anyway?" Henry asked, scanning the maze of corridors and hospital signs, an exasperated expression on his face. Peter knew how he felt—two days ago, he had been just as lost. Now, he was able to navigate the hospital like a regular. "The cafeteria is in the basement. Follow me—the elevators are this way."

Peter led the way while Henry followed. They walked in silence for several minutes before Henry finally got to the point.

"So, you're Natalie's boss. Is that right?"

"That's right."

"That all?"

Peter glanced at Henry. "Why do you ask?"

"Just a hunch. The way you two were acting in that room, for starters. Sounds like you've been spending a lot of time here. And I doubt many professors know how Natalie takes her morning coffee." Henry's eyes never left the corridor in front of them.

Peter shook his head. Clearly, there was no point in trying to deceive the man. "Natalie and I have been seeing each other for a few months."

Henry nodded. "I figured as much. You must have been behind that silly grin on Nat's face the whole time she was home last month. The girl was useless—so distracted I had to tell her everything twice."

Peter smiled and continued walking.

They reached the elevator and pressed the down button. "So, what's your story, Peter? Where are you from? Where's your family?"

Peter felt keenly aware of the fact that he was being interviewed by the family patriarch. "Right here in Dane County. My family farms 500 acres just outside of town."

"A farm boy?" Henry glanced over at Peter with new appreciation. "Well, that is a surprise. Looks like it didn't stick, though. Let me guess—you had enough of the early mornings and decided that being a professor might be an easier line of work?" Henry chuckled.

Peter accepted his ribbing with a good-natured shrug. "Not exactly. But if it makes any difference, I'm still out there every fall for harvest season."

Henry nodded his approval. "Good, good. I was a farmer's son myself. Couldn't wait to get away when I graduated high school. Moved into town and started working for an insurance agency. For ten years I worked my way up until I was one of the lead agents—suit, tie, the whole thing. And you know what? I was miserable. I hated working all day in an office."

The elevator doors opened, and the two men waited for its occupants to step out before taking their place inside. Peter regarded him with interest. "So, when did you get back into farming?"

"A few years after Natalie's mother and I married, I just sat down and told her I couldn't do it anymore. She told me to take all the money we had saved and use it to buy some land. She said she knew all along that I was meant for farming." He lifted his eyebrow skeptically. "Well, you know, women always say those sorts of things. They like to sound like they had it all figured out from the get-go. I don't know if she knew it ahead of time or not, but a few months later we found a 100-acre parcel and put our money down. Over the years, we've built it up to 650 acres and raised two daughters on it. Turned out to be the best thing I ever did."

Conversation ceased in the elevator, and Peter used the silence to ponder the man's words. When the elevator doors opened, they were greeted with yet another long corridor.

"Christ," Henry complained. "Where the hell is this place?"

Peter assured him that it was just around the next corner.

"So, you've taken up with my daughter," Henry declared, as if mulling over the point. "If I'm not mistaken, there are rules about this sort of thing at school, aren't there? Professors and students?"

Peter tensed. "Yes, sir, there are."

"I imagine you've given some thought to this?"

"Yes, we have."

Henry stopped and studied Peter closely. "So, tell me. What *are* your intentions with my daughter?"

Peter wasn't surprised by the question, but he didn't quite know how to respond. He had no doubt about his feelings for Natalie, or hers for him. However, she had gone through so much during the past few days—weeks, really—that he owed her more time before asking her to focus on their future together. Peter paused and then gave Natalie's father the best answer he could.

"I am Natalie's for as long as she'll have me."

Henry considered his answer. "All right," he said finally. "A little vague, but it'll do for now. But remember this. Natalie's the only one in this little arrangement that I am concerned with. If I see you doing anything to cause her pain, you'll have hell to pay. From me. Are we clear on that?"

Henry's face showed no signs of anger. His words were spoken in the same matter-of-fact tone he had been using the entire conversation. But the gravity of the message was clear, and Peter nodded respectfully. "I understand. I know how special your daughter is. I have no intention of hurting her."

"That's good, son." Henry stood up straighter. "All right, I see the cafeteria up ahead. You can go to class. I should be able to find the way back by myself." He dismissed Peter with a wave of the hand.

Peter said goodbye, thinking how much this man reminded him of his own father.

***

The next few days passed in a comforting routine for Natalie. Mornings began with a visit from Peter, followed by Natalie's parents, who accompanied her to her physical and occupational therapy appointments. At noon, Gina would stop by, cheering her with amusing anecdotes about Joey and work.

By late afternoon, Natalie rested, giving her parents time to return to their hotel for dinner. It was then they often crossed paths with Peter, who was returning from a full day of classes.

She was lucky, she knew. She had survived the accident and, with time, would recover from her injuries. She had the love and support of her parents, her best friend, and now Peter, something she could never have imagined only weeks before.

Still, something was wrong. Each day Natalie woke with an increasing sense of malaise, unable to muster up energy for emotions of any kind. She was irritable with others and impatient with herself, unable to concentrate on the simplest of tasks. In truth, she didn't feel like the same person anymore. She felt far away and empty, floating out of reach from the people she loved most.

***

Natalie was sitting up in bed, working the buttons of her shirt when Peter rapped lightly on her door. He peered inside.

"Hi. You decent?"

Natalie gave him a distracted smile. "Kind of. You can come in." She returned her attention to her shirt, her face set with determination.

"Going for the sexy look today?" Peter grinned as he entered the room, glancing at her half-open bodice.

"These damned buttons," she grumbled. "The occupational therapist says I need to do this myself, but it's almost impossible when the buttons are so small. Have you ever tried to button one-handed?"

Peter gave a sympathetic smile as he sat on the edge of her bed. "Let me help. It will be our little secret."

Natalie leaned back as Peter fastened the buttons one by one. Something so effortless and automatic would have taken her twenty minutes. Now, reduced to one arm and essentially no legs, she felt as helpless as a baby.

Peter glanced at her as he worked. "I don't think I've ever buttoned you before. Although if I recall, I was pretty good at unbuttoning…." He playfully slid his hand inside her shirt, touching her lightly.

Natalie blushed and pushed his hand away.

Peter accepted her rebuff good-naturedly. "You know, you're putting a serious crimp in my sex life. What am I going to do until you get back?"

"You'll figure something out."

He leaned over and kissed her. "Come back soon, okay?"

Natalie nodded, her face growing solemn. Tomorrow morning, she would be discharged from the rehab unit, her parents taking her back to White Falls to continue her recovery. Though nothing was certain, Natalie hoped to be back in Madison in time for the fall semester. Her heart lurched at the thought of being away from Peter for so long.

"Peter, I need to ask you something."

"What?"

"That professor from Chicago—Karla Livingston." She paused before continuing. "Did you sleep with her that night?"

Peter looked up in surprise. He reached out and smoothed a stray hair behind her ear as he answered. "No, Natalie. Nothing happened."

She nodded, considering his answer. Oddly, it did little to ease her mind. She persisted, a detached expression on her face. "But have you?"

He paused, considering his answer. "Yes," he said finally.

Natalie nodded. Her expression changed little.

Peter squeezed her hand to get her attention. "Hey, what went on with Karla happened before you and I became involved. It never meant anything."

"I understand. I shouldn't have asked."

He gave her a worried frown. "Whatever happened before us is irrelevant, Natalie. It has nothing to do with the way I feel about you."

Natalie said nothing. From her window, she could see a young mother holding her child's hand as they made their way through the parking lot. The knot in her stomach—always there, always reminding her—tightened at the sight of them.

Peter reached out and grasped her chin gently, turning her face toward his. "I want you to remember something before you go. It doesn't matter who came before you. It's only you now. You're the only one I care about. Do you understand me?"

"Yes."

Peter waited for her to respond, his face creased with concern. "Nat, please talk to me. I need to know how you feel about all of this."

She gazed at him sadly. "I love you, Peter. So much it hurts sometimes. And for months, nothing would have made me happier than hearing you say it back to me." She focused on her hands in her lap. "But now, after what I've done, it would almost be easier if you didn't love me, if you just left right now and didn't come back."

Peter shook his head in confusion. "After what you've…I don't understand. What could you possibly have done?"

Natalie let out a long sigh. It was still early, but suddenly she felt bone weary. "We made something together, Peter," she said miserably. "And because of my selfishness, I killed it."

Peter stared at her through narrowed eyes. "Are you talking about the baby? Natalie, you can't believe that you…."

Natalie cut him off, afraid that he might try to talk her out of what she so fervently believed. "When I found out I was pregnant, I was terrified. All I could think about was making it all go away."

She stopped and glanced out the window. The mother and her child were gone. "I tried to go through with it, but I couldn't do it. But not because I wanted the baby. All I ever wanted was you. Maybe deep down I thought that was the closest thing to you I would ever have."

Peter couldn't speak, his face awash with shame.

Natalie gave him a tortured look. "Don't you understand? The whole time—all I ever thought about was myself. I should have been thinking about our child, but I put it in danger instead. And now, having you here and hearing you say how much you love me—it just reminds me of what we made and how good it could have been."

Natalie's voice cracked. "I destroyed all that." She squeezed her eyes shut, willing herself not to cry, not to bring on more sympathy that she didn't deserve.

Peter shook his head, his hand slowly covering his mouth in disbelief. "Natalie," he began, his voice firm. "You were hit by a car. It was a horrible accident, and you're lucky that you survived it in one piece. I know you didn't mean for that to happen."

"No. But that doesn't make me any less responsible."

"How could you be responsible?"

"I never should have gotten on that bike. I should have been more careful at that intersection. The snow...how could he stop?" Natalie began to tremble as every event—every sensation—of that morning replayed before her closed eyes. *The vivid green of the traffic light. Her fingers, numb with cold despite the gloves she wore. The slush beneath her wheels as she forced her bike across the road. The blur of the late-approaching car. The look of terror on the driver's face. The shattering of glass. The explosion of pain. The darkness.*

Natalie opened her eyes. "If I had done one thing differently—anything—this would have been different. But I didn't." She sank back onto the pillows.

Peter sat on the bed and framed her face with his hands. He looked deeply into her eyes. "It was an *accident*. It was *no one's* fault. Even if you had been more careful, there's still no guarantee that this wouldn't have happened," he argued. *"Bad things happen.* We can't always control how things turn out."

Natalie slid her hand across the cast on her right arm, feeling its cold smoothness. She understood what Peter was trying to say, but felt unswayed by his words. Deep down, she knew that she had played a part in that accident. Frightened and confused about what to do about the baby, she let fate decide for her that morning. Now she had to live with the consequences.

"I can't change the way I feel."

Peter stood up from the bed and began pacing the length of the room. "If you're so interested in blaming someone, blame me. I fathered this child and then pushed you away when you needed me most. You rode into that intersection thinking you would have to handle this whole thing alone. If you let your guard down, it was *because of me*, not you."

Natalie bowed her head as his words sunk in, the smooth façade of detachment replaced by a turbulent mix of sadness and confusion. Peter gathered her in his arms, kissing her hair. "You shouldn't have had to deal with this alone," he whispered in her ear. "I'm so sorry I put you through that."

Natalie let herself be pulled into his embrace, absorbing the warm strength of his arms. Resting her head on his shoulder, she held on tightly with her uninjured arm. Without warning, an image of a child appeared in her mind. It had Peter's eyes. A tear escaped down her cheek. The knot inside her tightened in regret.

As they held each other, Natalie's mother stood unnoticed outside the doorway. She hadn't been standing there long, but long enough to finally understand what was behind her daughter's anguished silences. She turned away and headed back down the hallway, leaving the couple alone.

***

At Natalie's insistence, Peter left to teach his morning class, promising to return in the evening. There was so little time left. He was determined to spend as much of it with her as possible. On his way out, he passed by Natalie's mother sitting in the first-floor lobby.

"Good morning, Laura. How are you?"

She looked up in surprise. "Hello, Peter. Have you been up to see Natalie?"

Peter nodded. "I think they'll be taking her to therapy soon, but you should be able to catch her if you're going up now."

"I'm on my way," she answered, beginning to rise from the sofa. "How is she doing?"

Peter paused before replying. "It's been a tough morning," he admitted. "She's had a lot to deal with. I'm not sure how I would have done in her place."

Laura Brooks looked at him, an unreadable expression on her face.

"You're quite fond of my daughter, aren't you?"

"I love her," he replied without hesitation.

The older woman nodded but said nothing.

"If I could keep Natalie here with me, I would," Peter continued. "But, right now, she's better off in your care. I hope you won't mind if I visit her in White Falls."

"If that's what Natalie wants, you are welcome to visit."

Peter picked up on her guarded reaction. She was still unsure of him. Of course, if *his* daughter were involved with a man ten years her senior, he could only imagine how he would react. Probably throw the guy out the first door he could find.

Given that, he was grateful to Natalie's parents for being as open-minded as they had been. Peter gave her a tentative smile and said goodbye, determined to prove to both her and her husband the sincerity of his feelings for their daughter.

Chapter 22

·⟠·

Natalie's day began with back-to-back therapy sessions, followed by discharge meetings with medical staff to plan a smooth transition home. Prescriptions were written, visits from home health nurses arranged, therapy services scheduled in nearby Eau Claire, and a wheelchair reserved for pickup at the local medical supply company when they arrived in White Falls.

Natalie's parents made plans to go to her house and pack up what items their daughter would need during her months away from school. Summer clothes, toiletries, a favorite pillow and comforter—with Gina's help, they would assemble the items Natalie had listed and pack them into the car for their drive home tomorrow. Textbooks and class notes would be left behind. As much as she hated missing a semester, Natalie knew that she had more important work ahead of her before she could continue with her studies.

Natalie was exhausted when her mother finally wheeled her back into her room. However, upon entering, someone was waiting for her. Natalie sat up in surprise.

"Dr. McMann?"

Gordon McMann stood at the window beside her bed as she entered with her parents. He shifted awkwardly at the sight of the three people staring back at him.

"Hello, Natalie. How are you? Are these your parents?" His attempts at nonchalance were unconvincing. Everything he did was for a reason, and Natalie's heart lurched at the thought of what it could be.

Natalie glanced behind her and introduced her mother and father to the Psychology Department chair, a wary expression on her face. Mrs. Brooks wheeled her up to the bed with the intention of helping her tired daughter in, but Natalie declined. If she had to speak with this man, she felt better prepared to do so sitting upright in her chair than helplessly reclined.

His attempts at small talk soon exhausted, Dr. McMann gave Natalie a plaintive look. "Natalie, I was hoping to discuss a matter of importance with you. Perhaps there's a place where you and I could speak in private?"

Natalie nodded. "Mom, Dad, maybe this would be a good time to go to the house and pack things up. Would you mind?"

Her mother gave her a kiss on the forehead. "Of course, sweetheart. Don't overdo it, though. You've had a long day." She glanced at Dr. McMann as she said this. The tension between this man and her daughter was evident. Mr. Brooks gave his daughter a brief wave and followed his wife out, directions and packing list in hand.

Natalie watched Gordon as he circled the bed and sat down in the chair across from her. He moved straight to the point.

"I received your letter, Natalie."

Natalie frowned, almost forgetting the letter of resignation she had slipped into his mail slot the day of her accident. Everything about that day seemed hazy to her now, as if it had happened years before, not two short weeks ago.

"A lot has happened since then, Dr. McMann. I would appreciate it if you would disregard that letter."

"Actually, Natalie, I believe your letter makes a great deal of sense."

The lines on Natalie's forehead deepened in confusion, prompting Gordon to offer a benign smile. "Natalie, I'm afraid a rather disturbing situation has come to my attention—one that involves you and Dr. Spencer."

Natalie swallowed. "Oh?"

"It seems there is evidence of an inappropriate relationship between you two."

Natalie attempted to shift positions in her wheelchair but found it impossible to do so without help. She tried to relieve the pressure in her back and legs by slumping in the chair, with little improvement.

Gordon noticed her discomfort and stood up, offering a weak, "Perhaps I can help?"

Natalie waved him off. "No, I'm fine. I'm sorry, Dr. McMann, I'm not sure what you're talking about. Have you discussed your concerns with Dr. Spencer?" As exhausted as she felt at that moment, she looked at him unflinchingly.

"Of course," he replied. "And now I would like to hear your side of it."

"I'm afraid I have nothing to say, Dr. McMann."

Gordon stood up, his expression changing from pseudo-concern to impatience. He paced over to the windows. "Natalie, there is evidence of a sexual relationship between you and Peter Spencer. Surely you understand the seriousness of this charge and the sanctions that can be taken against you both."

Natalie's heart pounded in her chest, her throat so dry she feared her words might lodge in her throat. "You…say there's evidence. Does that mean that someone caught the two of us in an inappropriate act?"

Gordon studied her, a look of momentary respect in his face for the composure she displayed. In the end, though, it would do her no good. His response was cold and matter-of-fact. "Your car was seen parked overnight in front of Dr. Spencer's home on at least two occasions. On another occasion, the two of you were seen kissing in the front doorway of your own home."

He paused, as the full effect of his words sank in. "Discretion has never been one of Peter's strong suits." His winning card delivered, Dr. McMann waited for Natalie's reaction.

Natalie paled. The little strength she had mustered for this meeting felt like it had liquefied and run out of her body all at once, leaving nothing but a dried-out husk behind. After a long while, she returned his gaze, a blank expression on her face.

"What do you want?"

Gordon went straight to the point. "University ethics guidelines recommend both the immediate expulsion of the involved student and dismissal of the offending faculty member."

Natalie never wavered. "But you don't want to dismiss Peter, do you? You need him. He's too important to the department."

Gordon chose not to answer that statement. Instead, his expression reverted back to its original placid benevolence. "Natalie, I am well aware of Peter's exploits over the years. You simply got in over your head. It would be a shame for you to lose everything over such an unfortunate lapse in judgment, don't you think?"

A sudden revulsion welled up inside of Natalie. She could see now why Peter felt the way he did about Gordon. There was something so manipulative in the way he behaved. She felt violated just being in his presence.

Gordon continued. "As a gesture of goodwill, I am willing to make you an offer. In exchange for your complete silence on the matter and agreement not to return to this program, you will be granted a Master of Arts in Psychology."

Natalie frowned in confusion, trying to make sense of his words. "You...want me to leave the program and keep my mouth shut about what happened here?"

Gordon nodded. "And in return, we will allow you to graduate with a master's degree."

"But you already had my letter requesting withdrawal from the program. Why did you come here at all if that's all you wanted?"

"Because this ensures your silence," Gordon replied smoothly.

Like many graduate programs of its kind in psychology, UW offered a Ph.D. in Clinical Psychology. The degree required five years of course work and a dissertation, which was written and defended by the student during their fifth year of study. No master's degree was ever awarded during this period—the student simply jumped from bachelor's level to Ph.D. at the end of the five-year program.

However, if Natalie understood correctly, Gordon would bend the rules and award her a master's degree based on the courses she had already completed, so long as she agreed to leave the program without making waves.

She shook her head at the shrewdness of his proposal. As much as Gordon detested Peter—and she was sure he did—he was aware of Peter's popularity among students and the need to keep him on faculty to keep enrollment numbers up. Gordon couldn't afford to lose his star professor, so Natalie was the natural choice to be sacrificed.

"What if I don't accept?"

"Then Peter will be dismissed, and you will be expelled."

Natalie closed her eyes, a growing sense of defeat spreading across her face. What were her words? *I hope we don't regret this.* She and Peter had known all along the consequences of their affair being discovered. Now it was time to pay for the choices they'd made. Only, Natalie was not going to let him be fired for this. It was bad enough that she had lost their child. She wasn't going to let him lose his job, too.

"I accept your offer," she replied coldly. "What do I have to do?"

Gordon visibly straightened at the news. "Fine, fine," he answered. "Simply return home as you were planning to do. I will have my secretary complete the necessary paperwork and send it to the graduate college. You should receive notification of your degree in the next few weeks."

"No. I want something in writing now," Natalie interrupted. "I want your assurance that Peter will not be fired, and I will get that degree." She wheeled to the bedside table, each movement more painful than the last, and grabbed a notebook that sat atop it. Holding it out to Gordon, she demanded, "Write your proposal. I want both of us to sign and date it."

Gordon complied. In the next few minutes, he wrote out a brief summary of the points they had discussed. Then, after signing and dating it himself, he handed the notebook back to Natalie, who added her own signature.

The notebook on her lap, she said tersely, "Now get out."

Only after Gordon's footsteps could be heard fading down the hallway did Natalie let herself break down. Long denied tears streamed down her face, their passage accelerated by the muffled sobs that shook her body.

***

As he often did at the start of his shift, Joey looked in on Natalie before moving onto his assigned section of patients. Over the past few months, she had become a good friend to him, often offering helpful advice on matters regarding her roommate. Still, when Natalie was admitted to the rehab wing, Joey felt downright protective, checking in whenever he had a free moment and speaking with staff about her progress.

This evening, when he peeked into her room, Joey found Natalie distraught and slumped in her chair. He rushed to her side, but her only response to his repeated questions was a miserable shake of the head. With the help of another nurse, Joey transferred Natalie to the bed. He asked if she wanted to speak with her parents, Gina—*anyone*—but Natalie again shook her head and turned away.

Promising to return soon, Joey left the room, already reaching for his cell phone. He dialed Gina's number, tapping his fingers against the wall in impatience as he waited for her to answer.

"Hello?"

"Hey, it's me. Something's wrong…."

***

Natalie lay in bed, her position virtually unchanged, when her parents hurried into the room. Laura sat down beside her daughter, pleading with her to tell what had happened as

Henry hovered close behind, his face pinched with concern. But Natalie refused to explain. Her only response, uttered again and again, was "I want to go home, Mom. Please. Just take me home."

The next morning, Natalie was gently placed in the back seat of her parents' car, her boxes and suitcases packed into the trunk. Gina accompanied them to the curb, a look of heartbreak on her face, and waved to Natalie as they pulled away. Natalie spoke little during the trip, staring out the window when she wasn't lapsing into sleep. Mrs. Brooks watched her throughout the drive, deeply troubled by her daughter's lifeless expression.

Chapter 23

20 Months Later

"All right, everybody, I want those papers on my desk by Monday," Natalie called out to her class, raising her voice so it could be heard above the din of voices in the hallway. There was a collective groan from some of the students.

"But the dance is tomorrow night. Can't we have a little extra time?"

"You've known about this paper for a month, Jessica. Next time, don't put it off until the last minute." She smiled, unmoved by the expression of panic on the sophomore's face. As the students began to file out of the room, one girl approached her desk, an armful of books resting against her chest.

"Miss Brooks, what time can you be there tomorrow night?"

"I'm not sure. When do you need me?" Natalie packed her briefcase and began walking out, Erin close behind. She switched off the light as they left the room.

"Well, we need to get the refreshment stand set up, and Tanya says they still need a lot of help with decorations. I guess they couldn't get in the gymnasium last night to start decorating, so everything has to be done tonight and tomorrow."

As they made their way down the hall, Natalie braced herself against the occasional bumps and near misses that were inevitable this time of the day. Her limp was almost imperceptible—the long months of therapy now more than a year behind her—but she could still lose her balance at times. In fact, the only remaining vestige from the accident was not notable for its presence, but rather its absence—her bounce.

Friends had often teased that she bounced when she walked—each step beginning with a pronounced bend of the knee that released up sharply. Natalie just laughed it off at the time, but now she could feel the difference. Instead of the tell-tale spring, she now stepped cautiously, as if moving across an uneven surface.

"I'm sure you'll get a lot done tonight," Natalie reassured her, "but how about if I get there around 6:00?"

"Great." Erin gave her a grateful smile. Rounding the corner, they passed two of Erin's friends, also sophomores, who were in Natalie's morning psychology class.

"Hi, Miss Brooks," Carrie said enthusiastically. "We're just heading to the gym now. Do you want to see our decorations?"

"Sure," Natalie agreed. She wasn't in any particular hurry anyway.

The foursome headed out the side doors and across the parking lot to the gymnasium on the other side. White Falls High School was an old complex of buildings, built decades before the philosophy of "function over form" began to take precedence in school architecture. Natalie loved the quirky design. The top floor of the building, which housed the performing arts department, had attic spaces shaped like medieval turrets; staircases seemed to abound everywhere and often led to sections of the building in which only one or two classrooms were accessible; and, of course, there were the windows. Not the contemporary plate glass windows of today, but small, thick panes placed side by side, creating a translucent mosaic and blanketing the halls with an ever-changing light show of filtered colors.

Of course, the flip side to this charming turn-of-the-century design was a heating system that barely kept the building above sixty degrees in the winter, a spotty, room-by-room air conditioning system, and a gymnasium that was housed in a separate building from the rest of the school, requiring students clad in gym shorts to make brisk dashes to and from the main building, even in the dead of winter.

As they made their way to the gymnasium, the girls chattered on about decorations, refreshments, and, of course, their dresses and dates. Natalie was listening to Erin's excited commentary with amusement when Alyssa interrupted. "Um, Miss Brooks? Do you know that guy?"

Natalie turned and glimpsed a man headed in their direction but didn't process his image at first. He slowed to a stop a few yards from her, hands returning to his pockets, a self-conscious smile on his face.

Natalie abruptly slowed her pace, her eyes never leaving his. "Peter," she whispered.

The girls glanced from Natalie to Peter, and back again to Natalie. The color drained from her face, her expression one of absolute shock. Her legs continued moving of their own accord until she stopped herself a few feet away.

"Hi, Natalie."

He was just as striking as she had remembered. His face clean shaven, he looked healthy and tanned, as if he'd spent the summer and early autumn months outdoors.

Natalie stood there for a moment, at a complete loss for words. "What are you doing here?"

Peter shrugged his shoulders. "I was just passing by."

"Madison is three hours from here."

Peter conceded the point with a weak smile. "Well, it hasn't been the same there without you."

Natalie looked down. Her mind was racing, her heart beating so hard she could hardly take a full breath.

Peter tried again. "How are you?"

"Fine. How are you?"

"Fine." Peter answered back. His smile was beginning to look more forced by the minute. "Say, would you like to get a cup of coffee or something? Maybe we could catch up."

Natalie hesitated. "I...I don't know...."

"Of course, if you're in the middle of something, we could meet later."

"Miss Brooks," Erin blurted out, "don't worry about us. We can show you the decorations tomorrow."

Natalie was startled by the student's voice. She had forgotten that the girls were still standing there.

"No, now is fine," she answered him with a polite smile. "Girls, why don't you go on without me? I'll see you tomorrow night." She waved them off with a confidence that she didn't feel.

Reluctantly, the three teens turned and headed toward the gymnasium, but not before giving the pair one last glance and erupting into frenzied whispers about the stranger.

"Oh my God…"

"Did you see the way they looked at each other?"

"I'll bet they were lovers."

Peter chuckled at the comments and their completely ineffective attempts at concealing them. Natalie found herself coloring at the suggestion that they were once lovers. There would be plenty of gossip by tomorrow, no doubt.

"Tomorrow night?" Peter asked.

"Huh?" Natalie, still watching the retreating girls, spun around at the sound of his voice. Her head was beginning to feel like the pinball in an arcade game.

"What's happening tomorrow night?"

"Oh, it's the homecoming dance. I'm helping out."

They walked in silence until Natalie's car came into view. She headed in that direction, but Peter held out his hand to her. "Come on. My car's just over there. You can navigate."

Natalie spotted the silver Acura. A sudden feeling of dread rose in her chest. She did not want to ride in that car.

"No, that's okay," she said. "I'll drive." She avoided Peter's outstretched hand and instead led the way to her own car. She opened the back door and tossed in her briefcase, missing Peter's puzzled frown as he climbed in.

Taking care to avoid the late-departing students, Natalie turned onto the main road that led into town. White Falls had not yet progressed to the point of acquiring a Starbucks, or any cafe for that matter, so coffee drinkers had to be content with the corner diner or the bakery down the street. Natalie chose the busier of the two. The distractions might give her time to mask the expression of sheer panic she felt must be covering her face. On the other hand, it also meant that their conversation would be witnessed—and subsequently reported—to half the town by the end of the evening. Not much of a choice.

Peter was the first to break the palpable silence that had built up in the car. "This was a shock for you," he said. "I'm sorry."

Natalie shook her head and glanced at him, her expression sober. "No, I'm sorry for reacting like that. But you're right, this was a shock."

Peter exhaled heavily. "So, how are you? Really?" He repeated his earlier question, perhaps hoping for a more informative answer.

"I'm doing well," she answered, with a bit too much brightness. "I teach psychology at the high school. But I guess you already knew that. How did you find out about me?"

"I ran into Gina a few months ago. She told me how you were doing."

"She did?" Natalie frowned. "That's strange. She never mentioned seeing you."

"She's getting married in a few months, I hear."

Natalie nodded. Gina had been excitedly planning her wedding ever since her engagement six months ago. The wedding would be in the summer, with Natalie as her maid of honor. "Yes. You remember Joey, right?"

"Nice guy," Peter replied. "He worked in the rehab unit where you…" He let his sentence drop off.

"Right."

She turned the corner and parked along the side of the street that bordered the Hilltop Diner. "Here we are," she said, opening her door and stepping out. Peter did the same, climbing up onto the curb just as she rounded the car.

A heavyset woman in a Hawaiian print apron was cleaning the counter as they entered. She smiled and waved to Natalie, her towel flapping in the air with the motion. "Hi, hon. Sit wherever you like. I'll be right over."

"Thanks, Ruth. Just two coffees when you get the chance."

The diner wasn't as busy as she had feared. Besides a handful of regulars who preferred to sit at the counter, most of the tables remained empty. Still, she felt a few curious stares on the back of her neck as she and Peter passed by.

Natalie chose a booth in the rear of the restaurant. They both sat down. Moments passed as each one studied the other.

"It's been a long time, Peter." she said finally. "Why are you really here?"

Peter leaned back against the booth. "I just needed to see you, Natalie."

Natalie looked down in discomfort as he continued. "The way you left… No matter how I tried, I just couldn't understand what happened." He paused, perhaps in hopes of a response, but she offered nothing. "It's ironic. It took me months to admit how I felt about you. And I *know* you felt the same way."

She met his gaze, nodding silently.

"But you just walked away from everything. With no explanation. I was mad as hell at you for that."

Natalie was saved the need for an immediate reply when Ruth arrived at their table. She set down a silver pitcher of cream, flipped over two cups on the table and filled them with steaming coffee. When she was finished, she pulled out her order pad and eyed them expectantly. "Anything to eat?" she asked.

Natalie glanced at Peter, who shook his head. "No thanks, Ruth," she answered. "Just this for now."

Ruth wrote something in pencil, and then tore out the order sheet and laid it on the table in front of them. "Let me know if you change your mind." She returned to the counter, refilling diners' coffee cups along the way.

Grateful for something to occupy her hands, Natalie poured cream into both cups, remembering still how Peter liked his coffee. She emptied a packet of sugar into hers, stirring idly. "I'm sorry, Peter," Natalie answered. "I never meant to hurt you. You have to know that."

Peter waved off her apology. "I hurt you, too. That's not why I said it. It's just…you have no idea how much I wanted to forget you after that. I did everything I could think of to put you out of my mind. *Everything.*" Peter gave a humorless laugh. "But nothing worked. I guess that's the real reason I'm here."

Natalie looked up in bewilderment. "I don't understand."

Peter leaned across the table at her, searching her face. "We were right on the brink of something special, Natalie. And we let it slip away. I'm here to see if there's a chance that…we could try again."

Natalie stared at her coffee cup, her mind trying to absorb his words. She swallowed hard. "I don't think I can, Peter."

Peter sat back against the cushions.

"Is there someone else?"

Natalie shook her head. "No, it's not that. It's just…too much has happened, that's all. I'm not the same person anymore."

"I don't believe that."

"I'm not," she shrugged, a hint of sadness in her voice. She met his gaze, her face expressionless. "I've made a life for myself here. It's probably not much by anyone else's standards, but it's enough. But I don't have it in me for anything else. The other me is just… gone."

Peter looked like the wind had been knocked out of him. "She's not gone, Natalie. You can get her back. You told me that once, remember? And you were right. It just takes time and a little inspiration."

Natalie gave a faint smile. She vaguely recalled the morning when she had told him that. It felt like a lifetime ago. "And I suppose you're the inspiration?"

"That's the plan."

Natalie laughed under her breath. "You have a plan?"

Peter leaned over the table and took her hands in his. "I'm going to make you remember why you fell in love with me in the first place."

Natalie slowly pulled out from his grip. "Look, I don't think…"

He pressed on. "Nat, the least you can do is let me take you out while I'm here. All those months together, and we never even went out to dinner. I owe you that much." He paused, thinking. "What time is this dance tomorrow night?"

Natalie's eyes grew round. "Oh, no. That's for the high school students. I'm just there to chaperone."

"So, chaperones can't have a date?"

"Of course not. They're there to keep an eye on everybody else."

"So, why can't I be a chaperone?"

Natalie chuckled in spite of herself. "That would be a bit like the fox guarding the hen house, don't you think?"

He gave her a wounded look. "I take offense to that. There's only one hen that I'm after. The other ones are perfectly safe."

"There's nothing there for you to do." Natalie persisted. "You would be bored."

"You let me take care of myself. What time do you have to be there?"

"The dance starts at eight o'clock, but they need me to help with decorations at six."

Peter shook his head. "No, that's too early. Tell them seven o'clock. I'm taking you out to dinner first."

Natalie exhaled with impatience. He wasn't listening. "Peter, they need me before that. Besides, there's no place you'll be able to get reservations this late for dinner. All the students in town are planning to eat out beforehand."

"You tell them seven, and I'll have dinner reservations for us at five thirty," he replied evenly. "Ok? Now, give me your address."

Natalie shook her head. He never could take no for an answer. Then again, with her, he never had to—she could never deny him anything. Against her better judgment, she wrote out her address on a napkin and gave it to him, along with her new phone number. As she did so, a group of high school students filed into the diner, accompanied by loud conversation and laughter. They were on their way to the back of the restaurant before they realized that Natalie and Peter were seated at one of their usual tables.

"Hey, Miss Brooks! You're in our spot!" one said good-naturedly.

Natalie smiled and stood up. "It's all yours, Philip. We were just leaving."

The young man named Philip watched as Peter stood up, folding the napkin and slipping it into his pants pocket. He gave Peter a lingering look of appraisal, which Peter returned coolly.

"Have fun, kids," he said, removing a five from his wallet and tossing it onto the table as they left. Then, to Natalie's supreme embarrassment, Peter placed his hand on the small of her back as they moved down the aisle. That minute gesture held the attention of every student they passed. Natalie was unnerved, but to have removed his hand would have caused even more notice, so there it remained until they exited the restaurant.

"Was that really necessary?" she asked in irritation as they approached her car. "I have to teach these kids tomorrow. I don't have time for silly distractions."

"Who's distracting them?" Peter was all innocence.

"You. Now all they'll be talking about tomorrow is Miss Brooks and her 'mystery man'."

"*Mystery man*," Peter repeated. "I like that."

"I'm not surprised," she snapped. "You always liked being the center of attention." She recalled the day he visited her classroom, managing to distract her students so much they didn't hear a word she said. Peter had enjoyed every minute of it.

"Maybe, but you were pretty good at keeping me in my place."

"*Somebody* had to."

Natalie opened the car door and got in, not bothering to unlock his side until she was already seated. Peter slid into the seat next to her, appearing to enjoy her aggravation. "That's more like it," he said with a grin.

"What are you talking about?"

"You're starting to sound more like your old self again," he observed. "I think you just needed a suitable sparring partner."

"Oh, shut up."

Natalie made a U-turn in front of the restaurant and idled briefly until the traffic light turned green. She then turned onto the main road that led to the high school. As she drove, her mind drifted to the coming week when mid-term exams and papers came due. She glanced at Peter, whose long legs were folded up uncomfortably in her compact car.

"UW must be getting ready for midterms right now. How did you get away with leaving this week? Gordon must have had a fit."

"Gordon didn't have any say in the matter," Peter answered. "I'm not there anymore."

Natalie glanced at him before returning her gaze to the road. "What?"

"I resigned a year and a half ago."

That was when she'd had her accident. When she had returned to White Falls.

"You resigned? But why? Are you still in Madison?" The questions escaped from her mouth like rapid gunfire.

Peter fielded the questions one at a time. "Yes, I resigned. Why? I thought it best to resign before I got fired. And yes, I'm

still in Madison, but only until I find a new position elsewhere."
He looked at Natalie. "Did I cover everything?"

Fired? Natalie's car had turned into the faculty parking
lot, cutting short her opportunity to clarify his last statement.
She pulled alongside Peter's car.

"I'll pick you up at five o'clock," he said, reaching for
the door.

"Wait." Natalie put a hand on his arm to stop him. "You
can't leave me hanging like this. What happened?"

Peter gave a shrewd smile. "You'll find out the rest tomorrow night. Don't be late." He got out of the car without a
backward glance, leaving a very unsatisfied Natalie behind.

She watched his car move out of view, her mind a mess
of memories and emotions too tangled to process all at once.
For months after her return home, she had dreamed of seeing
him again. Or, more accurately, daydreamed. Each day of her
recovery, as she pulled herself painfully and unsteadily across
the parallel bars to strengthen her legs, she would close her eyes
and imagine him striding up the path to her family's farmhouse,
climbing the stairs to her second-floor room and sweeping her
into his arms.

Romantic, but unrealistic. Peter never came, of course,
nor could she blame him. She had left him, after all, giving Peter
little in the way of explanation or room for hope. As their time
apart grew longer, she resigned herself to the likelihood that he
had moved on, either finding someone new or at least a new one
each week. She certainly had fixed him, Natalie remembered
thinking. Thanks to her, he would never trust a woman again.

And now, a year and a half later, Peter was here. Natalie
was caught between two very different impulses—the desire to
run headlong into his arms and the protective instinct to run as
far away from him as she could, nursing the wounds that had
reopened just by seeing his face.

The parking lot was almost empty when she steered her
car toward the high school entrance and home. She fumbled with

her purse until she found her cell phone, dialed Gina's number, and waited.

Hearing Gina's recorded message, she left one of her own. "Call me when you get this. You've got some explaining to do...."

Chapter 24

Business was picking up at the diner, a steady flow of high school students and workers finished with their shifts at the local factory. Through the windows, Peter could see customers engaged in conversation or just reading the newspaper as they waited for their meals.

The kids from before were still there, clustered around the jukebox, their former boisterous behavior dampened by some technical difficulty with the change dispenser. Peter entered and sat down by the counter. Ruth approached him from behind, having just finished another coffee-refilling trip through the restaurant. She gave him a sideways glance as she rounded the counter, exchanging her empty pot for a full one that had just finished brewing.

"Forget something?" she asked.

"No," Peter answered with a smile. "Ruth, right? I could use another cup of coffee and some advice if you have a minute."

The other diners now completely forgotten, Ruth proceeded to fill his cup from the freshly brewed pot. She studied him with interest. "What's the problem?"

Peter found a pitcher of cream two seats over and grabbed it, pouring a healthy amount into his cup. He stirred as he spoke.

"You know that girl I was with?"

"Of course, I do. Natalie Brooks. Graduated with my nephew. She's back teaching at the high school."

Peter was impressed. Now here was a woman who knew her town inside and out. Just what he needed.

"Well, I'm taking her out tomorrow night. I would like to make it someplace special, but I don't know the area. Where's a good place to go for dinner?"

Ruth didn't need to give it much thought. "Mangiamele's, definitely. Italian food. Very romantic, if that's what you have in mind."

"That's what I have in mind."

"You won't get in there tomorrow night," interjected a voice from the stool next to him. It was Philip, one of the students he'd seen earlier. He leaned over the counter, pulled out a napkin from the metal dispenser in front of him and began to pull it apart, bit by bit.

Peter turned to him. "Why's that?"

"It's the homecoming dance. Everyone's going there. Me, I made my reservations three weeks ago," he said with importance before changing the subject. "Ruth, that change machine isn't working again. I'm out a dollar."

Ruth gave him an impatient glare. "I don't suppose you noticed the *Out of Order* sign on the top?"

"Huh?"

"Hey, Philip," yelled one of the other youths, still standing by the jukebox. "The sign on it says it's not working."

"Great," he muttered, rolling his eyes. "Ruth, can you…?"

Shaking her head, Ruth stepped over to the register to get some change.

Philip waited at the counter, staring at Peter. "So, is Miss Brooks your girlfriend?"

Peter ignored the question. "You're Philip, right?"

"Yep."

"Are you in Miss Brooks's class?"

"Yeah, I'm in her morning class."

"What do you think of it?"

Philip tossed the remnants of the old napkin aside and reached over for a new one. "Pretty good. I don't fall asleep in that one. Miss Brooks keeps it interesting. That Freud guy was a real piece of work, wasn't he?"

Peter smiled. "He certainly was."

"So anyway," Philip continued, evidently not as distracted from his earlier question as Peter had hoped. "You got a thing for Miss Brooks?"

Peter took a long sip of his coffee. "Something like that."

"She must have met you at college." Philip declared confidently.

This time, Peter *was* surprised. He knew word got around fast in small towns, but he had been here less than two hours. "What makes you say that?"

Philip pointed out the front windows to where Peter's car was parked. "You've got a UW parking sticker on your car," he said, "and I heard she graduated from UW last year. So, did you piss her off or something?"

Are all high schoolers like this? Peter wondered in amazement. Natalie must have her hands full with characters like this one.

Peter was saved by the reappearance of Ruth, who had been detained by several hungry customers at the other end of the counter. She handed Philip four quarters and waved him off. "Go on, and keep your voices down over there," she reminded him.

But Philip wasn't finished. "Flowers," he said with authority.

"Excuse me?" Peter glanced up from his cup.

"If you screwed up, you gotta send her flowers." Philip tossed the quarters up in the air, attempting to catch them in his other hand. He was only partly successful. Two coins fell onto the floor, spinning like wheels in separate directions. Philip raced after them and then returned to the stool, straddling it.

"Girls are suckers for flowers. No matter what you did, they'll forgive you."

"Is that so?" Peter smiled in amusement, coffee cup in hand. Even Ruth stood by, unable to resist his explanation.

"Seriously. A few months back, my girlfriend got all bent out of shape because I was talking to a freshman by the lockers. She said I was putting the moves on her. I wasn't really, but there's nothing wrong with keeping tabs on who's out there, you know?"

Peter nodded solemnly.

"So, I sent her some flowers—my girlfriend, not the freshman. It set me back a Saturday's worth of wages, but it was worth it, if you know what I mean." He gave a knowing smirk.

"Oh?"

"She was all over me after that. I was totally forgiven. It's like magic."

Peter laughed. "Okay, not a bad idea. So where do I go for flowers around here?"

"You need some forgiving, do you?" Ruth interjected.

"No," Peter grinned at her, "but I could use all the help I can get."

"Deininger's," Philip answered. "Just down the street. And don't forget the card that goes with it. They really like that part."

"Thanks, I'll remember."

"Okay, well, gotta go." Philip jumped off the stool, already glancing in the direction of the jukebox, where his friends still lingered. "Hey, what's your name?"

"Peter Spencer."

"See ya around, Pete. Good luck." And with that, he rejoined his friends.

Peter turned around on his stool, shaking his head with a smile. Ruth laughed too, a pleasant, hearty sound. "Can you believe kids these days?" she said. "Probably grow up to be a politician."

Peter took out his wallet and laid a five-dollar bill on the counter. Ruth picked it up. "Hang on. I'll get you some change."

"Keep it. And thanks for the advice."

Ruth beamed. If all her customers tipped like that, she and Homer could buy that RV and retire to Florida.

"Good luck," she said, adding, "oh, and tell Mrs. Mangiamele that Ruth sent you. She owes me a favor, and it might help with that reservation."

"I'll do that. Thanks again."

Exiting the diner, Peter found his way to Deininger's Floral, where he arranged to have a dozen red roses sent to Natalie at school the next day. Next, he would pay Mrs. Mangiamele a visit and see how far Ruth's name and a bit of charm could get him on such short notice.

***

Natalie checked the clock on the wall for what must have been the fiftieth time that day. Just three more hours and she could get out of here. All morning, she had felt as if she were in a fishbowl on display. Stray glances and giggles among the girls suddenly took on new meaning, whether they were actually intended for her or not. *That's life in a small town*, she reminded herself. Living in this community all her life, she knew as well as anyone that everyone's business was, well, *everyone's* business.

What made it worse was that her own attention was disrupted beyond repair. Every sentence she uttered, every question she answered, every point outlined in chalk on the board took twice as much concentration as usual. She couldn't get him out of her mind.

Natalie was going over questions for the upcoming midterm exam when the lunch bell rang. She was visibly startled by the noise, causing some of the students to laugh. She shook her head good-naturedly and wished everyone a good weekend.

Paula, a senior who was considered a shoo-in for Homecoming Queen, approached her with raised eyebrows. "Is your friend taking you to the dance tonight?"

Natalie reddened in surprise but managed to recover her composure. "As a matter of fact, Mr. Spencer *will* be coming. He has agreed to be another chaperone."

"Cool. I hear he's really good looking—you know, for an older man." Paula readjusted her backpack and followed the rest of the departing students out of the classroom. "See you tonight!"

Natalie was cleaning the chalkboard when a fellow teacher strolled in carrying a bouquet of red roses in a tall glass vase.

"I brought you something," Sarah said, grinning.

Natalie gave a puzzled smile until she realized who must have sent them. She shook her head in irritation. Of course, he would do something like this. "Thanks," she said sourly. Taking the vase, she scanned the room for a nondescript place to put it. She ended up shoving some books aside on a bookshelf, dusty from neglect, and sat the vase down upon it.

"Don't you want to know who sent them?" Sarah asked. "Read the card at least."

"I know who they're from."

Sarah sat down on the edge of Natalie's desk, watching her. "Could this have anything to do with that tall, dark, handsome stranger who was hanging around the parking lot yesterday?"

Natalie groaned. "Oh, this town! Can't a person have any privacy at all around here?"

"Not a chance," Sarah replied with amusement. "Besides, what did you expect? Weren't you with some of the sophomore girls when it happened?"

Natalie shook her head in resignation. Of course, she had expected this. She just hoped she would be wrong.

"So…" Sarah persisted. "Is this the guy from Madison?"

"Yes."

"The one you were involved with before the accident?"

"Uh huh." Natalie nodded. She glanced over at the flowers, which looked decidedly out of place in their dusty corner.

When she returned to White Falls, Natalie confided little about her experiences at school. To those interested enough to ask, she had returned home to recover from a car accident. But Sarah was the exception. The two had been former classmates, Sarah a senior when Natalie was just a freshman; not friends, exactly, but enough to exchange a friendly smile as they passed in the halls. Now that they were both teaching, the young women found it natural to strengthen the connection.

It came as a relief to Natalie, who spent the first few months with only her parents for company. She was grateful for the easy chaos found in Sarah's home, inhabited by her husband Jim and their two young children. In time, the women's friendship deepened to the point where Natalie entrusted her with some, though not all, of her story about Peter.

"So…" Sarah said, exasperated with the paucity of her friend's answers. "Why is he here?"

Natalie began rearranging the flowers, picking among the stems until she found his note. *"Looking forward to tonight. P."* She sighed.

"He's going to make me remember why I fell in love with him in the first place." She repeated his message word for word, as if not quite believing it herself.

Sarah gave a soft whistle. "Wow, you don't hear something like that very often. In fact," she frowned, "I've *never* heard something like that."

"Well, don't feel bad. It's not all it's cracked up to be."

Sarah was skeptical. "Okay, let me get this straight. You were crazy about this guy, things didn't work out, and now he's trying to get you back. And this bothers you because…?"

Natalie shoved the card into the pocket of her slacks, glancing at her friend in annoyance. "Because I don't *want* to fall in love with him again," she snapped.

Sarah paused, seeing the thinly veiled pain in her eyes. "I hate to point out the obvious, but it might be a little late for that."

Natalie shook her head and sat down at one of the students' desks. "Maybe," she admitted. "I just don't think I can go through it all again."

Sarah knelt beside her friend. "Did you ever think that you two might get it right this time?"

"I don't know, Sarah." Natalie twisted one of her rings up and down on her finger. "I just don't know."

Sarah watched her friend for a moment, then groaned as she stood up from a crouched position. "Nat, I don't know this guy from Adam. You're probably right. He's probably a real jerk and…"

"He's *not* a jerk."

"Okay, then maybe he's just not the right guy for you and…"

"He *was*," Natalie stammered, all too aware that she was now defending him from the very same arguments that she had made to herself the night before—a night filled with precious little sleep and far too many memories. "Sarah, there's so much you don't know, so many things that happened. I'm not sure we could get beyond it. Even now."

Sarah nodded. "Okay, I understand. If this is all too painful for you, maybe it's best that you stop things now."

"I can't," Natalie said miserably. "I have a date with him tonight."

"What?"

"He's taking me to the homecoming dance."

Sarah seemed unable to find her voice at first, her expression changing from perplexed to incredulous. A smile spread across her face and erupted into full-out laughter. "You're kidding, right?"

No response.

"You're *not*! Oh, this I've got to see!" She clapped her hands together gleefully. "And to think I didn't want to work the dance tonight."

Natalie rolled her eyes in exasperation and tried to explain in between her friend's bursts of laughter. "He wouldn't take no for an answer. You'll see. You'll meet him, and you'll understand what I'm dealing with. This man could charm the skin off a snake."

"Okay, okay," Sarah regained some composure, although her smile made it obvious that she was enjoying this conversation far more than Natalie. "It sounds like he's a very convincing guy. He must be used to getting what he wants."

"And right now, he wants me," Natalie replied.

"By the sound of it, you haven't exactly fallen into his arms," Sarah observed. "It must be driving him crazy that you're playing hard to get."

"I'm not *playing*," Natalie reminded her tersely.

"Good. Well, keep it up. There's nothing wrong with keeping him guessing," Sarah concluded. She changed the subject. "So, what are you going to wear?"

Natalie exhaled. "I don't know." It hadn't even occurred to her until now. "Just something for work, I guess. A skirt and blouse."

Sarah was unimpressed. "Perfectly reasonable, I suppose. I'm sure that's what Peg Kennedy is planning to wear."

"You're telling me I dress like the school librarian?"

"At work that's fine. For a night out, you need to dress your age. You're not sixty, Natalie. You're 27. You must have *something* fun in your closet, don't you?"

Natalie pondered a moment. "I'll see what I have."

"Good girl. Now let's go have lunch. Class starts in twenty minutes, and I'm starved. Oh, and move those flowers. That's just wrong to stick those beautiful roses in the corner like that."

Natalie put the vase on her desk and followed Sarah out to the teacher's lounge.

***

Natalie swept into the apartment and went straight to her bedroom closet, throwing her briefcase and purse onto the bed as she passed. Pushing aside the clothes she wore to school every day, her hands stopped at the few dressier outfits she had brought with her from her parents' house. Seeing her choices, Natalie groaned. Out of the four dresses, two were outdated, one no longer fit, and the last had a stain running down the bodice.

She sat down on the bed in frustration. Until now, it simply hadn't occurred to her that she would wear anything other than her standard work clothes. This wasn't her homecoming dance, after all. But now, Peter would be there. She hated to admit it, but she wanted to look her best.

As Natalie began to gather up the discarded dresses from the bed, her eye spotted a patch of white on the floor of her closet. Upon closer inspection, she realized it was a dry cleaner's bag that had fallen into the corner. Natalie let out a happy cry as she remembered its contents.

Inside was a black cocktail dress with off-the-shoulder sleeves. She almost hadn't tried it on that day at the department store, thinking it was too short and far too racy for her style. Fortunately, Gina had gone shopping with her and insisted that she try it. As it turned out, the style was perfectly suited for her—classic in design and color, yet just revealing enough to accentuate her delicate neck and shoulders.

Natalie purchased the dress for the wedding of a close friend from college. At first, she had been mortified at the thought of buying a black dress for a wedding. "Black is for funerals, isn't it?" she remembered asking all her friends, terrified that she would be the only one to arrive at the event dressed in black. But no, the saleswoman had assured her, wearing black to formal weddings was quite popular. Natalie fit in perfectly that night, and following the couple's happy event, the dress was relegated to the back of her closet, never to be worn again.

Until tonight. Natalie removed the dress from its hanger, examining it for any signs of discoloration or damage. Stepping out of her work clothes, she unzipped the dress and slid it on. It fit well, she thought with satisfaction, although a bit more loosely than the first time she had worn it. She placed a hand against her neck, wondering if she had any jewelry that might compliment the dress.

She went to her dresser, opened her jewelry box and peeked inside. Sifting through the strands of silver and gold, she found the silver bracelet her sister had given her two Christmases ago. The one that matched Peter's locket. *Where was it now?* she wondered. Shaking the memories from her mind, she fished through the tangle of chains and finally found a necklace that might work. It was time to leave the past behind and focus on the night ahead.

CHAPTER 25

Gina hung up the phone, almost as stunned as her best friend about Peter's appearance in White Falls. She had meant to tell Natalie about their brief encounter at Delaney's months before, but, in the end, she decided against it. The expression on his face that night told Gina all she needed to know. He had moved on and had little interest in revisiting that time in his life. There was no sense in hurting Natalie with this truth.

Gina had spotted him first. Glancing up from the conversation at her own table, she noticed Peter at the bar, beer in hand, as he surveyed the patrons around him. His appearance was little changed from the last time she'd seen him, with perhaps one exception—his expression was colder now, more distant than she had remembered. Gone was the gentle, affectionate countenance he wore whenever he was by Natalie's side. Now, he seemed almost predatory, glancing around the room as if in search of a conquest, which apparently, he just spotted at the table across the room, one inhabited by two young women barely in their twenties.

Gina spoke briefly to Joey and excused herself from the table. As she approached the bar, her mind raced with questions long unanswered. *Were the rumors true?*

When she reached his stool, Peter was already turned in the direction of the bartender, signaling for another beer. Gina touched his arm lightly to get his attention. "Peter?"

Peter swiveled around slowly to face her. For a moment, his expression remained unchanged before briefly widening in recognition. He smiled, though there was little warmth in his voice when he spoke.

"Gina, the roommate," he declared, shaking her hand and motioning for her to take the stool next to his. "How are you these days?"

Gina glanced over at her party, a threesome sitting at a table far from the dance floor. She nodded in their direction and then sat down beside him. "I'm good. How are you?"

Peter lifted his recently delivered beer and took a deep swallow before answering. "Couldn't be better." He replaced the bottle heavily onto the bar, punctuating the end of his statement.

Gina was silent for a moment as she watched him. By any outsider's opinion—certainly that of any unattached females in the place—Peter was as appealing as ever, his skin tanned, his hair longer. He was clean-shaven now, which added to his youthful appearance.

Peter caught her studying him and gave an amused smile.

"It's been a long time," Gina began. "Do you come here very often?" As soon as the words were out of her mouth, she cursed herself for such an unnecessary question. There was so much to ask, so much Natalie should know.

"Oh, now and again," Peter answered. He saw her looking again in the direction of her table. "Joey, right? You're still together?"

Gina smiled. "We're engaged. The wedding is in July. He's still working in the rehab unit where Natalie was...."

Peter cut her off. "Yeah...congratulations. He seemed like a nice guy."

"He is."

They remained silent for a few moments, each staring off into the distance. Gina tried once more.

"She's still in White Falls...in case you were wondering." Gina watched him to see if her words had any effect. Nothing. "She's teaching psychology at the high school. She likes it."

There was no change in Peter's expression. He never even turned his head. "Well, good for her."

"She's not seeing anyone, Peter. I don't think she has since..."

"That's no longer my concern, Gina," he answered, his caustic tone catching her off guard. "I think your party is starting to break up," Peter observed, pointing the tip of his bottle in Joey's direction before taking another drink. "Don't let me keep you."

Gina glanced over and saw that the couple she and Joey had come with were standing and preparing to leave. She caught Joey's eye and held up a finger for a few more moments.

"Are you okay to drive home? We'd be happy to give you a lift somewhere."

Peter gave her a patronizing smile and turned his attention back to the crowd. "I'm sure I can find a Good Samaritan if the need arises." The look on his face left little doubt in Gina's mind what the sex of that Samaritan would be. Still, for a fleeting moment, Gina thought she saw something in his eyes, something hidden beneath the cold bravado in his manner.

Rising from her stool, Gina gave him a sad smile. "I guess I'd better be going then. It was good seeing you, Peter."

"Bye, Gina. Take care of yourself." He extended his hand, grasping hers in a final handshake.

Gina walked away but stopped after a few steps. Peter watched her return with a puzzled expression. "She's never gotten over you."

There was a momentary softening in his eyes before they grew cold and unreadable again. "It was good catching up with you, Gina," he said. And before she could say anything else, Peter got up from his stool. Gina watched as he strolled across the room, the young women in the booth already making room for him to join their party. It was clear that he had found his prospective Good Samaritans who would get him through the night, or at least a few hours of it.

***

Friday was a full day. Peter returned to the hotel weary but excited, his mind overflowing with facts and figures.

He dropped the folder, thick with MLS sheets on farm listings onto the bed. Grabbing a cold drink from the mini fridge, he scanned a listing that seemed particularly promising. Under different circumstances, he would have spent the evening going over all the information, digesting it while it was still fresh in his mind. But tonight, he had more important things to do.

Stepping into the shower, he washed and redressed in the same khakis he had worn the day before, plus a crisp, white button-down shirt and blazer he had tossed into the car for good measure. He glanced at the clock—*4:05*. He didn't dare arrive to Natalie's early—no advantage in appearing too eager. He would just have to bide his time until it was time to go.

Peter turned on the TV but found nothing worth watching. He paced the room, feeling oddly nervous, as if this were a first date. Then again, he reflected with surprise, it was—and not just any first date, but one with high stakes. He considered for the first time the possibility of failure, of driving back to Madison alone.

He switched off the TV with impatience. He needed something to calm the butterflies, which were now colliding in his stomach with a distracting intensity. Rising from the bed, he decided to go to the lounge downstairs. Maybe there he could come up with a coherent game plan for the evening—suddenly "winging it" no longer seemed like such a good idea.

He had timed it well, judging from the noisy group of 20-somethings that were just leaving as he entered. Sitting down on the bar stool, he ordered a beer to quell his nerves.

Peter studied the room. There were few patrons in the lounge at this time of day. At the table farthest from the door were two men deep in discussion, about what he could only guess. Another man sat drinking alone, but given the frequency of his glances toward the door, was likely waiting for someone.

Out of habit, he reached into his pocket and felt for the familiar object that lay there, rubbing his thumb against it, as one might a worry stone. It was quickly becoming his talisman, and he would miss having it with him. Still, he hoped it would have a new home before long.

Barely a month ago, Peter had been driving home from the Farm and Fleet store, Tim's borrowed truck heavy with sacks of winter wheat seed they planned to get into the ground that week. He was three miles from home when he heard a muffled explosion in the engine and the truck began to lose speed. He coasted to the side of the road, swearing under his breath as he popped the hood. There, he was greeted with a golf ball-sized hole in the engine block.

Tim's phone went unanswered. Dawn, halfway into town to pick up Amanda from school, said that she'd grab him on the way home, but Peter didn't feel like waiting. He left the truck beside the road and began to walk, cursing his brother-in-law's piece of shit truck, while grudgingly savoring the autumn sun on his neck. A mile later, the glint of sunlight off metal caught his eye in the gravel on the edge of the road. He kept walking, but curiosity and boredom got the best of him, and he stopped to find the source of the reflection. Buried in the gravel and weeds was a small silver object, oval-shaped, attached to a rusted chain. Stunned, he held it in his palm, rubbing his thumb against the dirt-encrusted surface, its delicate filigree just visible beneath.

He didn't remember the last mile, only the flood of memories that flashed across his mind as he walked, his attention repeatedly turning to the pendant resting in his palm. This was a gift. An impossibility. Yet, here it was, within his grasp. And with it came a certainty he had not felt in months.

Dawn's truck pulled up alongside him just as he was reaching the gravel driveway to his house.

"I guess you didn't feel like waiting," she observed. Amanda, in the backseat, was already lowering her window and waving to him.

Peter looked up with surprise. He hadn't noticed their approach. "It was a good walk," he said absently, gripping the pendant tightly in his hand.

Dawn gave him a questioning glance, watching as her brother approached the car and tousled Amanda's hair.

"We're having pot roast for dinner, if you'd like to come over," she offered.

"No...." He shook his head, haltingly at first, then again with more resolve. "No, I have something important to do." He gave her a half-wave before turning toward the house, his steps quickening as he went. He bounded up the porch steps and unlocked the door, suddenly in a hurry.

With the help of directory assistance, he found the number of Henry and Laura Brooks in White Falls, Wisconsin. Pressing the numbers into his phone, he stood up from his chair and waited for an answer.

"Mr. Brooks? This is Peter Spencer from Madison. Natalie and I...Well, I could use your help."

***

Natalie was giving the finishing touches to her hair when the doorbell rang. She checked her watch in surprise—five minutes early? She laid down the brush, frowning at her reflection as she hurried past the mirror. Her heels clattered down the hallway, slowing her pace. She'd have to watch her step tonight in these things, she thought. Already just a bit off balance since her accident, Natalie had the double handicap of never having gotten the hang of high heels in the first place. Flats or boots suited her personality—and her natural clumsiness—much better.

Giving herself no time to think, she swung the door open.

"Hi," she said. Barely registering the image of the man on the other side, she turned around in search of her coat.

Peter watched her retreating steps with an intensity that would have unnerved her had she not been busy rifling through the closet.

He was still standing in the doorway when Natalie came rushing back, her coat half on. Peter moved to help her into her coat, but she inched away with a muttered, "I've got it."

Grabbing her purse, which hung from the closet doorknob, she straightened, motionless for the first time and feeling decidedly uncomfortable. When Peter made no attempt to move, Natalie's hand moved instinctively up to her face, where his gaze seemed to be focused most.

"What's wrong?" *Had she put on too much mascara? Lipstick on her teeth?*

"You're beautiful," Peter said. "I should have taken you out long before this."

Natalie looked down and swallowed. Her mumbled "thanks" barely audible.

They walked out into the brisk autumn air. For Natalie, whose nervousness intensified in the confined entryway with Peter, the open expanse was welcome relief. She headed for her car at the end of the sidewalk.

"I'm over here," Peter replied, his hand circling behind her and guiding her in the opposite direction.

Natalie felt acutely aware of his hand pressing on the small of her back. She tried to hasten her steps to move out of range, but her damned shoes kept her well within arm's length. When they reached his car, Peter sprinted ahead and opened her passenger door. Natalie hesitated for a moment before stepping inside.

As Peter circled the car and slid into the driver's seat, Natalie closed her eyes for a moment, inhaling the familiar scent that surrounded her. *His* scent. She could so easily fall tonight, Natalie thought with apprehension. *Be careful.*

* * *

"Mr. Spencer, we have your table right over here." Mrs. Mangiamele greeted him familiarly, her accented English adding to the charm of the elegant restaurant. She led the way into the dining room, which was already filled with couples, many dressed in their best evening wear.

Natalie felt the stares of the students they passed, some of whom openly smiled and called her name. After walking the full length of the room, Mrs. Mangiamele stopped at a small table next to the window. A candle flickered in the center. She handed them their menus and, with a mysterious smile, wished them a pleasant evening.

Natalie placed her napkin on her lap and surveyed the room again. She hadn't been here since her graduation from college, although by the looks of it, it hadn't changed much. One thing was certain—theirs was one of the best tables in the place.

"*How* did you get this reservation?" she asked, a ring of suspicion in her voice.

Peter sat back in his chair and gave an innocent shrug. "They had a last-minute cancellation."

Certain there was more to it than that, Natalie let the subject drop and scanned the menu. In a matter of minutes, the waiter was at their table, basket of bread in hand, reciting the evening's specials.

"Would you let me order for you?" Peter asked her.

Natalie would have answered an emphatic "no," but felt more constrained with the waiter there, a benign smile on his face. She hesitated, "I guess."

She listened with surprise as he recited a list of choices not unlike what she would have ordered—except the bottle of wine.

"I'm not drinking," she said after the waiter had left. "You should just order a glass for yourself."

"You used to enjoy wine with dinner," Peter said, frowning.

"Well, tonight I'm watching a gymnasium with four hundred kids." In truth, though, the kids posed far less of a danger to her than the very real risk of being in close proximity to him all night, her defenses further altered by alcohol.

Peter was unconvinced. "They don't seem like such a difficult bunch," he countered, glancing around the room. "Now, when *I* went to a school dance, things were a little more unpre-dictable."

Natalie smiled in spite of herself. She imagined him as a teenager, a flask of gin stuck in his coat pocket, spiking the punch when the teachers' backs were turned. Good thing that only soft drinks in cans would be served tonight. At least it might limit the damage from a few practical jokers in the bunch.

"I have no doubt," Natalie answered. "Speaking of," she continued, opening a subject that had consumed her for the past twenty-four hours, "Will you please tell me what happened with Gordon? Why did you quit? What are you doing now?"

The waiter returned with the requested bottle and poured a small sample for Peter to taste. Satisfied, he signaled the waiter to proceed. Natalie shook her head and covered her glass with her hand, so the waiter left after filling Peter's.

Sitting back in his chair, Peter observed, "One glass of wine isn't going to hurt anything, Nat. You don't get sloppy until you've had at least two." Getting the intended reaction, Peter grinned as he reached for the bottle and proceeded to fill her glass. "See? I haven't forgotten a thing. So, you enjoy the wine, and I'll tell the story."

The bargain sealed, Natalie drank slowly from her glass, not wanting to miss a single word.

Chapter 26

· ∞ ·

"You broke his *nose*?" Natalie said incredulously, her body leaning into the table as if searching for the missing piece of the story that would make it more believable.

Peter gave a sheepish smile, shrugging his shoulders. "I'm not entirely sure it was broken. There was a fair amount of blood, though."

She sat back. "I can't believe you did that. I can't believe he didn't have you arrested." Natalie pictured the scene—Peter standing over the shocked and bleeding form of Gordon, faculty members gaping in disbelief. That would be a departmental meeting they would never forget.

Peter took a slow sip of his wine. "He might have, but once Neil and the others heard about the way he coerced you into leaving, he probably knew he couldn't count on them as backup. After that, I just cleaned out my office and left. Neil and Jim ended up taking my classes for the rest of the semester."

Natalie considered his answer before replying. "We knew the risks we were taking, Peter. I never liked Gordon, but he had every right to ask me to leave."

Peter's expression transformed from placid to furious in an instant. "He *victimized* you. He came at you when you were at your weakest. If I had only known…if I had been there…."

"You would have lost your job," Natalie finished for him.

"I did anyway," Peter countered.

"But don't you *see*?" Natalie replied. "That was the one thing I wanted to *save*. I knew I had no future there anymore. But that was your job—your life. I just wanted to leave one thing intact from all of this."

Peter sat forward and took one of her hands, gripping it more tightly when she tried to pull away. "Don't *you* see that my life there only meant something if you were there with me?"

Natalie stared at him for a moment, at a loss for something to say. Just then, the waiter reappeared with their salads, and Natalie untangled her hand from his, grateful for the relative silence that followed.

The White Falls High School homecoming dance was a time-honored tradition for high school students of all ages. Held in the gymnasium, a warehouse-sized room with high ceilings and a built-in stage at one end, freshmen and sophomores were assigned the task of decorating, while juniors were responsible for organizing entertainment and refreshments. Seniors were freed of any obligations except to attend and supply the Royalty court, which consisted of nominated contenders for King and Queen. During the dance, the results of the vote were announced, and the winning King and Queen would take their places on elaborately decorated thrones. Except for the music and styles of dancing, little had changed from when Natalie attended high school there, which she found comforting.

Peter and Natalie opened the gymnasium door and were assaulted by the sights and sounds within. The room had been festooned with all things red, white, and gold, and the noise of students working on the last-minute touches was almost overwhelming. They stood for a moment in the doorway, taking it all in, before being spotted by two sophomores.

"Miss Brooks, you're finally here!" Sophomore #1 took Natalie by the hand, leading her into the room. "What do you think?" she asked excitedly.

"It looks great, girls. You've really…"

The second sophomore broke in, "Wow, you are gorgeous!"

Two more girls approached, attracted by the commotion. Peter stood a few paces back, watching with amusement as the girls competed for Natalie's attention. It was obvious she had made a strong impression on the students in her time here.

Glancing over in his direction, one of the girls spotted him and asked Natalie, "Miss Brooks, is that your date?"

Natalie saw his curious smile and blushed in spite of herself. He seemed as interested in her answer as the girls.

"This is Peter Spencer, an old friend who's helping me chaperone." Ignoring their skeptical faces, she continued, "How about putting him to work while I find a place to put our things?"

The hive of activity instantly centered around Peter as the girls listed off the heavy lifting and out-of-reach jobs that would be perfect for him.

"Thanks," Peter deadpanned, managing to send one last look over their heads at Natalie before he was spirited away in an excited sea of lavender, pink, and white. Natalie couldn't resist grinning. Sarah came up behind her and draped an arm around her shoulder.

"Well, well," she began approvingly. "You aren't sixty years old after all. Where did you find this number?" She motioned for Natalie to turn around for full effect. "You're a knockout. Is that him?" Sarah pointed to Peter, who was, by this time, carrying cases of soft drinks and placing them in a stack by the refreshment booth. "Nice."

Natalie misunderstood. "Yes, I'm sure the girls appreciate the last-minute help."

"No, I mean *nice*." The tone of voice made it clear that she wasn't commenting on his personality.

"Oh," she faltered. "I suppose."

"Does *he* like your outfit?" Sarah asked.

"I guess so."

Sarah put her hands on her hips, exhaling dramatically. "You aren't giving up a thing, are you? Well, that's okay," she conceded. "The night is young. Plenty of time…." Taking Natalie's hand, she led her to the refreshment booth where they began unpacking the cases hauled over by Peter.

***

The dance was well underway, and by all outward signs a solid success. New arrivals were announced by the screams of girls spotting their friends, followed by a period of gender-divided chatter and an eventual return to relative calm. Couples on the gymnasium floor danced to a mix of rock, pop, and the occasional country music number. Every five or six songs, the DJ put on something slower for couples needing an excuse to move a little closer.

Peter asked Natalie to dance several times, but she always had a ready excuse about being needed somewhere else. So, he strolled around, watching the students, helping with occasional tasks, but always keeping an eye on Natalie.

Eventually, Peter headed for an outside door in search of some fresh air and a reprieve from the loud music. Upon opening it, however, he realized that the door was not an exit but one which led to one of the interior hallways. Glass display cases lined the walls, and he found himself browsing at trophies and team pictures from years past. Baseball, basketball, football, along with many other sports, were represented for boys' and girls' teams. Toward the end of the hall was a display for softball. He glanced at it and had begun to turn away when he did a double take. There was Natalie, young and grinning, baseball cap perched atop her head, holding up a huge trophy with the rest of her team. Peter moved in closer, captivated by the excitement that radiated from her face.

Eventually heading back down the hall, Peter spotted another door that he hoped would lead outside. He was in luck. This exit opened out to a paved area with a basketball goal at one end. A small group of students, along with an older man, were playing a three-on-three game. Peter let the door close behind him and began watching the half-court game.

The man, who, at closer glance, was probably not much older than Peter, was calling the boys by name and insulting them with a good-natured familiarity that one might use with his own students. Seeing Peter, he called out, "You new here?"

Peter shook his head. "Just chaperoning for the night. I'm here with one of the teachers."

One of the boys offered which one. "Miss Brooks brought him. We saw you at Mangiamele's."

Peter acknowledged him with a brief nod, although by this time most of the kids were beginning to look alike.

The man stepped forward and extended his hand. "Jerry Anderson."

"Peter Spencer."

Jerry resumed dribbling, and then passed the ball to Peter. "Want to play?"

Peter caught the ball. He wouldn't mind a way to pass the time, and this seemed as good a way as any. "Sure." He passed the ball back to Jerry and removed his blazer, throwing it over a folding chair near the door.

Two teams of three formed, with Jerry and Peter each paired with two students. The first time Jerry's team had the ball, they easily drove down to the basket and scored. However, the next point was Peter's, who took a pass from his teammate and put it in off the backboard. Play continued in the same pattern, with the teams alternately missing some shots and making others. With the score 8-9, Jerry brushed hard against Peter on his way to the basket. Peter fell backwards, allowing free access for Jerry to rush to the basket and make the tying lay-up. A cheer broke out among the newly arrived students standing along the sidelines. Peter shot a glance at Jerry but said nothing. His teammates grumbled about the foul, but he leaned in and simply said, "Let's just take that final point."

And they did. After the hand-off, Peter dribbled the ball to the basket, dodging the increasingly aggressive Jerry guarding him. Passing the ball to one of his teammates, a shot was attempted but fell short of its target. Jerry jumped up to rebound, but Peter smacked the ball out of his reach, dribbling briefly and putting the ball up for the final, game-winning goal.

The spectators roared. "Coach Jerry! He shut you down!"

Jerry laughed and shook Peter's hand. "How about another one? This time one-on-one?"

***

Natalie was standing at the refreshment stand when Sarah grabbed her arm. "Come on, you've got to see this." Natalie followed, her eyes scanning the room, unsure of what exactly she should be watching for.

As they reached the far end of the gymnasium, she began to notice a few other students were headed that way, too. Exiting the building into the chilly night air, Natalie was struck by the sight that awaited her. Surrounded by dozens of kids, Peter and Jerry Anderson, JV basketball coach and PE teacher at White Falls High, were locked in a one-on-one basketball game.

"What's going on?" Natalie called to Sarah, barely making herself heard over the noise of the cheering kids around them.

"If I didn't know better, I'd say it was a duel," Sarah grinned. "Didn't Jerry ask you out once?"

"Yes, but..." The two men, coats off and sleeves rolled up, were playing ball like their lives—or at least their self-respect—depended on it. Fast starts, wheeling turns, sharp pivots, and plenty of aggressive bumping and charging characterized the game as each man shot, missed, and battled for each basket.

Jerry lunged over Peter's shoulder, managing to hit a lay-up in the process. The crowd cheered. As he ran back to the center line in preparation for Peter's next drive, he caught Natalie's eye. Peter took the ball and dribbled it past Jerry, managing to evade his attempts to steal it away. He attempted a shot, but Jerry's hand got there first.

Peter tried again, this time palming the ball midair and heaving it up for an off-the-backboard shot.

More cheers this time from the students rooting for Peter. As he passed by, Peter stared directly at Natalie, his expression strikingly similar to the one Jerry had just given her.

"*Oh my God,*" she said, putting her hand over her face. "You're right."

Sarah laughed, caught up in the excitement of the game.

Jerry's final drive took him up to the basket, but Peter was waiting for him. Peter blocked his first two shots, but on Jerry's third attempt, he slammed against Peter and sent him reeling backwards. This shot reached its mark and fell into the basket, winning the game 10-9. Students rushed onto the court, many to congratulate Coach Anderson on his victory while a few made their way over to Peter, who was getting up and dusting himself off. Weaving through the crowd, Natalie finally found him, smiling as the students slapped him on the back. As she approached, she noticed that his elbow was bleeding. "Peter, you're hurt," she frowned.

Peter looked at the scratch. "No big deal," he said off-handedly. He was out of breath and perspiring, but seemed no worse for wear. In fact, his face was alive with excitement.

"Come on, let's get a towel for that," Natalie said, leading him into the gymnasium.

Peter noted with satisfaction the firm grip she had on his hand. Finding some paper napkins tucked behind the concession stand, Natalie handed them to him, only then releasing her hold. Peter dabbed at the still-bleeding scrape.

"You see the game?" he asked with a boyish grin.

"I saw it," she said, all too aware of the point behind the competition. "You looked like a couple of overgrown kids out there."

"I would have beaten him if he hadn't fouled me three times."

Natalie rolled her eyes. She took his napkin and inspected the wound. Satisfied that the bleeding had stopped, she turned away in search of a trash can.

As she disappeared behind the refreshment stand, the strains of one song came to a close, replaced by a new one. Peter recognized it, closing his eyes as an image sprang to mind of a gypsy-scarved girl singing at the top of her lungs as she cleaned her room. It seemed like a lifetime ago.

Not for the first time, memories of her flooded his mind. From the night he watched her dance at Flannery's to their final painful hours together at the hospital, she had captivated Peter, body and soul. Natalie was his girl—he had no doubt. Yet, watching her walk away, Peter realized that Natalie still needed convincing. And there was precious little time left.

Couples moved onto the dance floor, each falling in step with the steady tempo of the song. Struck with a feeling of urgency, Peter strode over and took Natalie by the hand.

"Come on," he said. "This time you're dancing with me."

She attempted to pull away. "No, Peter. I don't dance."

"Of course, you do."

Natalie yanked her hand away with a force that surprised him.

"Not anymore. I *can't*," she whispered fiercely.

Peter was confused by her expression. Then, he understood. This wasn't anger, this was fear.

The music was loud, too loud for conversation. He stepped closer and whispered in her ear, "I won't let go. I won't let you fall." He held out his hand, but Natalie backed away a step. "It will be okay, I promise." His hand remained outstretched.

Natalie let him lead her onto the dance floor. As the dancers moved around them, Peter gripped her hand, his other hand resting on the curve of her back to steady her. She stepped cautiously, watching his feet while also watching out for the others around her.

Sensing her apprehension, Peter guided her movements, giving her time to recognize the comfortable rhythm to his steps. Before long, he felt her body relax as she moved in tandem with him. "See? You're doing fine. I bet you didn't know you could two-step."

Natalie gave a self-conscious smile. "I didn't."

"Stick around. There's more where that came from."

She laughed. "You're full of surprises, aren't you?"

"Yes, I am."

"Speaking of, that was some game. Anything behind that little performance tonight?"

Peter grinned. "I have no idea what you're talking about. By the way, what's the story with our friend Jerry? Something I should know?"

"He's asked me out a couple of times," Natalie answered.

"I figured as much. Did you take him up on it?"

"No."

"Good girl," he answered with satisfaction. "He's not your type."

"Actually, I was busy."

This wasn't the answer he expected to hear. "And if you hadn't been busy?"

Natalie laughed at his expression. "I probably would have said no."

Peter let it go at that.

The song ended, prompting some students to leave the dance floor. This time, it was replaced with one much slower in tempo.

Natalie's lighthearted banter evaporated as quickly as it had started. She mumbled an excuse about being needed at the refreshment stand and began to make her way off the floor.

No, not yet, Peter entreated silently. He caught up with her and gently took her hand, pulling her to a stop. "Just one more," he asked.

Natalie stood there, hand in his, acutely aware of what was at stake by returning to the dance floor. She wasn't ready for this, wasn't ready for the swell of emotions that threatened with each passing moment she remained in his grasp. She watched other couples file past them, their arms and bodies joining and moving in time with the music. Turning back to Peter, Natalie saw the plaintive look in his eyes and realized the utter foolishness in ever thinking that she'd had a choice.

The music swelled around them. Peter pulled her close, his fingers entangling with hers. His gaze never left her, but Natalie looked away. Reminded of the Greek myths she loved as a child, she knew too well the consequences of staring too long into his face.

The other couples swayed with the music, their movements conveying far more than any words could. Watching them, Natalie began to feel indescribably tired. Holding herself apart from Peter, when every fiber of her body ached to be held by him, took too much energy. Her body began to relax and, like the loosening grip of a drowning man, she let go, surrendering to the feeling that the music and closeness to him gave.

The dance floor was packed, couples surrounding them on all sides, yet Natalie had forgotten them. She rested her head against the soft cotton of Peter's shirt. Perspiration from the basketball game lingered on his skin and clothing, producing a powerful effect on her and evoking memories of the many nights she lay pressed against his chest as she was now. Natalie closed her eyes, her arms tightening around him. Peter responded to the change immediately, enveloping her body with his own.

In time, the music faded and the strains of a newer, faster song took its place. Natalie lifted her head from Peter's chest, drowsy at first, but then snapped to attention as she sensed the curious gazes of those surrounding her.

Sarah met the pair as they left the dance floor, a resolute expression on her face. In her hands she held Natalie's coat and purse. "*Go*," she said, a smile playing at the corners of her lips.

"What?" Natalie began, checking her watch. "The dance isn't over for another hour."

"If you two don't get out of here soon, you're going to start giving these kids ideas."

"What are you talking about...?" Natalie asked again, turning first to Sarah and back to Peter, who accepted the garments without argument.

Sarah ignored her question, instead addressing her next response to Peter.

"Take her home."

CHAPTER 27

Peter almost missed the turn onto Natalie's street. Her neighborhood was in a newer part of town, along the far western edge where there had been the predictable migration of businesses from a declining downtown. New chain restaurants and retail stores had also sprung up, along with a Walmart store.

"My father *hates* that place," Natalie had said earlier in the evening when they first passed by. "He would rather spend $50 more at the local hardware store than go there. He says it's a matter of principle."

Peter chuckled. His father had expressed a similar sentiment when the areas around Madison began to expand. "Same with mine. In his entire life, I think he visited only two stores—Verona Farm & Fleet and Miller's General Store. Going into a Walmart would have killed him."

But the drive home was mostly silent. Except for the occasional reminder to turn, Natalie watched out the windows, her expression unreadable. Peter noticed several apartment complexes lining the street. Most windows were darkened, but some still reflected a bluish, flickering light from the televisions inside. Natalie's complex was the last one on the left. The street dead-ended into a cornfield just beyond her parking lot. Presumably, a lack of building funds or demand had stopped further progress on her road.

Natalie directed Peter into the parking lot and pointed out a vacant spot near her building. Funny how he didn't remember any of this the first time, so intent was he on reaching her door earlier that evening. He pulled into the spot and turned off the engine.

The pair sat in their seats for a moment, the engine's silence only increasing their awkwardness.

"So," Peter began, breaking the uncomfortable silence. "We're here."

Natalie began to busy herself with collecting her purse and tightening her coat around her. "You could come in if you'd like. For a little while." She gave him a sideways glance, almost stumbling over the words.

Her discomfort was unmistakable. *For a little while.*

"Sure," he smiled.

Natalie opened the car door and crossed the parking lot to her building, Peter following close behind. After scaling the flight of stairs up to her apartment, she unlocked the door and entered the dark foyer. Only then did she turn and invite Peter inside.

The apartment was exactly what he would have pictured—warm, cheerful, and above all, functional. Natalie had filled the room with overstuffed furniture, handmade afghans, and potted plants in every corner. The artwork on the walls included framed posters by Monet and Van Gogh, black and white pictures of city skylines and a colorful map of the world. In one corner, a half-finished puzzle stood waiting for attention, while in another, an end table held a lamp and several framed photographs. Stacks of magazines and newspapers lay scattered across the coffee table in the center of the room.

Along the only wall not interrupted by pictures or windows was a bookcase filled with books of every subject. Peter could see that Natalie had finally gotten the chance to renew her love of reading. He moved closer to glimpse the selections—Psychology textbooks, Civil War history, classic literature, contemporary fiction, even a few dime-store romance novels. He pulled one out and showed her with raised eyebrows. Natalie smiled in spite of herself. "My mother gave that to me."

"Enjoy it?"

"Sure," she responded. "It's nice to believe in happy endings now and then."

Peter shot her a questioning glance, though she didn't seem to notice. He returned the book to the shelf and followed her as she continued her unofficial tour of the apartment.

"This is the dining room and kitchen," Natalie announced. "And down here," she said, pointing to the hallway, "is my room and the bathroom." She started to walk down the hall, but then appeared to change her mind mid-stride, colliding with Peter who stood close behind. Peter held his arms up to steady her.

"It's a nice place," he said. "I can see you've put a lot of yourself into it."

She ignored his comment, her manner uneasy. "So, would you like something to drink?" she rushed. "Some coffee or soda? I'm afraid I don't have anything alcoholic in the house." She slipped out of his arms without waiting for an answer, hurrying into the kitchen.

Peter watched her go, puzzled by her behavior. As he entered the kitchen, Natalie was pulling out the coffee and filters, placing it beside the waiting coffee machine.

"Coffee at this hour?" he joked. "You trying to keep me up all night?"

Natalie flinched, her arm knocking the opened can of coffee off the counter. A wave of tiny brown coffee grounds rained onto the floor. "*Damn it*," she cursed to herself, bending down to scoop up the coffee.

Peter knelt down in front of her. He took her hands, interrupting her efforts at cleaning. "Natalie, *what's wrong*?"

Natalie shook her head, closing her eyes. "I'm sorry. I'm just so nervous." She sat on the floor, her back against the cabinet. "Can you believe that? After all we've…" She left her sentence unfinished.

"Nervous—of me?"

Natalie hesitated. She seemed to be choosing her words carefully. "Of *being* with you," she answered. "It's… it's been a long time."

Peter absorbed the meaning behind her words. "You mean," he began. "You mean, not since we…" His voice trailed off.

"That week before Christmas. Pathetic, huh?"

Seeing her pained expression, Peter felt a rush of emotion. With all the fallout he'd experienced since their break-up, he hadn't considered the full extent of what she'd endured. In those fleeting moments, he pictured the months of slow, painstaking recovery, and the emotional toll it must have taken on her. Now, almost two years later, here he came, ready to pick up where they had left off. Of course, she would be ambivalent, even fearful. How could he have expected anything less?

Words failed him. Nothing could adequately express what he felt inside, so he just held her, letting his actions speak for him instead.

***

Natalie returned his embrace, grateful for the warmth and comfort it gave her. Grateful for a few moments where words weren't necessary. Gradually, with a predictability she had almost forgotten, she felt her body relax.

Peter pulled away, his expression sober. "Nothing has to happen, Natalie," he said. "I can leave now if that makes you more comfortable."

"*No*—I don't want you to go. I just don't know how much…I don't know how far I can…"

Peter kissed her forehead, brushing away a lock of hair that had fallen astray. He nodded with a gentle smile. Standing up, he held out a hand for her. "I think I'll take some coffee after all. We'll catch up. And you can kick me out whenever you've had enough of me."

Natalie exhaled, her face softening in obvious relief. She retrieved the broom and dustpan from the hall closet and began cleaning up the mess on the floor while Peter filled the coffee filter with what was left of the un-spilled coffee.

"Sit down," Natalie urged. "I'll be out in a few minutes." She motioned toward the living room and gave him a gentle push in that direction.

By the time Natalie brought the steaming mugs out to the living room, Peter was already several pages into one of her photo albums, which he had found on her bookshelf. He pointed to one picture with amusement. "You?"

Natalie handed him his coffee and glanced at the photo as she sat down. It was a shot of her in uniform when she played shortstop for the White Falls softball team. She grimaced at the pigtails, acne, and overbite that had not yet been tamed by braces. She took a short sip of the hot liquid before replying. "Guilty," she admitted with a blush.

"I saw your team's trophy in the school hallway," Peter observed. "I didn't know you played."

"I loved it," Natalie laughed. "I was a pure tomboy during those years. My mom was mortified."

Peter grinned. "Who's this?" he asked, pointing at an older woman in one of the photos.

"Aunt Carol, my mom's sister. See, there's my mom in the background."

"Is that the one from Virginia?" Peter asked.

Natalie glanced up in surprise. "How did you know that?"

"Your parents were visiting her when you had your accident. That's why they couldn't get to the hospital right away."

"I don't remember much from those first couple of days," Natalie admitted. "Gina told me you were there the whole time. She said that if she hadn't sent you home, you would have stayed there all night."

His expression turned grim. "I hadn't been that scared in a long time," he recalled. "I somehow had it in my head that if I stayed, nothing more would happen to you."

Natalie nodded, her eyes brimming with gratitude. "Hey, do you recognize that guy?" She pointed to a picture of a young man in a suit holding a baby, a serious yet proud expression on his face.

Peter was grateful for the distraction. "Your father?" he asked.

"Mm hmm."

"Is that you he's holding?"

"It must be," she replied "He's wearing a suit for work. He and Mom didn't buy the farm until I was three years old. After that, he never wore anything but jeans or overalls."

They continued browsing through the album and on through a second one, until they reached the last page. Peter closed the album with an audible clap and began to rise from the couch.

Natalie gave him a questioning look.

"Coffee's kicking in," he answered sheepishly. "Bathroom this way?"

She smiled and nodded. Peter disappeared down the hall.

Natalie got up from the couch and paced to the window. A feeling of restlessness swept over her. She shouldn't have had coffee so late at night, she scolded herself. Staring out the window at the darkness, she saw little but her own reflection and the half-moon up in the sky.

How many times had she watched out this same window, searching for answers? Haunted by actions she couldn't change, by decisions made in haste, Natalie eventually learned to forgive herself and leave the past behind. But now her past was back— forcing her to face the mistakes yet again and the one person she'd hurt most by them. Natalie wasn't sure where to begin.

"He loves you, Natalie. You can't just give up." Gina's words echoed in her mind, the same ones she'd uttered at the hospital that last night. *"He stood for hours in front of that waiting room window, just waiting for news from the doctor. He sat for hours with you after you came out of surgery. You don't do that unless you love someone."* But Natalie had lost so much in such a short time, and Gina's words couldn't touch her. It was

simply easier to throw everything away than to muster up the strength to fix what lay broken.

That same night, Peter had arrived. He was breathless and smiling, a bouquet of flowers clenched in his grip, complaining about some backup on the Beltline that had delayed him. What had she said to him? she wondered now. That it was over? That she didn't want to see him anymore? She couldn't remember the words, but the torn, bewildered expression on his face was burned into her memory.

Peter tried to get through to her, tried to understand what had changed. But it was no use. Her grief had erected a barrier between them as impenetrable as an iron wall. At some point, he must have glanced at the notebook on the bedside table, almost disregarding it except for Gordon's signature at the bottom and hers beside it. She remembered Peter peering at her, eyes narrowed in confusion and then in disbelief as he read the agreement in full. She offered him no explanation, no apologies. What must he have thought of her? The thought tortured her for months afterwards.

The next morning, numb with guilt and pain, Natalie went home for good, not even looking back to wave goodbye to her best friend.

Now, Natalie shut her eyes, mourning all the time they had lost. *No more*, she thought, shaking her head. Peter was a good man and he loved her. She would not waste another moment of their precious time together.

She turned away from the window, meeting Peter as he made his way down the hall. Wordlessly, she took his hand and led him into the darkness of her room.

Natalie reached up and cradled his face in her hands, drawing him down to meet hers. Peter returned her kiss tentatively at first, then with growing intensity, his hands winding deeply into her hair. Just once, he pulled away, gazing into her eyes as if to understand what she wanted to happen. Natalie's face was flushed, her breathing uneven. With a look, she answered his unspoken question.

Slowly, teasingly, Peter unfastened her dress and let it fall to the floor, kissing the newly exposed areas on her neck and shoulders with deliberate attention. While Natalie pulled at the buttons of his shirt, her hands suddenly hungry for the warmth of his chest, Peter's pace was decidedly unhurried. With methodical precision, he removed each of her garments until she stood before him completely exposed. Only then did he guide her to the bed and, with a brief curse about all the damned throw pillows in the way, laid her down.

Peter moved down her body with excruciating thoroughness. He left nothing unexplored, touching and tasting until she felt she would die from anticipation. When he finally moved inside her, Natalie cried out, as much from relief as from desire.

CHAPTER 28

—— · ⊘ · ——

The urgency that began their coupling evaporated into a pleasant exhaustion. Natalie lay curled on her side, Peter's body enveloping hers. He kissed her lightly on the back of her neck and stroked her hair, his fingers continuing a languorous path across her face and shoulders until the sheet stopped their movement. He marveled at how easily everything had come back to them. Despite their separation, each had remembered with tantalizing precision the touches and places that elicited the most pleasure in the other.

Peter sat up and scanned the room, taking care not to lose his hold on her. Throw pillows lay scattered in all directions on the floor. The patchwork quilt that once covered the bed now dangled uselessly along its edge. All that remained was a flowered sheet that she had pulled over them afterwards.

Except that now it was in the way. Peter pulled the sheet down and resumed his caresses over her newly exposed flesh. She made no sound, but he could feel her breath quicken in reaction, her stomach draw in reflexively as his hand made contact. He smiled. Playfully, he drew invisible shapes and letters on her stomach, eventually progressing to whole words that Natalie tried to guess, laughing quietly in delight.

In time, his hands drew farther downward, until he reached the site of her scar. Peter stopped, his finger tracing a path along the swath of tissue where the surgeon had repaired the accident's damage.

"Does it hurt?" he whispered in her ear.

"No."

"Is it sensitive?" he persisted.

"You could say that."

Peter smiled. "Should I stop?"

"Don't you dare."

Peter chuckled under his breath. He pulled her onto her back and renewed his explorations, this time with his lips, his face grazing her skin as he traveled.

Natalie reached out, cradling his face with her hand. "So soft," she whispered. "Why did you shave it?"

He shrugged. "Needed a fresh start, I guess."

Natalie's smile was sympathetic. "Did it help?"

"It didn't bring you back."

She said nothing.

Peter watched a cloud of sadness cross Natalie's face, regretting the turn of conversation. He didn't want to waste time with talk of the past. Not right now. Using distraction to his advantage, he bent to his task once more, slowly moving down her torso and leaving brief, yet charged, kisses behind for her to savor.

Eventually, he reached her abdomen. Peter pressed his lips against the scar, still pink and new, feeling the difference in texture between it and the surrounding tissue. Smooth and thinly stretched, it reminded him of a slender patch of new ice, fragile and shiny, in contrast with the frozen pond around it.

Natalie's barely audible sigh caught Peter's attention. Glancing up, he saw her eyes close, her face unmistakably content. Yet, for a moment, Peter's mind pictured her under darker circumstances—unconscious and opened up, a surgical team working to repair her damaged body. He withdrew his hand and sat up.

Natalie opened her eyes, startled by his abrupt response. She covered herself with the sheet. "It bothers you," she said eventually, more statement than question.

Peter turned and saw her stricken expression. "*God,* no." He reached out to smooth away the worried lines on her forehead. "Not in the way you think. You've just gone through so much. I should have been there to help you through it."

"I left you, remember? You didn't have much choice."

"If I'd had any sense, I would have followed you back here the next day," Peter countered.

Natalie shook her head. "No, Peter. You were right not to follow me. I needed time to pull myself back together." She touched his arm. "Every part of me felt like it was broken—inside and out. I wasn't myself for a long time after the accident. There was nothing you could have done."

"You blamed yourself for the miscarriage," Peter stated.

Natalie nodded.

Peter slid back into bed, his eyes searching her face. "But it wasn't your fault. You know that don't you?"

"I do now, but it took a long time. I ended up seeing a psychologist who was able to help me put the guilt aside, to accept that it was just an accident." She paused a moment, her face deep in thought. "It was the hardest thing I've ever done."

Peter sat motionless, waiting for her to continue.

"And if that wasn't enough, there was still the question of what I would do with my life." Natalie gave a short laugh, shaking her head at the enormity of it all. "I felt so adrift. All the things I had been working for suddenly felt meaningless. My doctor made me stop and think about what it was that I had loved most during my time in Madison." She paused. "Besides you, it was teaching."

Peter reached out and stroked her cheek. Pain reflected in his eyes. "I'm so sorry for all you had to go through. I'm so sorry for everything."

Natalie squeezed his hand. "I'm sorry too, Peter. This hurt us both. But I'm okay now. She searched his face. "Are you?"

Peter returned her smile, but it was tinged with sadness. It had taken him so long to realize what he had had with Natalie, only to lose her. Now, with the possibility of a second chance, he wondered if he was too late—if he had simply missed out on too much to ever be a meaningful part of her life again. A heavy feeling of doubt settled over him.

Natalie took his hand in her own, her voice gentle. "There's something I always wanted to ask you. Something in your eyes that I could never quite understand." She brushed her hand lightly across his face, her thumb tracing the outline of his brow. "Tell me about her," she whispered, never taking her eyes off him. "Tell me about Eve."

Peter's head lifted in surprise. "How do you…?"

"I was there when you dreamed about her. There were times when I could feel her in the room with us. Please."

Peter slowly sank back into the pillows beside her. He had never talked about Eve before; he wasn't even sure how to begin. He stared into the darkness, trying to pull his thoughts together. After a long pause, he began.

"Eve and I grew up together in Madison. Our families were very close. She was my sister's best friend. Our fathers had grown up together on neighboring farms, almost like brothers themselves. We went to school together, helped out with harvests together…you get the picture.

"For a long time, Eve was like my own sister. But, as I grew older, I started to see her in a different light. She was beautiful and outspoken, and she had this wild streak that I couldn't resist. She was also very sexually mature for her age, which, as you can imagine, was pretty appealing to a teenage boy." He smiled to himself and shook his head. "Of course, at the time I didn't know why she behaved the way she did, or why a thirteen-year-old girl would have that much knowledge about such things. I just felt unbelievably lucky."

Natalie's expression became grim.

"We were inseparable after that. But it wasn't until my senior year that she finally told me. Her father had been molesting her since she was eleven." Peter closed his eyes. "God, I wanted to kill him with my bare hands, but she just held onto me and wouldn't let go. I couldn't understand why she wanted to protect him. She acted like it was somehow her fault, too."

He took a long breath. "I was determined to get her out of there, to take her away with me when I went off to college.

But Will had no intention of letting her go. He went to my father and somehow convinced him that my intentions with Eve were less than honorable, that I was trying to steal her away from her family. The next day, my father sat me down and said that if I took Eve away with me, he would cut off the money and there would be no college.

"And I went along with it. Can you believe it?" Peter shook his head again, his face awash with shame. "It never occurred to me to defy him."

Natalie didn't move. With her eyes, she urged him to continue.

Peter's voice hardened. "Well, I couldn't take her with me, and I wouldn't leave her behind. So, I stayed at UW for the next four years while she continued to live with her family and that son-of-a-bitch."

"Did he ever…?" Natalie began cautiously.

"No, at least I was able to put a stop to that for her. One day, while Eve was in class, I paid her father a visit. He never touched her after that." Peter could still remember their encounter in the barn—up in the loft, of all places—where he had found Will stacking bales of hay. Peter had been so angry, so focused, that he scarcely remembered climbing up the rungs of the ladder. It hadn't even occurred to him to be scared.

Before Will had time to react, Peter grabbed the pitchfork away from him and pinned him up against the barn wall with it. He pressed the tines of the pitchfork against his neck until small circular droplets of blood began to form. *"I know what you did to her,"* he said, his voice little more than a growl. *"If you ever lay a hand on her again, I will slit your throat with this thing and watch you die."*

Will stood paralyzed, his eyes wide with terror as Peter spat the final words. After a few silent, staring moments, Peter released the pitchfork and tossed it to the ground in disgust. Will stumbled in his attempt to put as much space between him and Peter as possible. Peter climbed down the ladder, his eyes never leaving the older man's face. They never spoke again after that.

"Once I graduated, I took Eve with me to UCLA. I'd gotten an assistantship in the Psychology department there. It didn't pay much, but we were able to get a studio apartment together. Our families were horrified, of course, but we couldn't have been happier. We could finally start living our lives."

Peter turned onto his back and stared vacantly at the ceiling. His voice took on a lifeless tone as he related the rest. Natalie looked on with a worried gaze.

"Maybe it was the shock of being so far away from family and friends with nothing to keep her occupied. I'm not sure. But Eve changed after we moved there. She became restless, unhappy. If I came home late from a study session, she would accuse me of sleeping around. We began to argue. Not long after that, she got involved with a group of people that hung around the neighborhood. At first, I was glad that she had made some friends, but then she started going out with them at night and not coming home until two or three in the morning. I started finding pot and other drugs I didn't even recognize hidden in her purse and dresser drawers. I demanded that she stop seeing them, but she refused.

"This went on for months. I could see Eve changing in front of my eyes. She started losing weight. Her face looked tired and drawn all the time. I begged her to get some help. I even spoke with a colleague of mine and found a therapist who specialized in incest cases. But Eve wouldn't have anything to do with therapy. Not long after that, she moved out of our apartment. I came home from classes one day and her stuff was gone—clothes, pictures—everything she could carry, I guess. All she left was a note saying that she would be staying with friends. She didn't return any of my calls. She just disappeared. I almost went out of my mind.

"Then one night, she called." Peter closed his eyes, mentally recreating the moment, her final precious words. "It was her, but it wasn't. Her voice had this sing-song quality to it, like a little girl's, but she sounded scared at the same time. 'I can't make them stop,' she kept saying. 'I can't make the thoughts stop.'"

"I begged her to tell me where she was…." Peter stopped and shook his head. "But she just kept saying the same things over and over until she stopped talking altogether.

"In the background, I kept hearing the sound of wind rushing through the trees and suddenly I knew where Eve had gone. It was this look-out in the foothills where she and I would drive sometimes. You could park your car at the top and watch the sun set over the canyon. It was beautiful, but it was always windy. Eve loved that spot.

"When I asked if she was at the canyon, she hung up. I ran for my car, trying to get her back on the phone, but she never picked up again. By the time I got there, the access road was blocked off by a sheriff's car. I got out and pleaded with him, but he wouldn't let me through."

Peter could still recall the officer's guarded look that he would understand only later.

I think my girlfriend is up there. Please let me talk to her.

Sorry, sir, no one is allowed up there.

More pleas, growing more frantic and belligerent by the moment.

She needs me. I can talk to her. Peter began to step past the officer.

The officer maneuvered in front of him, holding up his hands.

She's not up there anymore.

Peter paused, still looking off into space. "She drove right over the edge." He imagined the carnage though he never saw it himself–the partially submerged car, roof and windows peeking out among the rocks and rushing water.

"The coroner's office listed her death as an accident or possible suicide. They said it was difficult to know for sure because of the high levels of opioids found in her system."

"I flew her back to Madison but didn't stay for the funeral. Eve's family blamed me for what had happened. Even my father wouldn't speak to me. Only my sister listened when I tried to explain. Eve never told her about being molested, but Dawn had suspected for a long time that something wasn't right. I guess, in a way, she wasn't surprised by the way things ended.

"I went back to LA and stayed. Dawn and my mother kept in touch with me, but my father and I didn't speak for years after that. He refused to take my phone calls and returned my letters unopened. I guess it was easier to believe his own son was responsible for Eve's death than his best friend.

"Funny thing was, I felt the same way. If I had gotten help for her sooner, maybe this never would have happened."

Peter went silent. A stillness descended over the room. He slowly returned from the past and, remembering where he was, turned to the woman beside him. He frowned when he saw Natalie's tear-stained face. "You're crying." he said with concern.

"I'm so sorry," she whispered.

"It was a long time ago, Nat. Don't cry."

"But you're still not over her. The dreams..."

Peter took her chin in his hand, his eyes holding hers. "The dreams have stopped."

She blinked, unshed tears escaping down her face. "How?"

"I let her go," he said simply. "I never realized how tightly I had been holding on to her memory. I guess I felt that if I couldn't do anything else for her, at least I owed her that. Except, living in the past isn't living, is it?" His smile was wistful. "You have to forgive yourself, or just stop trying altogether.

"So I let her go. I'll never forget her, but you're my girl now."

A sob rose in her throat, and she buried her face in his chest. "I love you," she breathed, her words grazing his skin as she tightened her hold. "I never stopped."

Peter wrapped his arms around her, overcome with a feeling of warmth and protectiveness. He was exactly where he belonged. Natalie was his home.

The remaining hours passed in a blur of wakefulness and sleep, of languid motion and contented stillness. They made love in the purest sense of the word, without fear of rejection, for the first time in their lives together. It was a curious feeling. Especially for Peter, who had spent his entire adult life fleeing from attachment. Now, his whispered endearments flowed out effortlessly, much to his love's delight.

Chapter 29

It was just past sunrise when Natalie made her way into the kitchen, taking a final glance at the sleeping man in her bed. She smiled at the discordant image: Peter's long frame, surrounded by pink afghans and lacy throw pillows. Clad in a terry cloth robe and slippers, Natalie stepped softly, not wanting to wake him. She started a pot of coffee, realizing too late her mistake in making only enough for herself. Old habits die hard, she thought. It would take time to get used to sharing coffee with him in the morning.

The new sun filled the window with its pale light. Natalie sat down in her favorite chair in the living room—an old, wooden rocker—cradling the warm cup in her hands and bending her face into the curls of rising steam. She recalled the Winnie the Pooh books her mother used to read to her as a child, how the bear would go to his "thinking spot" whenever he encountered something that perplexed him. Well, this was her thinking spot.

Natalie replayed the confessions of the previous night in her mind. So much had happened, so much they had both endured. Her accident, the loss of their child, Eve's tragic death —each one carrying enough pain to divide them forever. And yet, somehow, they had found their way back.

The sounds of movement in her room brought her back to the present. Peter was up. She listened, attempting to identify his actions from the sounds he made: sitting on the bed, fastening his belt, pulling on his socks and shoes. It was easy to picture him in her mind; his face was as familiar as her own. Such a captivating face, so much hidden behind those deep brown eyes. Until now. Breaking free from the trauma of Eve's death was a testament of his devotion to Natalie.

And her devotion? There was no question Natalie would do anything for him. But in this certainty, there was also some regret. For the last year and a half, Natalie's life had been here—her family, her friends, and a job that she loved and did well. Yet, there was nothing here for Peter. He needed a setting that could provide him with the teaching and research opportunities he had in Madison. To be with Peter meant following him to wherever those opportunities could be found. She would have to start over yet again.

"Morning."

Peter stood in the doorway, hair charmingly rumpled, and dressed in the khakis and white button-down shirt he had worn the night before. His smile was warm and guileless. "You look deep in thought."

Natalie smiled back. "Morning. How did you sleep?"

"Fine, once you let me," Peter said, lifting his eyebrow. He knelt by the chair, pulling her close and kissing her. Natalie's eyes opened slowly as he released her, barely managing to hang onto her coffee in the process. Had his kisses always made her feel so weak? She tightened her grip on the cup, surprised by how unsteady it felt.

"So, what were you thinking about?"

"You."

He grinned. "I like that. Tell me more."

Natalie brought the coffee cup up to her chin, not drinking, just finding comfort in its warmth. "I'm wondering what happens next."

Peter noted the faint lines of worry on her face. "I'm not sure," he answered. "A lot depends on you."

"Me?"

Peter stood up and held out his hand. "Come on," he said. "There's something I want to show you."

Natalie gave him a puzzled glance. "What, here?"

"No, not here. So go get some clothes on." He pulled her up from the chair, ignoring protests about her unfinished coffee.

"I'll get you some coffee later," Peter insisted. "This is more important."

Natalie scowled but headed down the hallway. As she busied herself with dressing, Peter went in search of coffee but found the pot almost empty. He swirled the remaining liquid around in disappointment.

"You didn't make any extra?" he called.

"I'm not used to overnight guests," she shot back.

Well, he couldn't very well argue with that one. Seeing her coffee cup on the end table where it had been abandoned, Peter picked it up and downed half the contents in one gulp. It was milky and sweet. He grimaced, remembering too late how she liked her coffee.

Natalie peeked her head out of the bedroom in time to watch him set down the cup.

"How can you drink it like that?"

Natalie laughed. "Serves you right for stealing my coffee."

She emerged a few minutes later, face freshly scrubbed and hair pulled back, her pajamas replaced by a warm, oversized sweater and jeans. She wore no makeup, a detail that did not escape Peter's notice. "There's my girl," he said appreciatively, taking her hand and pulling her toward him. "Ready?"

"Ready," Natalie answered. "But you still haven't told me where we're going."

"That's right," he said, a mysterious smile playing on his lips. "Just get in the car. I'll take care of the rest."

Natalie retrieved their coats from the closet on their way out, handing Peter's to him before stepping outside. The air was brisk and damp. They descended the stairs and made their way to Peter's car, where he opened her door and motioned her inside, obviously in a hurry to reach his destination.

As Peter started the car, Natalie tilted her head back, inhaling audibly. She sighed, a soft smile playing on her lips. "Don't ever sell this car," she said.

This was hardly the first time he had witnessed this mysterious reaction. "Would you mind telling me what it is about this car that affects you so much?" Peter insisted, his curiosity finally getting the better of him.

Natalie laughed. "It's *you*," she replied simply. "It's your smell. It reminds me of the first night I was in this car with you."

Peter remembered the drive home from Flannery's, the dreamy expression on her face as she dozed beside him. "But you were asleep."

"Smell is one of the most primitive senses we have, remember? You taught me that in Psych 101. I may not remember much about that car ride, but my body does. And I will never forget that smell."

Peter liked the sound of that somehow. That the connection between them had been hard-wired since their first night together. Mentally, emotionally, humans took far more time to make sense of the impulses that their bodies had already taken for fact. He reached out and playfully touched her nose. "I can't make any promises about the car. I may need to trade this thing in for something more practical in the near future."

At Natalie's frown, he bent the rest of the way and kissed her. "You still have me, though." Natalie accepted his kiss and shrugged, satisfied with the concession.

They drove for twenty minutes, leaving the downtown behind and moving deep into the large tracts of farmland that lay south of the town. Eventually, Peter spotted a road sign and, beside it, a mailbox with the name Garner. Natalie glanced at him questioningly but remained silent. He turned the car onto the gravel path, driving until he reached the farm beyond.

"Why are we stopping here?" she asked.

Peter turned off the ignition and was already opening his car door. "You'll see."

He neared the weathered wooden fence bordering the property, stepping up onto the first rail as he surveyed the extensive grounds. He glanced back as Natalie caught up with him at the fence.

"What do you think?"

Natalie gave him a puzzled frown. "About what?"

"This place."

"It's the Garner's farm."

Peter faced her with mild surprise. "You know it?"

Natalie laughed. "Of course, I know it. I spent half of my summers here. Maggie Garner and I were best friends from the time we were in grade school. I know this place as well as I know my own house."

No wonder he was so sure about this place. Peter shook his head, as if finally being let in on the whole story. He inched over so that Natalie could step up on the fence rail beside him. "Tell me more."

"Maggie and I would ride the school bus home together and take turns going to each other's houses. We played dolls and dress-up when we were younger, helped with chores, followed around her big brother and teased my little sister—everything." She pointed to the grove of trees that abutted the west side of the property. "We used to spend hours there when we were older." Peter could vaguely see the outline of a tire swing that hung suspended from one of the larger trees.

"Doing what?" Peter tried to picture her as a young girl, pony-tailed and in jeans, swinging from the tree.

"Oh, talking mostly—places we'd go, people we'd meet, what our husbands would be like, how many kids we wanted—you know—typical teenage girl stuff."

Peter smiled. "Did you ever dream of coming back here?"

Natalie smiled and shook her head. "God, no. We couldn't wait to leave and start a new life somewhere exciting. But," her expression became pensive, "dreams change, don't they? Sometimes home is exactly where you need to be."

Peter scanned the grounds that stretched out ahead of them. "So, what happened to Maggie?"

"She married her prince charming and moved to Cincinnati. Her husband is a stockbroker and she's a stay-at-home mom. See what I mean about dreams? Maggie was planning to marry a French diplomat."

Peter grinned. "I guess she's not planning to take over the family farm?"

"No, and neither is her brother. Todd's settled in Houston now. The Garners farmed here for thirty years, but I guess the work just got to be too much for the two of them. They retired to South Carolina a few months ago. It's a shame. Every year at homecoming, they had a huge bonfire on their property for all the high school kids. They hitched up the horses for wagon rides and served hot cider and s'mores. It was such fun. This year was the first time they didn't have it. The high school talked about holding one on the baseball field, but nobody really got behind it. It just wouldn't have been the same." Natalie stared off into the field, perhaps remembering the many homecomings spent here as a girl. She fell silent.

Several moments passed before he spoke. "I'm thinking of buying this place," he said matter-of-factly, his gaze still straight ahead.

Natalie gave a snort. "Right."

"I'm serious."

Natalie glanced at him, a frown replacing her smile.

"You can't be serious." Then, stepping down from the fence, she stared at him squarely. "You *are* serious."

Peter still hadn't moved from his perch at the fence. He gave her a sideways glance but continued to face away from her.

"Peter, this is a *farm*."

"I know that."

"A *working* farm," Natalie clarified.

"I know that, too. I'd be the one working it."

Natalie blinked. "But...but you're not a farmer. You're a professor."

He shrugged. "Well, like I told you, I'm kind of between jobs right now."

"You don't just stop being a professor, Peter," Natalie tried again. "That's a profession, not just a job. You don't walk away from something like that lightly."

Peter stepped down from the fence, smiling patiently at her look of alarm.

"I know I'm throwing a lot at you right now. Just hear me out, okay?" He took Natalie's hands, enfolding them in his, and told her his side of the story.

The first few weeks after she left were hell. Leaving Gordon's office, fist bloodied and half-crazed with anger, Peter fell into a trance of sorts—raw emotion replaced by a cold lifelessness. At first, there was a constant stream of phone calls, some curious, others genuinely concerned about his breakdown. Invitations went unanswered and messages built up on voice mail until it simply would hold no more. Only then did he finally obtain some measure of peace.

It was Dawn who broke Peter out of his self-imposed seclusion. Family dinners at the house provided a welcome distraction, and he was grateful for the genuine requests for advice from Tim about the farm.

Dawn knew that something was very wrong with her brother. While she didn't press him for answers, she wondered if it had anything to do with the young woman Amanda had once mentioned. It was the day that Andy was born. Peter and this girl—*Natalie, was it?* —spent the day with Amanda, taking her to the museum and out to eat. "He said they were just friends, Mommy, but he kissed her like Daddy kisses you," she had giggled. "Uncle Pete didn't see me watching. He thought I was asleep."

By the time the semester was over, Peter knew he wouldn't be returning to this school or any other. Teaching had long ago lost its allure, but this had settled it. He yearned for something that he could point to with pride, something he had produced with his own hands. Yet, the only thing that might have served that purpose—his book—lay in the same unfinished state it had been in since Natalie left.

Somehow, Peter had accepted that disconnect as the price of being an adult. He still remembered his father's words, *"Who really likes their job anyway? You do whatever you have to do to support your family."* But without a family, the words rang hollow in his mind.

So, he put his job search on hold, offering to help Dawn and Tim on the farm. Tim, trying to balance the demands of a growing yield and a growing family, gratefully accepted Peter's offer. The work was just as hard as he remembered from his younger years, but after a full day of milking, planting, cleaning stalls, and feeding animals, he fell into bed in a satisfied state of exhaustion. It was a feeling of accomplishment unlike anything he had had in a long time. At the end of the long summer, as he and Tim congratulated themselves on a successful harvest, Peter realized that the answers to his questions had been with him all along.

"I wanted something real," he explained. "That's the way I feel about farming."

Natalie was silent for a minute, the meaning of his words sinking in. "But here? Your family, your friends are all back in Madison."

Peter turned to her, an amused smile playing on his lips. "You're here."

Natalie shook her head. This was crazy. "I couldn't let you do that."

Peter tightened his grip on her hands, forcing her attention back to his face. "I don't care where I do this, Natalie. It could be anywhere. The only requirement is that you're there beside me. I've spent over half my life in Madison. I'm ready for a new adventure."

He paused. "You've been through a lot in the last couple of years, and you've finally found a place and a job that make you happy. Right?" He sent her a questioning glance. "Is this where you want to be?"

Natalie sidestepped the question. "You would do that for me?" she said, almost in a whisper.

He cradled her face with his hands. "I would do anything for you. Don't you know that by now?"

Natalie wrapped her arms around him. It was as if he had crawled inside her mind, understanding what she needed better than she did. Turning her face from the smooth folds of his jacket, she gazed at the fields with an entirely new perspective.

Peter cleared his throat, "There's just one more thing."

Natalie looked up, her expression wary. "What?"

He paused. "Well, I can't do this alone. And my guess is that people in these parts don't go in for farmers with live-in girlfriends. So... I'm going to need a wife."

Natalie didn't move. She just stood there, lines furrowing along her forehead as she searched his face for hidden meanings. A slow smile spread across his face as he saw her confusion. "Any chance you might be interested?"

Natalie swallowed. "You want me to marry you?" she replied, more statement than question.

"Do you think I came all this way just for a homecoming date?" Peter's eyes twinkled with amusement.

She didn't like being teased, not at a moment like this. "You told me once that you never wanted to get married. *Ever*," Natalie shot back.

Peter reached for her hands and brought them up to his chest. "You're right. I never did. But then you came along and everything changed." Quietly, a self-conscious smile on his face, he tried again.

"Marry me, Natalie. I want to spend the rest of my life with you."

Her heart was pounding so hard she could barely hear the words. She nodded slowly at first, then, as his smile warmed and spread across his face, more resolutely.

Peter's expression was one of genuine relief. "Yes?"

"Yes."

Peter lifted her into the air with a twirl, Natalie laughing all the while.

"Oh wait, I almost forgot." Peter released her back to the ground abruptly and reached into his pocket.

Natalie glanced down at the silver object he laid in her hand. It glinted in the morning sun. She gasped when she realized what it was.

"My locket! But how did you find this?"

Peter opened the clasp and fastened it around her neck. "It was just lying there, waiting for me along the side of the road. I almost didn't pick it up, but for some reason I did." He watched her as she opened it up, half expecting to see the blanket flower, but the compartment was empty.

"I had it polished and repaired. But whatever was inside they said they couldn't save. What was it anyway?"

Natalie smiled, closing the locket and gently stroking it with her finger. The metal, smooth and still warm from its contact with his body, was both soothing and electric. The blanket flower was gone, but its magic remained.

"It doesn't matter now. I have the real thing."

They strolled along the fence line, connected by one hand as Peter pointed with the other, telling of his plans for the coming planting season. His face was alight with energy and excitement. It was the same expression he had worn in the picture on the wall of his house—the one taken by Eve.

But this time, the smile was for her. And the future ahead, theirs.

Chapter 30

They found themselves back in the diner an hour later, hands still entwined, mysterious smiles on their faces. If Ruth noticed, she didn't say anything. "Sit where you like," she called from behind the counter. "I'll bring by coffee in a minute."

Peter led her to the back booth, the same one where they had sat just two days before. They were barely seated before Ruth came with coffee and a decanter of cream. Natalie untangled her hand from his to make more room on the table. She poured cream in both cups, pushing one over to Peter while she stirred sweetener into hers.

"So, what happens next?"

"Put my house on the market, walk the farm again—this time with you..." Peter launched into a point-by-point list of the seemingly infinite steps needed in starting up a farm: business plans, inspections, farm machinery, bank loans. He would begin with cash crops, while slowly growing their dairy operation. Maybe someday they could even expand into organic produce. Natalie's mind reeled at the scope of what was ahead of them, but, if anything, Peter seemed energized by it all.

Peter was in mid-sentence when Natalie spied her father, of all people, moving toward their table. She returned his gaze apprehensively as he slowed to a stop, wondering what kind of reaction they were in for.

"Hey, Dad… What are you doing here?"

"Herb and I have to work out the details for the Thanksgiving Day Parade. He's late as usual, but Ruth said you were here. Scoot over for your old man."

Natalie made room for him in the booth as her father sat down. He eyed them both expectantly.

"You remember Peter Spencer from Madison, don't you?"

"Of course, I do," he said, holding out his hand in greeting. "Peter."

"Henry."

He picked up a spare coffee cup from the table and poured coffee from the white decanter sitting on the table. He glanced at Natalie. "You look like you didn't get any sleep last night," he observed as he took a drink from the cup. Glancing at Peter, he remarked, "I suppose you had something to do with that."

Peter grinned into his cup as Natalie hissed, "Dad!"

"Oh, don't get your feathers all ruffled," he said dismissively. "It's none of my business how you two spend your nights. But you *are* going to make an honest girl out of my daughter, aren't you?" His eyes met Peter's.

"Yes, sir."

"She say yes?" Henry glanced at his daughter, who was looking positively confused at this encounter.

"Yes, sir, she did." Peter was openly smiling now.

Henry took another sip of his coffee, eyes alight with satisfaction. "Good, good. And how did she like the farm?"

"I think she likes it."

The two sipped their coffee while Natalie studied one man and then the other, feeling very in the dark. "All right, what's going on?" They looked up at once, their faces the picture of innocence. "You mean to tell me that you knew Peter was coming this weekend? You knew about the farm? You knew about his plans?" She glared at her father.

He shrugged, completely unrepentant. "Of course, I did."

Natalie shot Peter a fleeting glance. "And you didn't bother to tell me?" Peter sat up, raising his hands in self-defense, but it was her father who replied. "I learned a long time ago not to meddle in my children's business."

"Isn't that exactly what you were doing?"

Henry Brooks shifted in the booth, giving his daughter the full weight of his no-nonsense expression. "Your man Peter called me to ask for my blessing and my help in finding a good piece of land where you two could settle down. If you ask me, that wasn't any more than any father should have done." He paused, oblivious to the glances being exchanged across the table. "Besides, why would I tell you? I didn't know how it would all turn out."

Natalie pressed her lips together in irritation, returning her father's stare with one of her own. That they had planned this entire weekend without her knowledge or consent was mutiny, plain and simple.

Neither gave ground and, after a brief pause, Henry switched his attention to Peter, slapping both hands against the table.

"So, will you plant in the spring?"

And with that implicit invitation, Peter sat forward and began listing his plans in much the same way that he had with Natalie. Henry listened with interest, clearly pleased with the way this little project of his had turned out, while Natalie had little choice but to sit and watch in silence. Yet, as the minutes ticked by, her irritation slowly melted away. The two men clearly seemed to share a mutual respect. She listened to them trade ideas about crops, timetables, and machinery, their excitement unmistakable. No, not a bad way to start off at all.

Ruth came to their table, order pad in hand. "I see you found them, Henry," she remarked. "Herb's in front waiting for you. He's in the first booth."

"It's about time." her father began to slide out of the booth, then paused and turned to Natalie. Kissing her on the cheek, he said in a low voice, "I think you found yourself a good one, baby girl. Now don't go telling anybody about this until you deliver the news to your mother, okay?"

"Okay, Dad." Her smile was warm.

He stood up and traded places with Ruth. "Be sure to come for Sunday dinner tomorrow," he told them, extending his hand to Peter with a gruff equivalent of a smile. Peter shook it firmly before Henry headed up the aisle.

It wasn't until Ruth took their orders and left, her curiosity piqued but unsatisfied, that Natalie glared at Peter.

"So, you had this all planned out?"

Peter shrugged and offered a sheepish smile. "I told you I had a plan, remember?"

Natalie shook her head. This man had unapologetically enlisted her family, her students—her entire community—to win her back into his life. He would be a handful, to be sure, a constant challenge to the safe life she had built, pushing her to be the best person he knew she could be. And, in return, she would do the same for him.

Picking up her mug, she took a sip of coffee, taking in the full effect of the man in front of her. Her love, her world, her future.

She couldn't wait to begin.

THE END

Acknowledgments

Thanks to all those who have read the many versions of this novel and made it better with their kind and honest feedback.

Special thanks to Marijanet, who convinced me that this story deserved to be told. Without her encouragement, it might still be languishing in a lonely desk drawer.

About the Author

——— · ⚭ · ———

Suzanne Eisinger is a Midwest native who now divides her time between Vermont and Florida, trading in winter sports (she's an awful skiier) for walks on the beach. When she is not busy reading, hiking, or keeping up with the goings-on of her three grown-up kids, she is happily writing on her laptop, mug of coffee close at hand.

Suzie's freelance stories, poetry, interviews, and commentary have appeared in print and online publications throughout the US.